the MIGHTY DYNAMO

Illustrated by Marta Kissi

Kieran Crowley

MACMILLAN CHILDREN'S BOOKS

First published 2016 by Macmillan Children's Books
an imprint of Pan Macmillan
20 New Wharf Road, London N1 9RR
Associated companies throughout the world
www.panmacmillan.com

ISBN 978-1-4472-9978-3

Printed and bound by CPI Group (UK) Ltd, Croydon CR0 4YY

For Jack

and for Willow

*To 227FC, simultaneously the best and
worst team ever to play the game*

PROLOGUE

4 JANUARY

Noah Murphy, twelve years old and skinny as a greyhound, had been dreading this moment ever since he'd first heard the news two months ago. Bad things weren't supposed to happen during the holidays. Yet here they were, happening.

He squeezed his way across the living room, pushing past neighbours and relations, apologizing as he stood on toes and accidentally poked an elbow into Mr McFadden's ribs. A fire burned fiercely in the grate, the heating was cranked up high and Noah was hot, uncomfortable and in a very bad mood.

He swung open a window, letting in a cooling gust of crisp January air. It was a relief from the stifling heat.

The moment he opened the window, there were grumbles.

'Close it immediately, Noah. We'll catch our death of cold!' Aunt Margaret said.

Cold? Noah thought. There were rooms in hell that weren't as hot as this. But he closed the window anyway. He'd been terrified of Aunt Margaret ever since he was four years old and had broken a vase at her house. She'd spent ten minutes shouting at him about how clumsy he was, and he'd never forgotten it.

Noah took another look around. He hadn't been to many

parties in his life, but this was still the worst by far. A group of old people squashed into his home, supposedly to say goodbye to his father, but more likely just to scoff the free food. They stood around in clammy groups, chatting about the weather and their various ailments, spilling drinks and cake crumbs, and flaking cigarette ash on to the thin, worn carpet. Pot-bellied men checked their watches to see whether it was time to leave. Noah's grandmother, nearly ninety now, sat by the fire, shrunken into her armchair. She'd never got over the death of his mum, her daughter. She stared, watery-eyed, at the framed photo of her on the mantelpiece, ignoring everyone else.

Noah sighed loudly, and was rewarded by a disapproving look from snobby Aunt Margaret. Then she went back to scowling at the rest of the guests, looking at them as if she expected one of them to steal her purse at any moment.

Noah heard his father's deep voice above the hum of conversations.

'Boondoggle Bend. No, I'd never heard of it either. It's a little mining town in the Northern Territory,' he said. 'About a thousand miles from anywhere. I'll be living in a camp. It's no place for children, unfortunately, which is why they're staying here.'

Noah still couldn't believe he and his sister were being left behind while their dad went abroad for work. They'd spent most of the last two months arguing about it and even now, when his father was only two days away from travelling to the other side of the world, Noah realized he was still angry with him. He understood that his father needed a job. He understood that he owed a lot of money that needed to be paid off if they weren't going to lose their home. He even understood that working on the mines was the best-paying work someone his father's age could hope to find. What he couldn't understand was why he couldn't take Noah and his sister with him.

His dad had tried to put him off. He'd told him he wouldn't like it in Australia. That Boondoggle Bend was in the middle of nowhere and the camp he'd be living in didn't allow children. So what, Noah had said. They could live a couple of hours away and still get to see him once a month, which was better than seeing him once every eight months. It's dangerous, his dad had said. There are crocodiles and huntsman spiders. Noah had wanted to jump on the plane right there and then. That sounded far more exciting than life in his dreary hometown of Carraig Cruach in the west of Ireland. But, no matter what he said, he couldn't persuade his father to change his mind. He wanted them to stay at home with friends and family.

Though it's not like I have many friends anyway, Noah thought, and most of the family are a two-hour drive away. It isn't fair.

'It's only eighteen months, two years at most, Noah,' his dad had said. 'Then we'll be in the clear and everything can go back to normal.'

'Noah, put the kettle on for your grandmother,' Aunt Margaret snapped.

At least he wasn't going to have to stay with her. She'd offered to take them in because she thought it was the right thing to do, and Aunt Margaret was always someone who did the right thing, but she really didn't want to and when his father said no, the relief on her face was clear, even to someone like Noah, who wasn't very good at reading people.

He made his way into the kitchen. Two men, former workmates of his dad's, were so wrapped up in their conversation they didn't even notice his arrival.

'I couldn't do it. Go to Australia for a couple of years and leave my family behind like that? I wouldn't care how much debt I was in. Two kids and the poor mother dead. It's not right,' the chubbier of the two said, slurping his coffee.

'Isn't there anyone else who could take care of the boy?' the skinnier one said, pretending to be concerned about the fate of Noah's family. 'I know the sister's supposed to mind him, but she's only nineteen or twenty. She's still a kid herself.'

'Joe's brother is in America, so he's no good, and the grandparents that are still alive are in a nursing home . . .'

The chubby man suddenly became aware that his conversation was being overheard. He had the good grace to look embarrassed.

'Oh, Noah, hello. We were just . . . erm . . . Still playing the football?' He turned to his colleague. 'Young Noah's a brilliant footballer. The Messi of the West, his dad calls him.'

Noah ignored the man. He stalked across the kitchen and grabbed the kettle in a fury, knocking it against the edge of the cooker and leaving a deep scratch in the black plastic. How dare they talk about his family like that? They didn't know anything. He turned on the kitchen tap and let the water gush into the kettle. And football? His dad was leaving

4

and the man was asking him about football?

He stared out of the kitchen window into the back garden. The grass was long even though it was the middle of winter. A couple of years ago, it would never have needed cutting. Noah would have had all the grass worn away from playing football on it for a couple of hours a day. He'd loved the game then. The moment he'd finished school, he'd have been out there playing against imaginary opponents.

'Forgot how to boil the kettle?' Simone said, appearing beside him.

People said that his sister looked like their mam had when she was young, but Noah couldn't see the resemblance. His mother had never dyed pink stripes into her hair or had a silver stud in her nose, a ring in her lip and eyebrow, or a row of earrings in both ears. That was all Simone.

'They'll all be gone in a few minutes,' she said.

'Even Aunt Margaret?'

'She just said it's a long way back to Athlone. That's her cue. Then it'll just be the three of us again.'

'Not for long,' Noah said.

Simone glanced towards the kitchen door. The two men had departed. It was just her and her brother.

'This is hard for us, Noah. But it's going to be extra tough for Dad. I know you think he's abandoning you, but things are serious. He wouldn't leave if there was any other option.'

'But why couldn't he just get a job in Cork or Dublin or Galway like everybody else?'

'We've been over this again and again. This mining job pays

well. Far better than anything he could get here. We have two days left, Noah. Can you do your best to be cheerful? For Dad's sake. Don't make it harder for him.'

He knew she was right. She usually was. People in school always complained about their sisters, but Simone wasn't that bad. And now, instead of going to university like she should have been, she was staying home to look after him and working two jobs to help support them.

Dad stuck his head round the door. 'There you are. Her Royal Highness is leaving.'

Noah grinned. That's what Dad used to call Margaret just to annoy their mam. It always worked too.

'Hey, Dad, want to have a kickabout tomorrow?'

They hadn't played together in a couple of years.

'Sure,' Dad said, and beamed. 'I'd love to.'

'And don't let me win easily this time. I'm not a kid any more.'

'Noah, I stopped letting you win when you were seven. Every match we've played since then, you've won fair and square.'

The next two days went by far too quickly. One minute they were laughing and joking and eating toasted cheese sandwiches together, the next Simone – the traitor – was helping their dad put his bags in Mr McFadden's car for the trip to the airport. They stayed until the plane had taken off and then Mr McFadden had driven them back home in silence.

Noah lay in his bed that night, unable to sleep. His stomach was cold and clenched in knots. He tossed and turned for hours.

The house felt different now, emptier, and he hated it. He got dressed and went downstairs. Dawn was breaking when he sat down at the kitchen table. He sat there for the next hour, thinking and watching the sun rise. There had to be something he hadn't thought of, some way to bring his family back together. If only he could get some money himself and pay off what his father owed, then Dad wouldn't have to stay in Australia. But where was he going to get the money? He could win the lottery, but they wouldn't sell him a ticket until he was eighteen. Getting a job wasn't very likely either, not at his age. He wished he was smart. Then he could probably invent a game or an app and make a fortune. But he wasn't very smart, and wishing he was wouldn't change anything. There was very little he was good at, only one thing really. And then he remembered the flyer.

The one Stevie had given him.

The one about the tournament.

ARE YOU FOURTEEN OR UNDER?

DO YOU LOVE FOOTBALL?

DO YOU WANT TO PLAY IN THE SCHOOLS' WORLD CUP?

YES, THE <u>WORLD CUP</u>!

Qualification Competition in Dublin – June 12 to 16

**The winning school will represent their country
in the Schools' World Cup in Paris in October.
All expenses paid!**

Competition open for boys and girls!

**Scouts from major clubs will be in attendance so, even
if your team doesn't win, YOU could get a trial with a
professional club in Europe, the US, South America or an
even more far-flung part of the world.**

We will also have:
- **Training and football skills camps for younger children**
- **Professional footballers giving tips and tricks of the trade**
- **Penalty competitions**
- **Interactive video game – Soccer Blaster X**
- **Pop-up football shops**
- **Music, food and lots and lots more**

**Have you got what it takes to be the
new star of world football?**

Neymar Jr, James, Sterling, Götze . . . YOU?

**Entries must be made through your school. All details on our
website. Finalized squad list must be forwarded to us by 5 p.m.,
Friday 29 April. Any entries or amendments after that date
will not be considered without a doctor's certificate.**

CHAPTER ONE

25 APRIL

‘ If you're in the penalty area and you don't know what to do with the ball, put it in the net and we'll discuss the options later ’
                                                        Bob Paisley

There were only four people standing on the sidelines watching the football match, and Noah knew three of them. The fourth was a stranger. He was a broad-faced man with narrow eyes who had arrived early in the second half. Noah hoped he was a scout, but football scouts rarely came to this isolated part of Ireland. In fact *people* rarely came to this part of Ireland. If they did, they usually acknowledged their mistake, made their excuses and left as swiftly as they could.

It was permanently windy in the town of Carraig Cruach. And most days were cold. When it wasn't cold it was raining, although there were months on end when it was all three at once: cold and wet and windy. Arthur Slugsley, the man on the sideline, made another note as he tried his best to shield his clipboard from the lashing rain, which seemed to be pounding him from at least three different angles. Despite his jet-black, supposedly one-hundred-per-cent-waterproof poncho, and the umbrella that was almost whipped from his hand with every sudden gust of wind, he was sopping wet. Down in the dumps, but grimly determined to finish his work, Arthur managed to write:

> GOOD GAME INTELLIGENCE. SOMETIMES FRUSTRATED
> BY INABILITY OF TEAMMATES TO BE ON THE SAME
> WAVELENGTH. WOULD THRIVE IN A BETTER TEAM

This was in addition to some of the other things he'd already written about Noah Murphy. These included:

> VERY QUICK AND AGILE
> HAS GREAT SKILL AND CONTROL
> UNSELFISH – WILL PASS RATHER THAN SHOWBOAT

Noah was out on the left wing now, moving into space, just as he always did. Most people thought football was about skill and effort and it *was* about those things, but mainly it was about space and decisions. Finding space on the pitch in which to receive the ball and then making the right decision – when to pass, when to dribble, when to shoot.

Now he controlled a ball from Bestie and shimmied free of the man closest to him. It wasn't difficult for Noah to get away. Ever since the fourth goal had gone in, putting Noah's team, St Killian's, 4–0 up against Clydeabbey, the opposition had given up. It was almost as if they didn't *want* to be out there watching the goals flying in on this cold, wet, extremely miserable day.

Noah nutmegged the centre-back and faked a pass to the winger who was bombing into the area, before slamming the ball into the top corner himself to make it 5–0.

The goalkeeper fished the ball out of the back of the net with a heartfelt sigh. He was imagining being warm and dry in double Maths. The thought of being lulled to sleep by the steady drone of his teacher's voice was far more appealing than being stuck where he was right now.

Noah didn't celebrate the goal, his second of the game.

'You've won the match already. Why do you have to keep scoring? Are you trying to humiliate us?' the goalkeeper grumbled.

'It's nothing personal. That's just his way. He never stops,' Shieldsy, the tallest of Noah's teammates, replied. 'He's like the Terminator. If the Terminator played schools' football.'

'Can't you have a word with him? Tell him to take it easy or something.'

'He wouldn't listen. He just does his own thing.'

As he jogged back to his own half, Noah stole a glance at the sideline. The scout, if that's what he was, was making another note on his rain-soaked pad. Noah hoped it was a good one. He really needed it to be a good one, but, as Clydeabbey took their sixth kick-off of the day, his heart almost skipped a beat.

Oh no, he thought, not now.

A small figure was sidling up to Arthur Slugsley. A small figure Noah knew very well indeed. Unlike Noah, and every other person in the vicinity, Little Stevie, also known as IQ, was bone dry and almost cosy, buried as he was under layer after layer of oilskins. A wide-brimmed hat kept the rain off his face.

Noah's best friend in the world, his only friend, had been filming the match from the far side of the pitch, but he'd spent the last ten minutes edging nearer and nearer to the scout.

Slugsley looked down at the young teenager encroaching on his personal space. Even through the lashing rain, Noah could make out the look on the man's face. It was an unhappy mixture of confusion and annoyance.

With the World Cup qualifiers less than two months away, Noah knew that he had to impress the man on the sideline and he didn't need anyone messing things up by saying the wrong thing. And if anyone was going to say the wrong thing it was going to be Little Stevie Treacy.

Noah's jersey was stuck to him. The two ones that formed the number eleven on his back had begun to peel off and his navy socks sagged under the weight of water, exposing the tops of his shin pads.

'Wake up, Murphy,' came the shout from Liam O'Sullivan, the bullish left-back, as he slid the ball up the line.

Noah swore to himself. He'd lost concentration. That was stupid. O'Sullivan's pass was good, especially in these miserable conditions, and Noah took a touch, knocking the ball forward over the wet and muddy ground. He looked up, checking his options, as the huge defender, his face a furious red, thundered towards him. He'd had it in for Noah since the fourth minute of the game when Noah had turned him inside out twice in thirty seconds, before scoring the first goal. The defender was big and strong and fast, but he had no skill – though what he lacked in skill he made up for in intimidation – he was built like a son of the Hulk.

Noah caressed the ball with the outside of his right boot, sending it on a gentle parabola. It curled round the outstretched foot of the full-back and into the space between the two central defenders.

Jim Reynolds, the lightning-fast striker, had seen his teammate play a through ball like this before. Even though they disliked each other in real life, on the pitch they had a great understanding. Reynolds had started 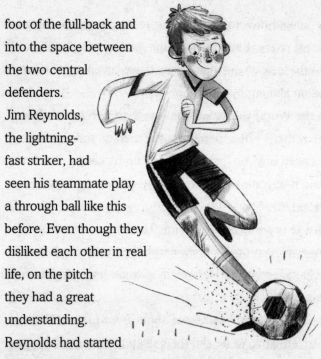 his run as soon as he'd seen Noah look up.

The centre-backs were slow to turn and Jim already had a couple of metres on them when the ball landed ahead of him, just in the right spot to take it in his stride. He cushioned it with his instep. Jim was in the penalty area with only the keeper to beat when Noah felt studs crunch into his ankle. There was a flash of nerve-shredding pain as his leg went from under him. For a second he was airborne and had a moment to consider the ugly, cold darkness of the sky, before he returned to earth with a splash as he landed in a puddle of dirty, icy-cold water. He heard the cheers of his teammates as Jim took the ball round the keeper and tapped it into the empty net.

'Get up. I barely touched you.'

Noah pulled down his sock and glanced at the six red stud marks on his ankle before turning his attention to his assailant. The defender was even more intimidating close up. He stood above Noah, leaning forward until Noah could clearly see the white pimple on the end of his square chin. The rest of his face appeared to have reddened up a notch, as if it was going to explode at any moment.

'Did you hear me? I told you to get up, you diving, whingeing, mammy's boy.'

Noah was used to being targeted in matches. He was one of the danger players, one to watch, which meant he spent half his time on the pitch getting kicked black and blue. He usually responded by partaking in some sneaky revenge when the ref wasn't looking – a little kick here, a sly dig there. He wasn't going to do anything now though, no matter how much he was provoked. There was too much at stake.

'I won't tell you a third time, you sh—'

'Take it easy,' Noah said.

'What did you call me?'

The alarm bells went off in Noah's head. He hadn't called him anything. The big bruiser was looking for a fight.

'If I wanted to call you something, I would have, but I didn't, so back off,' Noah said.

'Get him, Brick,' someone shouted.

'Your name is Brick?'

'Yeah, what's it to you?'

'Nothing, but your friends must really hate you if they call you Brick. It rhymes with too many things,' Noah said.

15

'Like what?'

Noah struggled to his feet as the referee *peep-peep-peep*ed on his whistle. Brick must have figured out one of the rhymes because the next thing Noah saw was his opponent's fleshy fist hurtling towards him. And then all hell broke loose.

PLAYER PROFILE

Name: Noah Murphy

Nickname: None really. Sometimes people call me Moses. You can probably figure out why.

Age: 12

Position: Central midfield, but as long as I get a game I don't mind where I play.

Team you play for: St Killian's is my school team. I used to play for CC United, which was the only football club in town, but it closed down last year so now it's schools' football or nothing.

Training schedule: St Killian's train on Wednesday evenings, but I do a lot of extra training myself. For the last few months, I've been getting up at 6 a.m. on school mornings to practise shooting with both feet and to improve my touch. I usually do that for an hour or two. I do a few exercises as well to improve my speed and spring. I don't eat sweets or any sugary stuff, and I make sure I eat plenty of fruit and drink lots of water. Three times a week I go jogging around the local football pitch. When I get the chance to use the internet, I go on YouTube and watch a lot of football videos to learn new skills.

Player you're most like: Fàbregas, I think.

Favourite player: Arjen Robben. He's outstanding.

Favourite goal: Zlatan's goal against FC Breda. Look it up on YouTube. It's amazing.

Messi or Ronaldo: Messi

CHAPTER TWO

'The Baggio brothers, of course, are not related'
George Hamilton

'Wow, that eye's going to look fantastic tomorrow,' Stevie said chirpily.

Noah's left eye had swelled up. A ragged fingernail scratch ran down one cheek and even though he'd had a shower after the match there was still a smear of caked blood beneath his nose.

'It's already turned into quite a shiner,' Stevie continued, 'and that mark on your face looks pretty sore too.'

Noah had left the dressing room to find Stevie waiting for him outside, just as he'd expected. The rain had eased off to a drizzle, but his friend was still in his oil slickers and hat. His mother had told him not to get wet, and unlike most of their classmates Stevie usually did what he was told.

'I'm fine,' Noah said, sounding a little more surly than he meant to.

He was still annoyed at having been sent off. It wasn't like he'd done anything wrong, but the referee wouldn't listen. There had been seven punches thrown and he'd been on the receiving end of each of them. They'd hurt too. Brick might not be much of a footballer, but he could certainly throw a solid right-hander.

They strolled out of the changing rooms, which were tucked in beside the football pitch at the back of the school grounds, then walked past the school itself and down the long driveway that led to the front gates. There was no one else around. Most people didn't need a second invitation to go home once the school day was over.

'I've got some fantastic footage of the fight. Want to see it?' Stevie asked.

'Much as I'd love to see myself getting beaten up, I think I'll wait till later to have a look. What did you say to that man?'

'The scout?'

Upon hearing the word 'scout', Noah felt a flutter in his stomach. It was a mixture of nerves and excitement.

'He told me to go away and stop annoying him, but everybody says I annoy them so I wasn't going to let that hold me back,' Stevie said. He anticipated Noah's next question. 'He didn't actually say he was a scout, but he definitely was. No doubt about it. He was writing stuff about you and it's not like we get journalists covering our matches.'

'Did you see what he wrote?'

'I barely came up to his elbow so I couldn't really make too much of it out, but I definitely saw your shirt number and the letters EXC were right beside it.'

'EXC? What does that mean?'

'It means he was writing something good about you. A word

beginning with EXC has to be good news. I mean what are the options? Excellent. Exciting. Exceptional?' Stevie grinned.

As hard as he tried, Noah couldn't think of any other words.

'There is excruciating, of course,' Stevie said, his grin fading. 'Like excruciatingly bad, but it's highly unlikely he wrote that down. And there's a word that means poop, but surely he wouldn't . . .' Stevie blushed.

'I hope he doesn't blame me for that stupid fight like the referee did. If he tells his club I'm a troublemaker they'll never give me a trial,' Noah said.

They walked along in silence for a couple of minutes before Noah spoke again.

'Thanks for the effort, Stevie, but you shouldn't have gone up to him. Your mum probably wouldn't like it if she knew you'd been talking to a stranger.'

'Wouldn't like it? Hello? Have you met my parents? They only warn me about the dangers of the world fifty times a day. Don't talk to strangers, Stevie. Don't drink milk after the best-before date, Stevie. Last week they said: Don't go out without sunscreen, Stevie. Sunscreen? It was raining.'

Noah smiled. Poor Stevie had the strictest parents ever. Still, he wouldn't have minded that. He wouldn't have minded at all. Sometimes Stevie didn't realize how lucky he was.

'Anyway, you don't need to worry about me,' Stevie said. 'I took a picture of the car he came in, wrote down the car registration then took a secret photo of him on my tablet and emailed all the details to my own account so that if I do go missing the authorities will know who to look for.'

The littered streets were still slick with rain when Noah took a turn Stevie hadn't expected. They usually carried on until the end of Shoulders' Lane where Stevie went left and on towards his estate, which was by far the nicest one in town.

'Hey, you're going the wrong way,' he called.

'I'm meeting Simone. Today's shopping day,' Noah said. 'See you tomorrow.'

Stevie gave him the thumbs up. 'I'll have all the match stats ready for you,' he shouted after him.

There was a solitary girl standing by the gates of St Mary's school, but it wasn't Noah's sister. He'd never seen this particular girl before. She looked a little lost. She had fair hair and a nose that was slightly too long for her face. He would hardly have noticed her at all if she hadn't been wearing a replica football shirt over her green school uniform. Noah knew his football jerseys, but it still took him a few moments to recognize the team because it was such an unusual one to see around these parts. It was from MLS, the American league. Columbus Crew. Yellow with some black stripes.

The girl caught him staring at her. She seemed to take it as a challenge and stared back.

'Nice jersey,' Noah said.

'Nice black eye,' the girl replied.

A sleek maroon car approached, pulling up to the kerb with a whoosh. The passenger door opened and the girl jumped in. As the car took off, Noah found himself waving goodbye. He didn't know why he did it and he knew it looked odd, especially

21

when he saw the girl shake her head at him as if she felt sorry for someone who was so obviously pathetic.

He made his way into the school and strode down the empty corridor checking each classroom in turn for his sister until he heard voices coming from the last room on the left.

Simone was dressed in her cleaner's uniform of baggy overalls, and when Noah reached the door she was on her hands and knees scrubbing the linoleum floor, doing her best to remove an ink stain that had proven to be extremely stubborn.

Before the hello had left his lips, Noah saw two final-year girls approach her from the back of the otherwise empty class. One, with red hair, had a wastepaper basket clasped between her freckled fingers. The other, taller girl, was blonde and tanned, and carried herself with an astonishing degree of self-importance. She was Jacinta Hegarty, Noah's school principal's daughter. Noah didn't know her very well, but he'd seen enough to know she wasn't a nice person.

'You know, I really admire you, Simone. I don't think I'd be able to your job,' Jacinta said in a voice that sounded sweet but was filled with nastiness. 'Not that I ever would, of course. I mean, cleaning up someone else's mess? That's got to be humiliating.'

She turned to her companion and knocked the wastepaper basket from her hand. The contents – a tuna sandwich, some crumpled copybook pages and a half-finished pink Slurpee drink – fell to the floor. The thick Slurpee spread slowly across the surface of the lino.

'Ah, Fiona, look what you've done now,' Jacinta said reproachfully. 'And just after Simone had done such a good job cleaning the floors.'

Noah couldn't hold back. 'You did that deliberately,' he cried. 'Clean it up yourself.'

'It's OK, Noah,' Simone said evenly. 'I've got it.'

Jacinta Hegarty turned her gaze on Noah. She looked him up and down, and from the unpleasant expression on her face Noah guessed she didn't approve of what she saw. He didn't care what she thought. No one treated his sister like that.

'You've brought your own little pet bodyguard. Isn't that sweet?' Jacinta said. She sniffed the air. 'Whoa, he stinks. If you're too poor to buy soap and groom him, Simone, you could at least tell him to wash himself with some of those detergents on your cleaning cart. I won't tell Mrs Power you're taking them for your personal use. *It'll be our little secret.*'

Noah's face was almost purple with rage. If Hegarty had been a boy, he was certain he'd have punched her on the nose by now.

'Jacinta Hegarty and Fiona Quigley! What are you two still doing here at this hour? You don't come in on time in the morning and you won't go home in the evening. Clear out now or I'll give you some work that'll keep you here until ten o'clock tonight.'

The woman who had appeared at the door was the St Mary's principal, Mrs Power, a stick-thin woman with long, black hair. Her words had an immediate effect and the two girls grabbed their schoolbags and scarpered from the classroom as quickly as they could.

Mrs Power sighed and turned to Simone. 'That girl is turning out to be just as bad as her father. The last thing this town needs is another Hega—'

She stopped mid-sentence when she saw Noah. He was still annoyed, but his rage was slowly subsiding.

'What are you doing here?' she asked him.

'That's my brother, Noah,' Simone said, getting to her feet. 'I asked him to meet me here.'

'What happened to your face?' Mrs Power asked.

'Oh. It's nothing,' he mumbled. 'I fell.'

'It must have been a spectacular fall. What class are you in, Noah?'

Mrs Power spat the question at him. She was being nice, but she had a sharp way of being nice, and it unnerved him. He felt as if he was being interrogated and a wave of guilt washed over him even though he hadn't committed any crime.

'Mr Moran's class,' he said.

'Getting top marks like your sister always did, I hope.'

'Not always,' Noah mumbled. *Never* was a more accurate answer. He was a solid C student.

'Well, study harder, then,' she said.

After he'd answered enough questions to satisfy her curiosity, Mrs Power strode back to her office in double-quick time, moving with the speed of someone with one hundred things to do, but only enough time to complete ninety-nine of them.

Noah spent the next few minutes helping Simone clean up the spilled Slurpee. Once she'd finished her work, they left the school and went to the supermarket at the end of town, only a couple of hundred metres from the terraced house they called home.

Shopping was the least favourite of Noah's chores because it meant he got to see shelves of delicious and tempting food they couldn't really afford. Noah had been lost in thought on the walk to the supermarket. Simone was the sort of person who always stood up for herself. He'd never imagined that she'd let someone talk to her the way that Hegarty girl had. He wasn't planning on saying anything, but suddenly found himself blurting out the words as Simone was trying to choose between two different brands of tomato ketchup.

'Why did you let her away with it?'

'I need the job, Noah,' she said.

'But—'

'No buts. I need the job. I can't afford to have any complaints made against me so I'm going to keep my mouth shut and just keep working.' She placed the cheaper bottle of ketchup in her basket and turned to her brother. 'Are you going to tell me what happened to your face this time?'

'I got in a fight.'

'What did I tell you about fighting?' she continued.

'That it's fun and I should do more of it.'

She gave him a withering look.

'It's not that bad,' he said. 'Anyway, you should see the other guy.'

'What did you do to him?'

'Nothing. He hasn't got a scratch on him. I took your advice. I didn't react at all. That's not easy, you know.'

'You really didn't lay a finger on him?' she asked. Her voice was filled with suspicion.

'I'm telling you, Simone, he looks better now than he did before. Punching my face gave him a really good workout. He had a very healthy glow afterwards.'

She grabbed him by the chin and twisted his head left and right to assess the damage. One or two of the nosier shoppers began to look in their direction. Noah tried to break free, embarrassed by the attention, but his sister had a grip like a steel clamp.

'So, who was it this time? Another argument with Jim Reynolds?'

'No.'

'One of the McCooleys?'

'If I'd fought a McCooley, I'd be in a body bag right now.'

'Who was it, then?' Simone asked.

'A guy called Brick,' Noah said.

'Fighting people isn't enough for you, huh? Now you've moved on to inanimate objects.'

The outside of the Murphy home had seen better days and those better days had been quite some time ago. The house was in need of several coats of paint and the tiny front garden had more weeds than lawn. Dad was the one who'd always kept it tidy.

As the dull grey of the afternoon transformed into the slightly duller grey of the evening, Noah sat in his small and, it has to be said, messy bedroom. The posters on the walls were of footballers from a variety of different clubs. Unlike almost every other football fan in the world, Noah didn't follow any team in particular. He loved the game, not the clubs.

He was still annoyed by the fight with Brick, but *more* annoyed by the way in which that Hegarty girl had treated his sister. He got to his feet and lifted the mattress with his left hand, reaching underneath it with his right, fingers moving along the bed springs until they located what he was looking for.

Technically, it wasn't even Noah's notebook. It had belonged to his mother. He had found it when they were clearing out an old wardrobe a few months after she'd died. There were pictures of the 1980s pop stars Duran Duran on the cover. He opened it up and flicked past the pages she'd filled in over the years – names of songs she liked, phone numbers of friends in college, a glued-in picture of Simone as a baby and then a small sketch she'd done of Noah playing football in the back garden when he was only five or six. Underneath she'd written the words *My Mighty Dynamo*. He ran his fingers across the page, but then, just as the image of her face popped into his head, he thumbed through a few more pages until he found the one he was looking for.

He'd written the words the day his father left for Australia. He read them again now, as he did every week.

> I will do everything I can to become a
> professional footballer. No matter what it
> takes. I might not be good enough, but I
> will not fail because I didn't try.

Beneath that he'd written the things he would do when he started earning lots of money.

> I will buy a new house for my family.
> Dad will not have to work abroad.
> I will pay for Simone to go to university.
> I will buy a 52-inch television.

Stevie was the only one who actually knew about Noah's ambition to be a professional footballer, but Noah had never told him the reasons why. It wasn't because Stevie couldn't keep a secret, he could, he was the most loyal friend in the world, but for some reason Noah found it impossible to talk to him about this.

The rest of the notebook's pages were filled with the names of football clubs from all over the world. Noah was in the process of writing to every single one of them, telling them about his skills and talent and asking for a trial.

He was still waiting for an invitation, but he'd only written to one hundred and fifteen clubs so far. There were thousands left. He knew the chances of getting a trial this way were slim, but he wasn't despondent. Even if the scout who'd watched him today decided against recommending him, he knew there was a great chance of being spotted at the World Cup qualifying tournament. In just over six weeks' time, he could be signing a contract with a professional club. Then things would be the way they were meant to be. He'd have enough money so Dad could quit his mining job and come home and Simone could tell Jacinta Hegarty where to shove it. The idea of it all working out made him excited.

Which is why he was so upset when everything went badly wrong the next day.

CHAPTER THREE

6 I didn't really want to be involved in a normal
football club 9   Eric Cantona

The tired and mostly miserable pupils of St Killian's Boys
were arriving for another day of school and the corridor had
begun to hum with the sound of one hundred and fifty different
conversations. Noah, who'd been up at dawn to practise with
his weaker left foot, was in the middle of a huge yawn when
Stevie ran up to him, wheezing a little.

'I got the analysis done,' Stevie said, as someone barged
past, knocking him into a locker. 'Sorry.'

'Don't apologize – he bumped into you,' Noah said. 'What
analysis?'

'On yesterday's match,' Stevie said brightly.

'Great.' Noah smiled. His best friend was the only person
who thought about football more than Noah did, and he didn't
even play the game.

Stevie took the tablet from his school bag and switched it on
just as a sudden hush fell over the crowd of students. It takes a
lot to get a couple of hundred teenagers to shut up all at once,
but that's what happened. They all froze for a moment, unsure

of what to do, until someone made a move and the rest parted like a shoal of fish that had spotted a great white heading in its direction. The sense of fear was palpable.

'McCooley,' Little Stevie whispered.

Kevin McCooley was the toughest person anyone in the school had ever had the misfortune to encounter. He was the youngest of three brothers and, by reputation, the meanest of the lot. His older siblings, a set of twins, had left St Killian's the previous June, just months before Noah had started in the school. There was a rumour that there'd been a party in the staff room to celebrate their departure and it had only come to a halt when one of the teachers remembered that another McCooley was starting at the school the following September.

'He shouldn't be called Kevin. It's too misleading. Kevins are nice, normal people. Not like him,' Stevie had said the first day they'd seen him in school.

It was almost impossible to believe that McCooley was the same age as Noah and Stevie. He looked a lot older. His hair was wild and stuck out from his head in seven separate clumps. His face was permanently set in a scowl and he exuded a sense of menace that made every last pupil and teacher nervous of him.

'It was like being trapped in a room with a psychotic lion,' Mr Moran had been overheard saying when he'd spent an hour after school giving Kevin McCooley detention. It was a mistake no teacher would ever make again.

Most people weren't foolish enough to mess with the McCooleys, not with their reputation. There had been a report

31

in the local newspaper about Kevin's mother being sentenced to six months in jail for beating up two of her neighbours when they complained about the loud rap music she was playing at four in the morning. One of them had been forced to give up his career in the army after the assault.

'It's the twenty-first century and we're still scared of bullies. It's ridiculous,' Stevie whispered.

Kevin McCooley slowed his swagger and his head swivelled in their direction. His eyes narrowed to black beads and he growled. A low rumble at the back of his throat. It wasn't very loud, but it was definitely a growl.

Noah focused on his shoelaces as if they were the most important things in the world. McCooley stared at him. Noah couldn't see him staring, but he could feel it. The wild-haired teenager's eyes were burning into him with a laser-like intensity. McCooley muttered something to himself, then walked on.

'Imagine what he'd be like if we'd actually done something to annoy him,' Stevie said, his voice a little squeakier than it had been a few moments earlier.

'There's something seriously wrong with him,' Noah said as he watched McCooley shove a little kid out of the way.

The contents of the younger boy's bag spilled all over the corridor's floor, but nobody dared move a muscle to help him. As McCooley disappeared round a corner, the bell rang, calling them into class.

'I'll show this to you after school,' Stevie said, putting his tablet into his bag. 'Those punches you wanted to see have been captured perfectly. When the blood gushes from your nose you can put the video on slow motion and it's like watching one of those BBC nature programmes. The red is really deep and rich.'

'You know when I said yesterday that I'd watch it later, Stevie? I actually meant I'd never watch it.'

'Oh, right, well, not to worry. The stats are good. Your passing percentages were by far the highest. Over ninety which is excellent on a wet, muddy pitch.'

'Great. How long did it take you to do all that?'

'Oh, not that long. Between the analysis, creating the database and reading the data from the monitor I'd put on your arm it was only about three or four hours.'

'Three or four hours? You're mad. If you spent that long studying . . .'

'I'd be top of the class? I am top of the class, Noah. I always am. And I spent three hours studying last night. See you at lunch.'

Noah headed into his classroom, two doors down from Stevie's. He took his usual seat just in front of Michael Griffin. An hour later and Noah was struggling to keep his eyes open during a Geography class when a voice crackled over the ancient PA system.

'Can Noah Murphy make his way to the principal's office at once.'

His first thought was that it was a family emergency and his heart began to thump wildly. He couldn't face that again. But then he remembered that the principal came to the door in person for emergencies. No, a call on the PA meant one thing: Noah was in some kind of trouble. He just couldn't figure out

33

what it was that he was supposed to have done.

The office wasn't huge anyway, but Mr Hegarty's bulk made it look even smaller. He was a big man, far too big to be healthy, and the chair creaked beneath his weight, the sides of his bottom slipping over its edges like silly putty. Mr Hegarty fought back the urge to belch, scratched his nose instead and pretended to read a file on his cluttered desk. He set the file down and opened a bright red packet of *Grudz*, a sweet that Noah had never seen anywhere other than in his headmaster's hand – they certainly weren't stocked in any of the local shops. He popped three of the brightly coloured sweets into his mouth before he glanced at Noah.

'Mr Murphy,' he said between chews that turned his lips a pinkish red. 'You know why you're here, of course?'

'No, sir.'

Hegarty sighed. 'I have a report on yesterday's match. What have you got to say for yourself?'

'About what, sir?'

'About the fight you started.'

'The fight I started?' Noah was astonished. 'I didn't start anything. I was the one who was attacked. Look at my face.'

He pointed to the blue-black bruise and the scratch on his cheek. Hegarty shifted in his seat trying, and failing, to get comfortable.

'That doesn't prove anything,' he said. 'It may suggest that you'd be a terrible boxer, but being beaten up doesn't mean you didn't throw the first punch.'

'Anyone who was there will tell you that I wasn't the one who started it. Ask them, sir.'

'I've spoken to the people I need to speak to and I've made my decision. You dragged the school's good name through the mud.'

'But, that's not right, I—'

'Are you questioning my authority, Mr Murphy?'

'No, sir,' Noah said.

'Good. Now, I can't have my pupils going around attacking others whenever they feel like it. We're not animals, after all. There are consequences to your actions and in this case the consequence is a punishment. Since you disgraced yourself playing football, I've decided that the punishment should be football related.'

That didn't sound good. That didn't sound good at all. Noah was trying to think of some form of protest, something he could say to change his principal's mind. Detention he could handle, extra homework he could handle, but a football-related punishment?

'You're banned from playing for the school team until the

beginning of the next school year,' Mr Hegarty said.

Noah's world collapsed in a single moment. His heart sank to his stomach with a great whoosh, then continued its descent until it hit the floor. Noah was so shocked that he wasn't even sure if he'd heard his principal correctly.

'W-w-what?' he stuttered.

He didn't hear Mr Hegarty's reply. He saw the man's lips move, but the sound that came out made no sense to him. It was like listening to someone speak while you're underwater.

Noah grew light-headed. He felt extremely odd. As if all this was happening to someone else, as if it wasn't real. He shut his eyes. For a moment, he thought he was having an out-of-body experience.

He opened his eyes again and everything came back into focus.

'. . . It gives me no pleasure to do this to you,' Mr Hegarty was saying with a smile. 'But your behaviour hasn't given me any other option. When you wear the St Killian's crest on your jersey, you're not only representing yourself, you're representing every pupil and all this school holds dear. Attacking Clydeabbey players does not form part of our core values and further-more . . .'

Banned from the school team for something I didn't do, Noah thought.

It was so unjust it couldn't be true. All that extra training, everything he'd sacrificed had been for one reason: to get to the World Cup qualification tournament.

And now Mr Hegarty was going to take his chance away.

Just like that. Because he'd decided he could. Noah couldn't let it happen. He *wouldn't* let it happen. He found his voice again.

'That's not fair,' he said, just about holding back the urge to shout the words.

'I never said it was fair. I said that it was a punishment,' Hegarty said.

'Well, give me some other punishment.'

'Sir,' Hegarty sneered.

The way he said it reminded Noah of Jacinta, Hegarty's daughter, the previous evening.

'Give me some other punishment, *sir*. Please. One that hasn't got anything to do with football. I need to play in that tournament. I just . . . could you change it to something else? Anything else?'

'Of course I could,' Mr Hegarty said, 'I just don't want to.'

It was an enormous effort for Noah to remain polite. The shock had worn off completely now and it had been replaced by blood-boiling anger. He wanted to pick something up and smash it into little pieces.

'But . . . but, you can't ban me,' he spluttered. 'I've told you I didn't start the fight.'

This has to be some kind of pathetic joke, he thought.

'My report says that you did and my decision is final.'

'But . . . but . . . but –'

And then it hit him and he wondered why he hadn't thought of it earlier. He had an escape route.

'I can prove I didn't start it. I didn't even throw a punch,' he said.

The headmaster's eyebrows knitted together. Suddenly, he didn't seem as certain of himself. He shifted uneasily in his seat.

'You can? How?' he asked.

Stevie nearly had a heart attack when he heard his name being called out over the public-address system. Every pair of eyes in the classroom zoomed in on him. It made him feel threatened, like a cornered animal. He hated being the centre of attention.

'Woooooooooo, Li'l Stevie's in trouble,' Hawk Willis said.

Hawk Willis always has to have something to say, Stevie thought, plunging his hand into the depths of his schoolbag to retrieve his asthma inhaler. He found it and took a couple of steadying puffs.

'C'mon, Stevie, man. Time to face the music. We always knew the law would catch up with you one day,' Hawk continued.

Even the teacher smiled a little at that one. Stevie had never been called to the principal's office before. He'd never been called out of class. As far as he could remember, he hadn't ever missed a single second of school. Even when he needed to go to the bathroom, he'd hold on until lunch or break-time.

'Steven, you'd better not keep Mr Hegarty waiting,' the teacher said. 'And don't forget to take your school bag with you. He requested that you take your bag.'

Stevie stood up. His legs wobbled.

'Are you OK, Stevie?' the secretary asked a few minutes later as he waited outside the principal's office.

He nodded briefly then took another puff of his inhaler.

'Can I get you a glass of water? It's not any of your allergies, is it?'

'No,' Stevie gasped.

When she was satisfied that he wasn't going to collapse in front of her, the secretary told Stevie he could go through to Mr Hegarty's office.

'Steven Treacy. How much trouble have you got yourself in this time?' the principal said as Stevie took his first tentative steps into the office.

Noah thought Stevie was going to burst into tears.

'It's a joke, Mr Treacy. The humour is derived from the fact that you're never in trouble, unlike your compatriot here.'

Until that moment, Stevie hadn't even noticed Noah was in the room. His best friend looked in worse shape than he did. All the colour had drained from Noah's face.

'I've been told that you may possess some footage of yesterday's football match, specifically the part of the match that descended into a disgusting display of violence,' Mr Hegarty said.

'Y-y-y-es, sir. I have it on my tablet.'

Stevie opened his bag, took out the tablet and switched it on.

'Can I have that, please,' Mr Hegarty said.

His use of the word 'please' suggested he was asking politely, but his tone indicated it was a command. Stevie passed it across without another word. It looked much smaller in Mr Hegarty's huge hands. The principal switched it off immediately, the red light at the top blipping three times before fading out.

'Hey, aren't you going to look at it?' Noah asked.

'No, Mr Murphy. I'm confiscating it. Tablets that have been used for non-school purposes are subject to one week's confiscation.'

Noah looked at Stevie. If there was one person who knew the school rules it was his best friend. And Stevie never broke those rules. He wouldn't risk it. He wouldn't have brought a tablet to school if there was any danger of getting in trouble for it.

Stevie seemed reluctant to speak, as if he was torn between being loyal to Noah and not daring to disagree with his headmaster. Eventually it appeared that friendship had won and he nervously spoke up.

'Mr Hegarty, sir, ahm, the tablet *is* used for school purposes. I'm doing a project in Mr Moran's class.'

Mr Hegarty stared down at Little Stevie who shivered under the man's gaze.

'Well, Mr Treacy, we're talking about a football match and that's not a school project, now, is it?'

Noah was stumped. He looked at Stevie who stayed silent for a moment as Mr Hegarty leaned back in his chair. There was a creak and a flash of concern crossed Hegarty's face as the chair sounded as if it was about to snap in two. He slowly edged it forward until all four legs were safely on the floor again.

'Now, if you gentlemen—'

'If you don't mind, sir, it *was* used for school purposes. At the football match, I mean,' Stevie said in a voice barely above a whisper. His eyes were as wide as a couple of buttermilk pancakes.

'Are you saying I don't know the rules, Mr Treacy? The rules of my very own school?'

'N-no, no, of course not. Definitely not,' Stevie stammered. 'Well . . . what I mean, ahm, what I'm saying is . . .' He wiped sweat from his brow with the back of his sleeve as Hegarty continued to glare at him. '. . . I think there's been a mix-up, sir. The match was a school match and, you know, for insurance purposes the players were considered to be at school. And I was filming it for the benefit of the school team.'

Mr Hegarty glared at Stevie with a look so terrifying that Noah had never seen its like before. Stevie withered right in front of his eyes.

'But, of course, that's just my personal opinion, so, heh heh, what do I know?' Stevie gulped.

'Exactly,' Hegarty said. 'What do you know?'

He opened his desk drawer and placed the tablet inside, then slid the drawer shut.

Noah decided to give it one last try. 'Sir, if you could just look at it for one minute you'll see that I didn't start the fi—'

'I can ban you for as long as I want, Mr Murphy. The school board will back me and it's not like you have the resources to challenge any decision. Do you want to play for this school again before your eighteenth birthday? Because if you don't all you have to do is continue talking.'

He turned his attention to Stevie.

'One week, Mr Treacy, one week and you'll get your device

back. When the period of confiscation is up, I will examine the footage and if your account proves to be correct then the ban will be lifted.'

'But the closing date for entries for the World Cup qualifiers is in three days,' Noah said. 'If I'm still banned then the coach won't be able to put me in the squad and they don't allow changes unless it's a medical emergency. Next week will be too late. If you just look at the video now—'

'Are you really still talking, Mr Murphy? After what I just said?'

Noah shook his head. There was no doubting that was the end of the matter for now. He knew that saying anything else would be a complete waste of time. His principal wasn't going to change his mind. If he was going to get out of this mess, he had to find another way.

'Right, you two, get back to your classes and learn something,' their principal said.

After they left, Mr Hegarty picked up his mobile phone and dialled a number he chose after searching through his contacts. It took a few rings before the call was answered.

'Hello, it's me,' Hegarty said. 'It's done. He's off the team.'

Out in the corridor, Stevie was worried about his friend. He'd never seen anyone who was this pale yet still alive. There were corpses and ghosts with healthier complexions than the almost-translucent Noah. He wanted to say something, to tell him that it'd be all right, but Noah would know that he was just being sympathetic and he hated sympathy. Stevie was still searching for the right words when Noah spoke.

'He's not going to get away with that. I'm playing in that tournament. I'll do whatever it takes.'

'What are you going to do?'

'Whatever. It. Takes,' Noah said.

'OK, but that's not actually clarifying anything. All you're doing is repeating some words.'

Noah smiled. It wasn't his natural smile and, to someone who knew him like Stevie did, it looked a little deranged. 'I've got an idea,' he said.

'An idea? What kind of idea?' Stevie asked, a little nervously.

'A plan to get me back on the team.'

'A plan? Really?' Stevie said. 'You do know I'm the one who comes up with the plans. That's the way it works with us. You're the action man; I'm the thinker. This messes up our whole relationship dynamic.'

'Relationship dynamic? What are you on about, Stevie?'

'Nothing. Forget it. So what's this plan you've come up with in less than thirty seconds? I'm sure it's really well thought out.'

'Oh, don't worry,' Noah said. 'It's a good one.'

It wasn't a good one.

PLAYER PROFILE

Name: Steven Treacy

Nickname: Little Stevie; IQ; Titch; Midge; Hobbit

Age: 12

Position: I don't play organized football. I'd love to, but I'm not good enough.

Likes: Sports science and match analysis. Computers. Reading. Reading. Reading.

Dislikes: There's not much I don't like. To each their own.

What you like about football: It's only the greatest game ever! I love everything – the crowds, the excitement, the goals. I love the tactics: you have a team playing 4-3-3 and a central defender moves up to midfield and you're attacking with 3-4-3. I love all the skills and tricks, especially the ones the old Brazilian player Ronaldinho used to do. He was ace. I've never told anyone, but I practise them myself every night. Haven't mastered any of them yet, though.

Favourite player: I like Neymar Júnior. Alexis Sanchez is excellent too. And what about Carli Lloyd? It doesn't get much better than a hat-trick in a World Cup final! I like managers too, like Jürgen Klopp and Pep Guardiola.

Favourite goal: That goal when Sergio Agüero won the title for Manchester City years ago. It wasn't the best goal ever, but it was the most exciting one I've seen. I was jumping up and down and I don't even follow City.

Messi or Ronaldo: They're both great.

CHAPTER FOUR

'Football is not about justice. It's a drama – and criminally wrong decisions against you are part and parcel of that'

Pete Davies

'Don't do it,' Stevie said.

It was night-time, a clear and dry night for once, and the sky was sprinkled with hundreds of stars. Noah knew that Stevie was only trying to stop him from doing something he considered to be very, very stupid indeed, but it was easy for Stevie to warn him off. His life was simpler.

He doesn't have to worry about the things I have to, Noah thought.

Noah had spent the last few hours trying to prepare himself. Deep down he knew what he was planning might be filed under the word idiotic and if his sister knew what he was up to then she'd have been furious with him. That's why he hadn't bothered telling her.

It had been almost twelve hours since the meeting with Principal Hegarty, but instead of calming down he had found himself getting angrier and angrier. Even if he had started that fight on the pitch, like the principal claimed, the ban would have been harsh, but when he was the innocent one it made things far worse. Still, he had wavered slightly before he left the house, wondering if what he was about to do was worth the risk. He'd read what he'd written in his mother's notebook again:

I will not fail because I didn't try.

What he was going to do this evening wasn't exactly what he meant when he'd written those words, but he was still going to do whatever it took.

'Noah, please don't do this,' Stevie said for at least the ninth time. 'You're not behaving normally. This isn't the kind of thing someone like you undertakes.'

'Stop going on about it, Stevie,' Noah said. He was dressed from head to toe in black and held a black and yellow beanie hat in his hand.

They passed by the pubs on Tarbuckle Lane, or Hangover Street as it was known locally. A couple of middle-aged men stood outside dragging furiously on their cigarettes.

Noah was growing more and more exasperated with his friend's attitude. He wished he'd never told Stevie about the plan – mentioning it had been a big mistake – but he needed to borrow Stevie's phone if it was going to work and he hadn't been able to come up with a fake reason as to why he needed it quickly enough. That was the trouble with doing things in a bit of a temper – you didn't always plan properly.

'You're not thinking it through,' Stevie whined.

He was having to move fast to keep up with Noah and it was taking its toll on him. Unlike his friend, Stevie was far from fit and his asthma always seemed to hold him back.

'I don't have to think about it. I'm not like you, Stevie. I can't sit around analysing things from every angle until morning comes. I have to follow my gut.'

'Nobody makes plans with their gut.'

'Course they do,' Noah said.

'Only people who make huge mistakes.'

They passed by Dee's Diner, the town's worst fast-food place and a byword for food poisoning. According to one of the local wits, you got a free gift with every burger – a trip to the hospital.

'Listen,' Stevie said. 'If you get caught, then the football scout won't recruit you. There's plenty of talented guys out there to choose from, you know. You need to be better than all of them. You said yourself they won't want someone who's trouble. If they hear what you've been up to, they won't want to touch you with a barge pole.'

'What's a barge pole?' Noah asked.

'It's a long pole that's used to propel a type of boat down a riv– Stop distracting me. I'm not just being cautious, Noah. I'm trying – Noah? Noah? Are you listening to me? Right, I've had enough. We can either do this the easy way or the hard way. Your choice.'

He jogged past Noah and then turned round and placed the palm of his hands against his friend's chest in an effort to stop him from moving any closer to the school.

'What are you doing, Stevie?'

Noah kept walking. Stevie's feet slid across the surface of the footpath as he was pushed backwards. He hadn't even slowed Noah down for a moment.

'I'm stopping you from making a fool of yourself,' he puffed as he glided past Hawk Willis's house.

'Just to be clear, is this the easy way or the hard way?' Noah asked.

Stevie moved aside as Noah continued to stride forward.

'I really should consider joining the gym,' Stevie said. 'That was remarkably feeble.'

He sped up again in an effort to keep pace with his friend. Noah knew that Stevie was only trying to help, but he didn't want any help. This was something he had to do by himself.

'Think of the consequences,' Stevie said.

'If I don't do this, then the consequences will be worse.'

'So you don't get to play in the tournament. It's very disappointing, but you're young and there's lots of clubs—'

'Do you know most of the major clubs recruit players at the age of eight or nine these days? I might be too old already,' Noah said. 'I have to take this chance.'

Stevie stopped in his tracks. 'Too old? Noah, you're twelve.'

'Ryan Mason joined Spurs when he was seven.'

'And Didier Drogba didn't become a professional until he was twenty-one,' Stevie said. He couldn't understand why Noah was so determined to make it as a professional footballer all of a sudden. His friend had always talked about it as something he'd like to do, but in the last couple of months it had become an obsession.

'Yeah, well, I need this.'

Part of him wanted to explain why, to tell Stevie that he needed it to make things better, but he couldn't. He held it all back. It was easier that way.

'Just wait a moment, Noah. What happens if you get caught? At best you get expelled, at worst you get sent to a young offenders' institution. You'll probably end up sharing a room with a guy named The Bludgeoner. You'll want to fit in with that crowd to avoid some terrible beatings so you'll get one of those awful forehead tattoos. When you get released, you won't be able to get a job with a tattoo like that so you'll drift into a life of crime. Your family will disown you and you'll have no friends. You'll end up eating nothing but junk food so you'll be obese before you know it. And you're sure to lose your teeth in a fight so—'

It was Noah's turn to be stopped in his tracks. 'What *are* you on about?'

'I'm not really sure. I think my imagination got away from me there, but, still, my point remains the same: you're going down a bad road, Noah.'

Noah knew that Stevie was only trying to protect him, but boy, was it annoying.

They'd almost reached the end of the town now. Only every second streetlight seemed to be working and just to make things gloomier a bank of clouds drifted across the sky extinguishing the stars like someone snuffing out candles. Stevie shivered and pulled his jacket closer around him as they took a left past the library and headed towards the end of a quiet street. All the businesses along the row were shut for the night. There was no sign of life. A few of the premises had metal shutters to stop people from breaking in. Graffiti had been sprayed across their ridged surfaces. Noah and Stevie reached the school's entrance. The barred metal gate preventing their progress was more than two metres tall. A stone grey wall, just as high, ran round the perimeter of the school.

'See, you won't even be able to get in. That gate's locked at six every evening without fail and the wall's too high to climb. We might as well go home now and try to come up with a better plan. I'm sure there are lots of other things we can do,' Stevie said.

Noah didn't appear to hear him. He ran his fingers along the wall as if searching for a secret button, then he looked up at the gate.

'I think I can get over it,' he said.

'Noah, don't do it. Mr Hegarty will find out if you've been in there. Someone will see the sensor light or an alarm will go off. Something will go wrong.'

'No, it won't. I'll get in the window, head for his office, film the tablet's video on your phone and leave straight away. Nobody'll even know I've been there. I'll be in and out in less than a minute.'

Stevie began to shake his head. 'Very bad plan,' he muttered.

'Then I'll put the clip of me getting beaten up online. After that it's just a matter of getting the video to go viral. People love watching others getting hurt, so that'll be no problem. When everyone in town sees that I didn't fight back and shouldn't have been banned, then Hegarty will be forced to put me back in the squad.'

'There are so many variables and uncontrollable events in that scenario I don't know where to begin.'

'If you're saying it won't work, you're wrong. Now please go home, Stevie. Your mum will go mad if she finds you're out at this time of night.'

'It is rather late, but she's at her book club and Dad's watching his World at War programmes so I think I'll be OK,' he said.

'Wish me luck,' Noah said.

He hopped on to the gate, grabbed one of the metal bars and easily hauled himself up to the top. As he swung over the other side, the hem of his jeans got caught on a small metal spike. He wriggled free, ripping the end of the jeans, then dropped to the ground on the far side of the gate, landing softly.

Noah put on the beanie hat and pulled the ends of it down, stretching it over his face until it covered his head completely. Stevie's eyes widened when he saw the square yellow figure with the stick arms and legs emblazoned on the hat.

'You're breaking into the school while wearing a SpongeBob SquarePants hat?'

'It's the only one I could find. I don't normally wear hats,' Noah said.

'I'm going to upgrade this from Very Bad Plan to Worst Plan Ever.'

Noah had cut out holes for his eyes and mouth, but they were slightly askew so that he could only use one or the other at a time. He had to choose between breathing or seeing.

'Go home, Stevie. Go home before you get into trouble.'

Noah was already scarpering up the long path that led to the school. As soon as he was out of sight and the sound of his footsteps had begun to fade, Stevie realized how quiet it was when he was alone. It gave him the creeps, which as far as he was concerned was only one step down from the heebie-jeebies. Tree limbs creaked even though there was no wind. He could hear his own breathing and the sound of his heart gently beating against his chest. He didn't like being here, not one little bit. What if his father suddenly decided to check on him? If he found out he wasn't in his room, he'd be on to the police immediately. What if the police started searching for him? He'd seen half an episode of *CSI* once. With their resources, they'd have him tracked down in minutes. And they'd find him helping Noah break into the school. Nobody would believe he'd tried to stop him. His life would be over. Over! Sure, Noah was only trying to fix an injustice, but good luck arguing that when you get to court. Legally, the case would be on very shaky ground.

Calm down, Stevie, he told himself. You're freaking out. Nothing's going to go wrong – you just worry too much. You always have. But when he heard another noise, which made him jump, he gave up on trying to be brave. He pushed the gate open and followed Noah up the path. It was only when he was halfway towards the school building that he realized that the gate should have been locked.

CHAPTER FIVE

*‘ They're the second-best team in the world and there's
no higher praise than that ’* Kevin Keegan

Noah stopped when he reached the hedged area that surrounded
the school's vegetable garden. The garden was tucked away in a
corner within sight of the main building. He'd heard something.
He ducked down low so that he was well hidden from sight. The
yard where they played football at lunchtime was empty. He
was sure whatever it was he'd heard had come from beyond the
prefabs, the temporary buildings on the other side of the yard
from the school. He was wondering if it was just his imagination
when he heard the wheezing off to his right.

'Stevie,' he said. 'Over here.'

'Where's here? It's not exactly bright tonight.'

Noah moved to the edge of the garden, into the space
between the two thick hedges that acted as an entrance. His
friend smiled with relief when he saw Noah's outline in the
darkness, and followed him in.

'I heard something. I think there might be someone out
there,' Noah said.

'Then why are you talking so loudly?' Stevie whispered

furiously. 'What if it's a roving gang of axe murderers?'

'And they've decided to wait for victims in a closed school, late at night, in a town in the middle of nowhere, in the hope that someone just might turn up?'

Stevie took a blast on his inhaler. 'OK, fair point, but what if it's Kevin McCooley or one of his brothers?'

Noah hadn't thought of that. The last thing he wanted was to get caught, but the second last would be a run-in with the McCooleys. In the moment's silence they heard footsteps. Noah and Stevie ducked down behind the hedge. It would be enough to hide them from anyone's view unless the intruders had a sudden fancy to do a spot of night-time gardening. A few seconds later, they heard low, mumbling voices.

Before Stevie could stop him, Noah was crawling on his hands and knees across the cold ground. He reached the gap between the hedges and leaned out for a better look. There were two of them coming from the football pitch behind the prefab. As they passed the entrance to the main building, they accidentally activated the sensor light. The beam of light radiated about ten metres, but didn't quite reach the vegetable garden. It did reveal the two intruders, though, and Noah recognized them at once. He wasn't sure of their names, but they were in his year at school.

'It's that Dublin guy and that friend he's always hanging around with,' Noah said.

The two boys in question – Darren Nolan and Sunday Anishe – hadn't realized that there were some people lurking in the undergrowth and they reacted badly when they heard Noah's voice and saw the masked figure in black lying on the ground.

They screamed like babies.

When Stevie heard the screams, his reaction was involuntary: he screamed too.

'Quiet,' Noah shouted, removing his SpongeBob beanie.

Stevie stopped immediately and Sunday's and Darren's screams petered out to a whimper.

'Darren. Sunday. It's me. Steven Treacy.'

Their horror-struck faces relaxed immediately. Neither of them could imagine anyone or anything that was less frightening in this world than Little Stevie Treacy.

'IQ. You nearly gave us a heart attack,' Darren laughed with relief when Stevie emerged from his hiding place.

'I didn't nearly have a heart attack,' Sunday said. 'I wasn't scared at all.'

'Then why did you scream?'

'I was joining in and being a part of things,' Sunday said. 'Nobody likes to be left out.'

'Sunday and Darren, this is Noah,' Stevie said.

'We know him,' Sunday said. 'We were in the school trials with you, but you were the only one from our year who made the team.'

'Oh, yeah, I remember you now,' said Noah.

The truth was he barely recognized them. He'd guessed that Darren was originally from Dublin because he had an accent, and he sometimes saw Sunday around town and thought that he was a football fan because he always seemed to be wearing a Nigerian football jersey with the name MUSA on the back, but if he was asked to list one other thing he knew about either of them he'd have drawn a complete blank.

'What are you two doing here so late at night?' Stevie asked.

'What are you on about? It's only quarter past nine,' Sunday replied.

'You know what I mean.'

Sunday and Darren glanced at each other, as if they were trying to decide whether or not they should tell him their big, dark secret.

'It's just—' Darren began.

'Don't tell him. We'll look like cowardly fools,' Sunday said.

'Stevie's cool. He won't tell anyone,' Darren said.

Sunday shrugged his shoulders and raised the palms of his hands up, as if to say, I warned you – now I'm out of it.

'We're neighbours, Sunday and me. We both live on the College Wood estate. About two weeks ago, we saw this guy, a couple of years older than us, picking on a little kid. The kid was crying—'

'He was bawling his eyes out. Snot was flying out of his nose. Darren and me went over and said to the bully: "Man, if you don't leave that child alone you will have to deal with us." He walked away and we thought that was the end of it.'

'Except it wasn't. The next day he came back with about fifteen friends.'

'What did you do?'

'We ran as fast as we could till we were out of sight. We heard that he was going to get us the next time he saw us, so we

57

decided to lie low for a couple of weeks until it all blows over,' Darren said.

'If it blows over,' Sunday said.

'So now we avoid going out around the estate. When we get sick of being stuck at home, we sneak out here and have a kickabout. We played too long tonight and lost the ball when it started getting dark. We'd just given up searching for it when we bumped into the two of you.'

'Who threatened you?' Noah asked.

'They called him Whacker or something like that.'

'Whacker Ryan,' Noah said. 'I know him. He has the brains of—'

'An addled sheep,' Stevie said.

'So, what are you doing here?' Darren asked.

Stevie explained their situation as the newcomers listened intently.

'That is stupid,' Sunday said when Stevie had finished relaying his tale.

'I know. How could Hegarty have me kicked me off the team for something so minor?' Noah said, glad of the support.

'No, not that. That's bad luck because playing in a World Cup would be amazing. Your *plan* is stupid,' Sunday said.

'Thank you,' Stevie said, throwing his hands in the air. 'I'm glad someone agrees with me. I've been trying to make him see sense for the last half hour.'

'So, that's why you've got that *Spy Kids* vibe going on,' Darren said, nodding at Noah's clothing.

'I don't care what anyone says. I'm going to get back into the squad.'

'By breaking and entering? You'll get expelled.'

'Only if I get caught. And I won't get caught.'

'No offence, Noah. You're a good footballer, but you never struck me as someone who was particularly bright.'

'You say no offence, Sunday, but it is kind of offensive.'

'I think my pal here is saying that you might not have thought it through. Even if you do manage to get in you don't know the alarm code, so the alarm will go off. One of the key-holders lives in that estate over there,' Darren said, pointing towards the back of the building. 'If he's quick, you'll have less than two minutes to find Hegarty's office in the dark, then somehow unlock his door. What are you using to unlock the doors?'

'I left one of the windows in my class open after school,' Noah said. 'I pretended I forgot a book and sneaked back in when the cleaners were there, then made it look like the window was closed.'

'Do you think they don't check all the windows are shut before they leave?' Sunday asked, a little scornfully.

Noah had had enough of them. They were just standing there talking and being pessimistic. It was a waste of time when what was needed was action. He took off, rushing past them, racing towards the school entrance.

He felt someone's hand grab the collar of his jumper. Noah was stunned. He was fast himself *and* he had a head start, which meant the guy who'd grabbed him was very quick indeed.

'Just stop it, mate,' Darren said, as Sunday caught hold of

Noah's arm. Noah tried to shrug them off, but their grip was too powerful. He struggled on, slowed down almost to a snail's pace, but still dragging himself towards the school's front door.

'Use your head, Noah Murphy. Don't be an idiot,' Sunday said.

Noah was still a good fifteen metres away from his target when, without any warning, he began to feel ridiculous. The red mist that had been hanging over him for the last twelve hours evaporated suddenly and he saw things clearly. No matter how unjust Hegarty had been, what he was trying to do now was wrong. He wasn't the sort of person who broke into a school. It wasn't who he was. The last bit of fight drained from him and he stopped struggling.

'I . . . er—' he began.

He felt himself moving backwards as Darren and Sunday hauled him away from the door. He tried to tell them that he wasn't going to go through with it, but now one of their arms was across his face and all that escaped from his lips was a series of unintelligible squeaks.

'We can't let you do it. You seem like a decent guy. Can't let you get yourself into that sort of mess,' Darren said.

The heels of Noah's trainers scraped along the tarmac as the dual force of Darren and Sunday pulled him backwards and soon he found himself back in the vegetable garden again.

Darren released his hold on Noah. 'Don't run. You know we'll catch you.'

'You're fast. You must be the fastest in our year,' Noah gasped.

'I'm quick, but I'm no Hawk Willis,' Darren replied, just as the sensor light blinked off.

Before anyone else spoke they heard the rumble of a car in the distance. It came to a stop, the engine still running. And then they heard a creak as the metal gates at the end of the driveway swung open. They looked at each other. Somebody was coming in.

They weren't doing anything wrong, perhaps a bit of light trespassing, no more than that, but instinct told them to hide. They immediately ducked down behind the hedge, keeping well out of sight.

Noah caught a glimpse of the car as it whizzed past the entrance to the garden and pulled up right outside the main door, activating the sensor light again. He knew who it was at once.

'Hegarty,' he whispered.

Noah's stomach began to churn when he realized what trouble he'd have been in if the lads hadn't stopped him. He'd have been caught red-handed breaking into the office

by Hegarty himself. They'd saved him.

Three of the four teenagers used their fingers to create tiny gaps in the hedge. They peered through as their principal climbed out of the car, then belched and broke wind simultaneously. Sunday clamped a hand over his mouth to stop himself from laughing. Noah and Darren bit their tongues, but Stevie remained stony-faced. He'd never found bodily functions to be amusing and he wasn't about to start now when they were right on the verge of being in a world of trouble. Mr Hegarty unlocked the front door and disappeared into the school.

'Let's leg it,' Darren whispered.

'I'm with you,' Sunday agreed.

'If I get out of here safely, I promise I will never, ever do a foolish or dangerous thing for as long as I live,' Stevie whispered.

They were just about to make their move when they heard another car approach the gate. A moment later a red Ford Fiesta drove past the garden's entrance and Stevie's expression changed. He recognized it immediately. He pushed himself forward between Sunday and Darren and prised his own viewing gap in the hedge. The car door of the new arrival opened and Arthur Slugsley, the man Noah and Stevie had presumed was a football scout, got out. Noah glanced at his best friend and knew that they were both thinking the same thing: *What is he doing here?*

Slugsley looked around impatiently, his eyes darting this way and that. A minute later the principal emerged from the school. He had a small package under his arm.

'Mr Hegarty?' Slugsley asked.

'Mr Slugsley,' the principal replied. 'We finally meet in person.'

Slugsley reached inside his overcoat pocket and took out a thick brown envelope and a package of a similar size to the one Hegarty held. The principal's face lit up when Slugsley handed them over. He laid the package down on the car bonnet and handed the one he'd removed from the school to Slugsley. Hegarty opened the brown envelope and flicked through the contents.

'This isn't the full amount. It isn't even ten per cent of it. What's going on here?' Hegarty said, his voice rising.

'Your work isn't over yet, Mr Hegarty. When our project is successful, you'll receive the rest,' Slugsley replied.

'But that's over a month away.'

'With all due respect, Mr Hegarty, how is that my problem?'

Hegarty's cheeks puffed in and out. He looked furious.

'We'll be in touch,' Slugsley said.

He was back in the car and had driven off in less than ten seconds, as if he couldn't wait to get out of there. Hegarty watched him drive away, then turned his attention to the envelope again. He looked inside and made an unpleasant face.

'*Ah-choo!*'

The sneeze was out of Stevie before he'd realized it was on its way. He didn't even know he was allergic to the hedge.

The principal looked in their direction immediately.

'Who's there?' he boomed.

The four boys held their breath.

'Show yourselves now. Don't make me come over there,' Hegarty continued.

Little Stevie began to stand up, but Noah caught him in time and dragged him back down.

'What are you doing?' he whispered.

Hegarty walked towards them. He was big and bulky, but he was moving quickly. He shoved the envelope into his pocket. Noah wasn't sure what to do. There was only one way out of the vegetable garden and if they moved now Hegarty would spot them. There was no way he couldn't. They were trapped and it was his fault. Darren and Sunday would have been at home ages ago if they hadn't had to stop him from breaking in.

'Listen,' he whispered. 'No point all of us getting in trouble. I'll go down there and distract him. When he's giving out to me, you lot sneak off.'

'Great, that's a good plan,' Stevie wheezed.

'No, it's not,' Sunday said. 'You didn't force us to be here. We're all in this together. Nobody moves.'

'Right, that's a good point too,' Stevie agreed.

Noah smiled. They were good lads. Still, that didn't mean he had to do what they told him.

Hegarty was only ten metres away now. He was puffing with the exertion.

'If I have to come in there the punishment will be double what it will be if you come out here now,' he panted.

Noah got to his feet. He was about to accept his fate when the sensor light blinked out. Mr Hegarty had moved too far away from it and it wasn't picking up any motion. The yard was plunged into darkness again.

The four lads didn't need a second invitation to escape. They turned and ran along the side of the hedge then sprinted down the driveway, Noah pulling Stevie along by the arm.

'I can see you. I know who you are and your parents will be receiving a call from me first thing tomorrow morning,' Mr Hegarty bellowed, even though he couldn't see a thing.

He turned and rushed back towards the light, hoping to activate it and catch a glimpse of the intruders. Unfortunately for him, he tumbled forward and landed on the tarmac, ripping the knee of his best trousers. He scrambled to his feet again and rushed towards the school. The light burst into life. Mr Hegarty looked back up to where he guessed the boys had headed, but there was no sign of anyone. They were gone.

PLAYER PROFILE

Name: Darren Nolan

Nickname: Dar; Nolester. They're rubbish nicknames. I'd like something better, but it's not like you can give yourself a nickname, is it? That'd be embarrassing.

Age: 12

Position: Right-back is where I play. Lots of people think it's boring, but I like it. You get to attack and defend, cross the ball, put in tackles and you're always involved in the game.

Likes: Twister ice cream and Charlie Higson books.

Player you're most like: Don't know, but it'd be deadly if people thought I was like Seamus Coleman. He's class.

Favourite player: Tough one. I never saw Maradona or Zidane play because I'm too young, so I suppose it'll have to be someone from the last few years. I like some of the Borussia Dortmund players and I support Spurs, St Pat's, PSG, Juventus, Valencia, Santos, Boca Juniors and New York City FC, so it'll probably be someone from one of those clubs. I dunno, maybe – hang on, not any of those – Gareth Bale. Yeah, that's who I'll go for – Gareth Bale. A Spurs great, even though he doesn't play for us any more. And Harry Kane is unbelievable. Oh, I nearly forgot about Paul Pogba – he's excellent too. There are just too many good players to choose from.

Favourite goal: Lionel Messi's goal in that Copa del Rey final against Athletic Bilbao. He dribbled past everyone from the halfway line. It was AMAZING.

Messi or Ronaldo: MESSI!

CHAPTER SIX

'Ian Rush, deadly ten times out of ten, but that wasn't one of them'

Peter Drury

Noah barely slept that night. There were too many thoughts running around his head. Why was the scout meeting Hegarty at the school late at night? What was in the envelope? Was it money? And, if so, what was he giving him money for? It didn't make any sense as far as he could see. In the end, though, he decided there was only one question he needed to worry about: how was he going to get back on the team? There were just over two days left before the World Cup competition deadline. He had to do something now.

There hadn't been time to discuss his options on the way home the previous night. Sunday and Darren had said their goodbyes and raced back to College Wood while Stevie had spent most of the journey fretting about Hegarty calling him into his office the following morning, despite Noah's assurances that he couldn't have recognized them.

'Of course he recognized me,' Stevie had said. 'I have a very distinctive running style. I was called into his office for the first time yesterday. I broke into the school tonight. I'm on a

67

downward spiral, Noah. I'll be in a biker gang by next Tuesday the way things are going.'

Distinctive running style or not, Hegarty didn't call them into his office, so Noah assumed they must have got away with it. He didn't hear a word any of his teachers said in class that morning. He spent the whole time thinking of ways to get back into the team. By lunchtime he'd come up with a total of zero. Luckily, Stevie had come up with three.

'The entry forms for the tournament have to be in by five o'clock on Friday. Option one is go straight to the source,' Stevie said.

By source, he meant Noah's former teammates. Which is why at lunchtime that day Noah called an unofficial meeting of the St Killian's squad in an empty classroom while Stevie stood guard outside in the corridor. Only eight of the players turned up and Noah guessed from the looks on their faces that most of them were only there out of politeness.

'I know you don't want to miss the tournament, Murphy, and I'm sorry that you're going to, but what are we supposed to do about it?' Bestie Keenan said.

He was a midfielder with exquisite skills; sometimes he'd dribble the ball past a player, then go back and do it again and again, just for the fun of it.

'I was thinking you could have a word with the coach.'

'A couple of us mentioned it to him already, but he said his hands were tied and he couldn't put you back in the squad even if he wanted to. It's Hegarty's decision,' the tall centre-back Rob Gillespie said. 'Sorry, mate.'

'Maybe you could tell him that you won't play in the tournament unless he puts me back in the team?' Noah said. 'You could go on strike to show your support.'

Before anyone had the chance to reply, they were distracted by the sound of a scuffle outside. And then Jim Reynolds was at the door. Stevie the bouncer was no match for the powerful forward.

'Why on earth would we want to go on strike?' Reynolds asked.

'Hey, Jim,' Noah said a little warily. 'Because we're a team and we're supposed to stick together?'

At the best of times, Reynolds was a disagreeable character, but on a day like this, when someone he disliked was in trouble, he was unbearable.

'Don't "hey" me,' Reynolds said. 'You've been kicked off the team and now you're trying to wreck things for everyone else by dragging us into it. Some teammate you are. You're the one who messed up, so take your punishment like a man.'

'I didn't mess up. I didn't start that fight,' Noah said. Jim was getting under his skin, but he was trying not to show it. 'You all saw the guy attack me.'

'We'd love to help you,' Sean McDonagh said. 'But we were celebrating Jim's goal. We didn't see what happened.'

'And I can't see further than two metres without me glasses,' Terry Sweeney said.

'You heard them, Murphy. They didn't see it and nobody believes a word you say anyway. Now get lost, this is our classroom, not a crèche for little kids.'

Noah tried his best to change their minds over the course of the next few minutes, but in the end he had to give up. It was no use.

'Looks like we're on to option two,' Stevie said as they strode down the corridor a few minutes later.

Noah couldn't blame his teammates. They all wanted to play in the tournament too. Maybe they didn't need it the way he did, but who'd want to miss out on the chance of playing in a World Cup? He'd been asking too much of them. The way Hegarty had been acting lately, anyone who backed Noah was likely to be banned as well. At least they'd been pleasant and honest about it. He liked most of his teammates; Jim was the only one who'd got under his skin. Ninety per cent of the goals he'd scored were from Noah's passes. Whoever replaced him in the team wouldn't be able to replicate that. He was sure of it. Jim needed him even if he didn't realize it.

He's a grade A moron, Noah thought.

Option two was just as successful as option one. Stevie had managed to get a phone number for Brick, the Clydeabbey player who had pummelled Noah, hoping to persuade him to contact Mr Hegarty and confess that he had been the one who started, continued and then finished the fight. To Noah's surprise, when he rang Brick he found that he was more than willing to say all that to Hegarty. The only problem was he wanted to be paid two hundred euros to do it.

'I don't have two hundred euro,' Noah said. 'And, you know what, even if I did I wouldn't give it to a balloon-headed idiot like you.'

'Very diplomatic. That's bound to win him over,' Stevie whispered. He added in an enthusiastic thumbs up for good measure.

'No, wait, sorry, I didn't mean to call you an idi—'

The line went dead.

'That went well,' Stevie said.

'What's option three?' a deflated Noah asked.

Option three involved Simone ringing Mr Hegarty and trying to persuade him to reverse his decision. She was more than happy to try especially since she had almost been as outraged as Noah when he told her what had happened, although he had neglected to mention his attempt to break in to the school. That wouldn't have gone down well at all. When she met Noah and Stevie at the coffee shop where she was waitressing that afternoon she seemed down in the dumps and admitted that her attempts had failed.

'I don't want to say anything bad about your principal in front of you, but that man is a horrible, miserable excuse for a human being,' she said.

'Glad you held your tongue,' Stevie said as he eyed up a caramel slice.

'What's the next option on the list?' Noah asked.

'That's all I have, I'm afraid,' Stevie said. A customer called for attention and Simone went to get him another cup of coffee.

'You can come up with more ideas, Stevie. You're the smartest guy I know.'

'That's true. I am exceptionally smart.' He thought for a moment. 'What about a court injunction?'

'What's that?'

'We ask a judge to stop Mr Hegarty from kicking you off the team while the court reviews the case against you. My dad says the law moves as quickly as a lazy glacier, so with any luck the tournament will be over before the judge makes his decision. It means you get to play.'

That sounded like a very good idea to Noah, but when Simone returned she shot it down immediately.

'Sorry, Noah. Injunctions cost an absolute fortune and we just can't afford one. We can't even afford to get our boiler fixed.'

'I could get a part-time job to help pay for it.'

'There's not a job in town that would pay you enough money to go to court in the next twenty-four hours,' his sister said.

Noah began to pace up and down the small shop much to the annoyance of some of the customers. This is torture, he thought. He had to find a way into the tournament. There had to be something he hadn't thought of yet.

And then, out of nowhere, an idea popped into his head. He was stunned by its arrival and moments later when his surprise wore off he realized that he was impressed too.

'It's a schools' competition,' he said.

'It is,' Stevie said, not quite sure where Noah was going with this.

'Hegarty's the principal of our school – that's why he can ban me. But he's not the principal of every school.'

'You mean—'

'What if we set up our own school? You could be the principal and you could make sure I was in the squad.'

When Stevie heard Noah's words, he stopped dead.

'That's genius,' he whispered. A faraway look came into his eyes.

Noah had seen that look before. It meant that Stevie was in deep thought. He was blocking out all sights, sounds and smells to stop anyone or anything from distracting him.

'Everyone be quiet. Stevie's thinking,' Noah called out.

The cappuccino machine hissed. Cups clinked. Conversations continued. Nobody paid Noah the slightest bit of attention.

He took a seat across from an elderly lady. He remained there for a couple of minutes biting his nails until Stevie snapped out of his trance.

'Anything?' Noah asked hopefully.

'Don't know yet,' Stevie said, his voice flat and low. 'I've got to go home and see if I can work this out.'

'You do that. Go home and do whatever it is you have to do,' Noah said. 'I can bring you cups of tea, biscuits, law books, towels. Whatever you need.'

Stevie didn't seem to hear a word Noah said. He wandered out of the shop almost in a daze. As he watched Stevie leave, Noah crossed his fingers and hoped against hope that his friend would be able to come up with something.

The elderly woman he'd been sitting across from leaned towards him and smiled.

'If you're just going to sit there like a big lump with a gormless expression on your face, then you might as well make yourself useful. Here's a fiver. Get me a milky coffee and a scone with raspberry jam,' she said. 'And don't even think of stealing me change. I know how much it costs. To the exact penny.'

Noah sighed as he headed towards the counter. I really have to get out of this town, he thought.

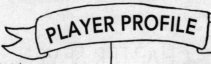

Name: Sunday Anishe

Nickname: Happy. My dad's friend came up with it after an old TV programme theme tune – 'Sunday, Monday, Happy Days'. I hate it. My brother's nickname is Thor. That's much cooler.

Age: 12 ¾

Position: Left-winger

Likes: Southampton. They're my favourite team. Nobody else in school follows them; I like that. Superhero films. Astronomy. Physics. Pizza.

Dislikes: My nickname. Chips.

Player you're most like: The Brazilian player Bernard, if he wasn't as fast as he is. I'm not a slowcoach, but I'm not very pacy either.

Favourite player: My father always tells me Jay-Jay Okocha was the best player in the world, but I like Ahmed Musa. He was brilliant against Argentina in the World Cup back in 2014. He's been my favourite player since.

Favourite goal: The old Southampton legend Matt Le Tissier scored some unbelievable goals. Hard to choose which one was the best. I look at a lot of goals on the internet.

Messi or Ronaldo: Messi. Ronaldo is good, but Messi is unbelievable.

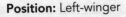

CHAPTER SEVEN

ONE DAY, NINETEEN HOURS AND FORTY-THREE MINUTES TO TOURNAMENT DEADLINE

'*The person who said winning isn't everything, never won anything*' Mia Hamm

'I told him we should set up our own school and enter a team in the competition and Stevie said it was a genius idea and he's practically a genius himself so that's genius multiplied by genius, which makes it like, I don't know, one of the greatest ideas ever. Up there with the invention of fire and stuff like that.'

'Nobody invented fire, Noah,' Simone sighed. 'And we'll just have to agree to disagree on the school idea.' She thought that setting up a brand-new school sounded like the most far-fetched plan she'd ever heard, but at least her brother was in a better mood now that he had some hope again.

'You'll see, Sim. When Stevie gets here and shows us his plans, you'll be the one apologizing to me.'

No matter what his sister said, Noah was feeling optimistic about Stevie's chances of getting him back into the tournament. And his mood had improved even more when he'd spoken to his dad for almost twenty minutes on Skype earlier. He'd cracked up laughing when his father had told him a story about his lunch being stolen by a red kangaroo. It was the first time they'd had a laugh together since Christmas and it made Noah more determined than ever to bring his dad home.

It was a couple of minutes before nine o'clock and the pasta was bubbling in a big pot on the hob.

The smell of Bolognese is possibly the nicest smell in the world, Noah thought.

He was really looking forward to eating a decent home-cooked meal. Then the doorbell rang.

Noah was surprised. Apart from a monthly inspection from his Aunt Margaret they rarely had visitors, especially at this time of night.

'Who's that?' he wondered aloud.

'That's my friend, Dave. He's here to fix the boiler and in return we're going to give him his dinner. Be nice,' Simone said, smoothing down her hair.

Dave? Noah had no idea who that was.

It turned out that Dave was ridiculously tall. He seemed to stretch up to the heavens, or he would have if the hall ceiling hadn't got in the way. He was the biggest human being Noah had ever met. The hairiest too. He had a huge mop of curly brown hair and a beard that could only be described as magnificent. If Noah had been asked at that moment to describe Dave in one word, then that word would have been 'yeti'.

It was only when Simone elbowed Noah in the ribs for the third time that Noah realized he'd been gawping and that his sister had been speaking to him.

'What did you say?' he asked, blinking furiously.

The yeti stuck out an arm, took Noah's hand in one of his

great meaty paws and shook it gently.

'Nice to meet you. I'm Dave,' he said through the beard.

The few patches of skin that were visible were as white as alabaster. It was difficult to tell Dave's age beneath the tangle of hair, but he sounded as if he was around twenty, which Noah was fairly certain was Simone's age. It was only when they began to head towards the kitchen that he noticed Dave was carrying a bunch of fresh flowers.

'Why are you bringing flowers to do some plumbing work?' Noah asked.

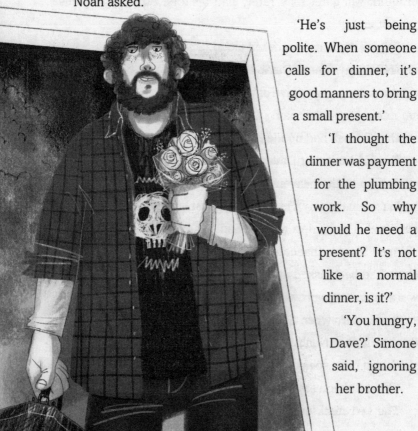

'He's just being polite. When someone calls for dinner, it's good manners to bring a small present.'

'I thought the dinner was payment for the plumbing work. So why would he need a present? It's not like a normal dinner, is it?'

'You hungry, Dave?' Simone said, ignoring her brother.

Dave grinned. 'I'm always hungry.'

I'm not surprised, Noah thought. All the energy required to move a body that size? He must eat a wheelbarrow full of porridge for breakfast.

Dinner was good. Better than anything Noah had tasted in ages. He would have licked his plate clean if he thought he'd get away with it.

'Did you know that you're the first person I've ever met called Noah?' Dave said in between mouthfuls. 'Is it because of the ark?'

'No, it's not because of the ark, Dave.'

Noah had heard that one before. There were plenty of jokes about his name from people who thought they were funny and original. They weren't either of those things.

'Sorry, that was dumb,' Dave mumbled into his beard. 'I'm such an idiot sometimes.'

Noah smiled. Despite having an unerring ability to say the wrong thing, there was something likeable about this huge guy.

'Simone said you're a plumber,' Noah said, changing the subject.

'Not really. I mean I do some handyman work, but I wouldn't say—'

'Stop annoying him, Noah,' Simone interrupted.

'I'm not annoying him. I only asked him a question. You don't mind, Dave, do you?'

'No, no, ask away,' Dave said.

'Take no notice of my sister. She talks to me like she's my mother sometimes, but she's not.'

'Your mam's not going to join us tonight?' Dave asked.

Simone and Noah looked at each other. Neither of them knew what to say. They were distracted by the sound of Dave's jaw dropping open and the smack as he slapped his forehead with his hand.

'Your mam's not here because she's dead. Grace told me not to mention it. I'm so sorry,' he said. He looked genuinely distraught.

'It's all right,' Simone said sympathetically. 'Anyone can make a mistake.'

'Not anyone. Just me. I always say the wrong thing when I'm nervous. Always. I don't mean to. It just sort of pops out before my brain has time to stop it. Like with the ark thing. I didn't mean to insult you . . . I'm sorry. I think I should go,' Dave said, edging his way out of the chair.

It took him some time to unfold his limbs and Noah couldn't help but gawk again.

The awkward moment was forgotten when they heard a crash followed by a huge yelp coming from the back garden. Noah was the first to react. He was out of the door before Simone had managed to shout at him to stop.

'Noah, don't. It could be a burglar.'

It wasn't a burglar – it was Stevie. He'd been making his way to the back door through the small garden and in the darkness had managed to stumble into two wheelie bins, one of which had somehow landed on top of him, pinning him to the ground. That wasn't the reason he'd almost fainted, though. The reason for that was the sudden appearance of the big, hairy unknown face that now loomed over Noah's shoulder.

'Don't worry, Stevie. It's just Simone's friend, Dave,' Noah said.

'Oh, thank goodness for that. For a moment I thought it was something – Well . . .'

'Inhuman?' Dave said as he easily lifted the wheelie bin off Stevie and set it right side up again.

'No, no, no, I mean it was—'

'Don't worry, I get that all the time,' Dave chuckled. 'One of the lads at work even calls me Yeti.'

'I don't see that,' Stevie said a little too hurriedly as he clambered to his feet.

'Me neither,' Noah said. 'Can't understand why anyone would think that.'

'What's going on out here?' Simone asked as she arrived in the back garden. 'Stevie? What are you doing sneaking round the back in the dark?'

'I'm on a covert mission, Simone. Can't be spotted out in the street unless I want to be grounded until my twenty-fifth birthday.'

'Your mother doesn't know you're here?'

'My mother still tries to put toddler milk in my breakfast cereal. She'd have a heart attack if she knew I was here. Still, I must say I find all the sneaking around exhilarating. I never thought it would be my kind of thing, but after the other night—'

He stopped in mid-sentence when he saw Noah shake his head rapidly. The last thing Noah needed was his sister finding out what he'd been doing at school.

'Right, er, anyway, the reason I came here disturbing your evening is . . .'

Stevie took out a bundle of typed A4 papers from his backpack. They were bound together with a silver bulldog clip.

'What's that?' Noah asked.

'This is your salvation. I've figured out a way to get you into the tournament.'

CHAPTER EIGHT

'The future of football is feminine'

Sepp Blatter

'I told you we'd be setting up our own school,' Noah shouted as Simone bundled him back indoors before the neighbours complained about all the noise.

This was brilliant news. A way to get back into the tournament. He could hardly contain his excitement. Energy surged through him like a jolt of electricity. He wanted to sprint around the kitchen high-fiving everyone.

'Our own school?' Stevie chuckled. 'No, no, no. That's ridiculous and impossible.'

Noah wasn't impressed by his sister's I-told-you-so face.

'But when you came up with that off-the-wall idea earlier it did spark the synapses,' Stevie continued. He pointed at the folder he'd taken from his backpack as they all settled round the kitchen table. 'That's a printout of the Schools' World Cup qualifying tournament rules.'

'How is that going to help?' Noah asked, his excitement fading a little. He couldn't see where Stevie was going with this.

'Well, I've spent the last six hours thinking about our

83

problem. We've been focusing on the unstoppable force that is our principal. He, and he alone, has the power to get you back in the squad. But for some reason, yet to be determined, he doesn't want you there. Your school idea made me realize that the only way to solve this problem is to remove Principal Hegarty from the equation.'

'You want to kill our principal?'

Simone sighed. Even Dave shook his head sadly.

'Yes, Noah. I've hatched a grisly murder plan,' Stevie said. 'Meanwhile, back in the real world, I read through the rulebook again and again until I discovered something. Something interesting. The rules say that you have to play for a school in your area, which means you have to play for a school in Carraig Cruach.'

'That's the problem, Stevie. The only school in Carraig Cruach won't let me play for them,' Noah said.

He was becoming irritated now. He didn't like all this talk of rules and regulations. He wanted action.

'Except that it doesn't specifically say that you have to be enrolled in that school.'

'What difference does that make?' Noah asked.

'Well, if the rules said that you had to be a student at the school you represented in the competition then you could only play for St Killian's,' Stevie said.

'But I still have to play for a school in the area and since the only school in Carraig Cruach is our school, then the only team I can play for is St Killian's.'

He couldn't understand what Stevie was trying to say.

'Except St Killian's isn't the only school in the area.'

Simone laughed. 'I like the way you're thinking, Stevie.'

'Thanks,' Stevie said with a smile.

'Oh, right, yeah, good one, little dude. I get it now,' Dave said a few moments later. 'Do you think it'll work?'

'Will what work? Am I the only sane one in the room? St Killian's is the only school here. Unless there's some imaginary or invisible school I've missed. What's going on?'

'Noah, think about it. There's more than one secondary school in Carraig Cruach.'

As far as Noah was concerned there was nothing to think about. It must be all the thinking that Stevie did that had caused him to go mad. He'd always said that thinking too much was bad for you. The only thing he couldn't figure out was why Simone and Dave were playing along with it. It was clear that the only school in town was St Killian's. Sure, there was the girls' school, St Mary's, but that . . . No, wait, no, that couldn't be what he meant.

'Stevie, are you saying what I think you're saying?'

'Depends on what you think I'm saying.'

Noah looked at Stevie. Stevie looked back at him. He looked at Simone. Simone looked at him. He looked at Dave. Dave was probably looking at him, but his hair was hanging over his eyes so it was hard to tell. Noah's eyes widened until widening them any more would have caused his eyeballs to pop out and roll along the dusty linoleum.

'What? You can't be serious.' Noah threw his hands up in the air. 'No, no, no, no, no. Are you really saying that you want me to play for a girls' school?'

That was it? That was the big plan Stevie had spent hours coming up with? It was ridiculous. He was wrong about Stevie being practically a genius. This plan proved that. It was the opposite of genius. It was . . . Noah realized he didn't know what the opposite actually was, but whatever it was, Stevie's plan was definitely it. Yet, at the same time, it was the only plan they had.

'Explain it to me again,' he said, biting at his fingernails.

'The rules don't state that you have to attend a school to play for it. As long as it's in your school area, you're eligible. The organizers probably expect that you'll play for your own school because, you know, normally you would, but whoever wrote the rules wasn't precise enough. They're also ambiguous when it comes to the competition because it doesn't actually say that girls' schools *have* to enter the *girls'* competition,' Stevie said.

'Why would they need to say it? It's just common sense. Girls play in girls' competitions. Boys play in boys' competitions. And I can't play for St Mary's because – in case you hadn't noticed – I'M NOT A GIRL.'

'That's just a technicality,' Stevie said.

'Being male is just a technicality? There's something wrong with you. Something seriously wrong.'

'Look, Noah,' Stevie said, using his calmest tone, a tone so calm it could have soothed a hippo with a toothache. 'I know you're not a girl. You don't need to be a girl.'

'Noah, just listen to Stevie,' Simone said.

Noah's head had begun to hurt. He rubbed his temples.

'OK, this is what I'm proposing,' Stevie began. 'Every school in the country is allowed to enter the tournament. St Mary's haven't entered, so their place is going spare. We take that place. We form our own team and play under the name St Mary's. We are not girls. We don't need to be girls. We don't have to pretend to be girls. All we have to do is get a team together in a day and a half and enter the competition before the deadline passes. Since the rules don't say girls' schools have to play in the girls' competition, we enter the team in the boys' competition. There's lots of boys' schools called St Mary's, so we'll keep our fingers crossed that the organizers won't even notice. Anyway, technically we won't be breaking any rules. Then in six weeks' time you'll play in the tournament.'

Noah took a deep breath and let Stevie's words sink in. It seemed to make sense, but there had to be something he was missing.

'Mr Hegarty's head will explode when he finds out,' Noah said.

'Like a pumpkin that's just been hit with a six-kilo sledgehammer, little dude,' Dave said.

Noah quite liked the idea of getting under Hegarty's skin, but he wasn't so keen on the consequences that would no doubt follow.

'I'll never be able to play for the school again if I do this. He'll make sure I won't. But at the same time . . .'

'There's only just over one day left before the squad lists have to be sent off so unless you've got some other fantastic 'idea up your sleeve then this is going to be your only shot.'

'All right,' Noah said. 'Let me get it clear – we'd be playing for St Mary's School for Girls, but we'd be in the boys' competition.'

'That's it.'

Noah thought about it for a moment. It sounded like a plan. Except there was something wrong. He couldn't quite put his finger on it . . .

'We don't have any players,' he shouted. 'That's what's wrong. How can I play an eleven-a-side football match by myself? We need more than one player, Stevie. We need a team. And guess what? We don't have a team.'

'Don't get stressed, Noah. It'll be fine. We'll ask some of the other lads in school,' Stevie said.

'Don't get stressed? Of course I'm stressed. Who are we going to get? All the good players are in the St Killian's squad. None of them are going to leave and join us. You saw how they reacted when I asked for help. Anyway, they have half a chance of winning in a team that's played together for a year and a half, not one that's been patched together six weeks before the tournament starts.'

'Maybe they wouldn't join, but there are others who would. Carraig Cruach isn't that small a town and there are plenty of kids who'd love to play in a big tournament. They'd have a chance of playing in the World Cup. That's amazing. And there's plenty of them who'd want to play with you. They look up to you.'

'They look up to me?' said Noah, surprised and a bit chuffed.

'Oh yes, they think you're fantastic,' Stevie said. That was a white lie on his part. The only one who really looked up to Noah was him. 'We could get Darren and Sunday. And some of the guys who kick a ball around the yard at lunchtime.'

'My brother, Tony, is football mad,' said Dave. 'I'd say he'd be a definite to play. Although he's only in primary school, he had to stay back a year. Would that be a problem?'

'Not one that I couldn't solve,' Stevie said.

'He might even have a friend or two who'd be interested.'

'Is Tony as big as you?'

'Nearly my height. A lot skinnier, though.'

'He could be good in the air,' Noah said.

'We could ask some of the local businesses to sponsor the team for equipment and things like that,' Simone said.

The mood in the room was improving rapidly.

'And I know a rep for a sportswear company. Elaine Stokes. She's really nice. She might be able to get us a few jerseys on the cheap,' Dave said.

Noah wondered if he was feeling all right because part of him had started to think that this might actually work. It'd be tough and they had very little time to get organized, but you never knew unless you tried. And if it was the only way to get into the tournament then he had to go for it.

'Wait, aren't we forgetting something?' Simone said. 'Something important.'

'I know what you're thinking and I was about to get to that. It's possibly the most important thing of all,' Stevie said.

Noah was perplexed again. They were always talking about things that he hadn't quite figured out just yet. He wondered if they did that just to confuse him.

'What's the important thing?' he asked. 'And just give it to me straight. None of your riddles this time.'

'We can't just play for St Mary's because we feel like it. The principal has to sign the entry forms. We have to get her permission,' Stevie said.

'You mean that if Mrs . . .'

'Power,' Simone said.

'If Mrs Power says no, then we can't enter the competition?'

'That's it,' Stevie said. 'She's our only hope.'

'Well, what are we doing sitting around chatting? Let's get over there and ask her now,' Noah said, grabbing his coat.

He rushed out of the kitchen door. In less than three seconds he was back.

'Ahm, where does she live?'

'We're not going to visit her now. It's far too late. We'll go to the school first thing in the morning,' Simone said.

There was so much to do if their crazy plan was going to work that Noah wanted to get started immediately. But no matter how much he begged and pleaded he couldn't persuade his sister to change her mind. He'd have to wait until the morning.

Dave said he'd make sure Stevie got home safely and an hour later Noah was lying in his bed, once again with far too many thoughts running around his head. He was convinced that with so much to consider there was no way he was going to fall asleep, but a few minutes later he was snoring and Simone had to call him three times the next morning before he woke up.

CHAPTER NINE

THIRTY HOURS, SEVENTEEN MINUTES, FOURTEEN SECONDS TO TOURNAMENT DEADLINE

'Tense and nervous are not the words, though they are the words'   Chris Kamara

Stevie paced up and down the almost empty corridor of St Mary of the Immaculate Conception School for Girls, his perfectly polished black shoes *click-clack*ing on the floor.

'Any chance you could stop doing that, Stevie?' Noah said.

'Sorry. I'm just a bit anxious.'

'Me too,' Noah said. He had hardly any fingernails left after the last few days. 'I wonder what's taking her so long.'

They'd been in the school since eight that morning and Simone had been in the office with Mrs Power for almost twenty minutes already. At first Noah had been confident that Mrs Power was going to say yes to their proposal – after all, he thought, it was no skin off her nose whether they played or not – but the longer Simone stayed in the office the more worried he'd become.

Eventually, when his patience was just about to snap, the office door opened and Simone emerged. Noah couldn't read her expression. She wasn't smiling, but at the same time she didn't look particularly upset either.

'Are we in?' he asked.

'She didn't say no,' Simone said. 'But she didn't say yes either.'

'What does that mean?' Noah asked.

'It seems that she dislikes Mr Hegarty. She didn't say it outright, but I get the impression that she thinks he's a horrible man, a buffoon, and she'd really enjoy upsetting him. You may not believe it, but she has a great sense of humour.'

'Then why won't she agree to what we asked?' Stevie said.

'She wants to talk to you before she makes any decision,' Simone said to Noah.

'Me? Why would she want to talk to me?'

'I don't know, but you'd better get in there because she has lots of things to do and only about five minutes to spare,' Simone said.

Noah was getting used to being in principals' offices. He didn't think he'd ever get used to Mrs Power, though. He couldn't decide if he really liked her or was really frightened of her. She was much smaller and looked a lot more frail than Hegarty, yet she exuded an authority that was at odds with her appearance.

'Welcome, Noah. Your sister has explained your plan to me,' she said, indicating that he should sit down. He did so immediately even though he'd have preferred to remain standing.

'It's not really my plan – it's my friend Stevie's,' Noah muttered.

'Speak up,' Mrs Power said sharply. 'No one likes a mumbler.'

Noah sat straighter in his chair and spoke a little louder. 'Sorry, what I was saying was I can't take credit for the plan, because it—'

'Let's hurry this up, Noah,' Mrs Power said, a touch impatiently. She glanced at the clock on the wall behind Noah's head. 'The gist of it is that you want to play football for my school in some world league competition and you need my signature on the entry form. Is that correct?'

Noah nodded as quickly as he could in order to keep things moving at a pace.

'I admire creativity when it comes to problem solving and a little mischievousness is very good for the soul so I must admit I like the idea of you boys playing for a girls' school,' Mrs Power said, her fingers tapping furiously on her desk. 'On the other hand, some parents may disapprove of this kind of thing and I do have to consider how St Killian's might respond too. It's important for schools in the town to have a good relationship with each other.'

'Is your answer no, then?'

'The scales are in the balance, young man, and if they remain in the balance then I will say no. I need a very good reason from you if we're going to tip them towards the yes side. Tell me why it's so important for you to play in this tournament.'

'I like football,' Noah said, realizing as soon as the words were out of his mouth how feeble they sounded.

Mrs Power arched an eyebrow. 'You like football?'

'I really like it,' Noah said.

'You really like it?'

'Really.'

I'm an idiot, Noah thought.

She looked at him for a moment, then smiled sympathetically. She got to her feet.

'Thanks for coming to see me, Noah. Unfortunately, I have to say no on this occasion. Now, if you'll excu—'

'You can't say no,' Noah blurted out.

'I can't?'

'No, I mean, yes of course you can. Say no, I mean. It's your school after all. And you're Simone's boss and I'm not a pupil here. And I didn't mean to shout. Sorry about that. So, to sum up, you're in charge,' Noah said, 'but please don't say no.'

To his surprise, Mrs Power sat down again.

'Tell me why I shouldn't,' she said.

Noah opened and closed his mouth. This was difficult. All of a sudden his throat felt dry and scratchy.

'I'm a very busy woman and the clock is ticking,' Mrs Power said.

Noah couldn't hear the clock ticking because his heart was beating so loudly. He had to give her a good reason for signing the form, but he didn't know where to start.

Mrs Power began to shift uncomfortably in her seat. He knew she'd leave now unless he said something. Anything.

'My father is in Australia,' he said.

That wasn't where he wanted to start, but those were the words that had popped into his head and once they were out there he thought it best to keep going. He must have said something right because Mrs Power settled back into her chair and despite the occasional stumble the story soon began to flow.

He didn't tell her about his mam, even though she probably already knew all about what had happened to her. He didn't want to talk to anyone about that, so he told her about his father instead. He told her that his dad had been out of work for a long time and it was only a few months ago that he had been lucky enough to find a job in the mines in Australia. Noah explained that Simone had given up her place at university to remain at home with him and now she was working two jobs to pay for food and bills while their dad's wages paid the mortgage.

'She should be at college. She's very clever,' he said.

'She was the brightest in the school when she was here,' Mrs Power said.

'I need to make enough money so she can give up work and start studying. And then I can bring my dad home. The only

95

way I can earn money like that is by becoming a professional footballer.'

It was uncomfortable saying all those things to a stranger when he hadn't even said them to his best friend, but it felt good too, as if a weight was being lifted from him.

'I don't know much about football,' Mrs Power said. 'But I can only imagine that there are thousands and thousands of young boys who want to be professionals. The odds of making a living at it appear to be very slim.'

'Yeah, very, very slim, almost impossible,' Noah agreed, 'but I have to try. What else can I do? I'm too young to get a full-time job. I'm not smart enough to start my own business. This is all I can do for now. If you were me, you'd try too, wouldn't you?'

'Yes, Noah, I would,' Mrs Power said with a smile.

She opened a drawer in her dark wooden desk and took out the form Simone had given her.

'You're going to do it,' he said.

He jumped from his chair and took half a step towards her, ready to embrace her in a bear hug until he remembered who she was and where he was. Instead of continuing, he just stood there awkwardly with a huge, slightly stupid grin on his face.

'Now, before I sign this, there's something I'm going to need you to do for me.'

'I'll do anything you want me to do,' Noah said.

PLAYER PROFILE

Name: Margaret O'Connell

Nickname: None. People call me Maggie, but it's not really a nickname, is it?

Age: 12

Position: Forward. But I'm not one of those who tracks back and does all that tackling and stuff. I save my energy so I can score amazing goals.

Likes: Football. Ice cream. Burgers. Big Bang Theory.

Dislikes: Moving. I've moved to four different towns in the last five years because of my dad's work. You get sick of it. Getting to know new people all the time is a pain.

Player you're most like: I'm unique. One of a kind. Take the best qualities from any player you can think of and I have them all. I'm not being arrogant, just honest. If you asked me if I was any good at music, I'd be honest too – I'm rubbish and I sing like a crow. But when it comes to football there's no getting away

from it – I'm going to be great.

Favourite player: Me. I'll be your favourite player too. Just give it a few years. I also like James Rodríguez.

Favourite goal: I love World Cups more than anything, so even though they weren't the greatest goals ever scored I went crazy when the US women's team beat Japan 5–2 in the final. In the men's World Cup when John Brooks scored the winner for the USA against Ghana with less than five minutes to go, I screamed the house down. I loved John's celebration too. He was just so stunned to have scored. My mom's American and we had a crazy time supporting both teams. #USWNT #USMNT

Messi or Ronaldo: Ronaldo. All day every day.

CHAPTER TEN

Noah wasn't sure. He wasn't sure at all.

'A girl,' he said for the third time, his voice rising a little higher every time he said it. 'She said there was a new girl in school called Maggie O'Connell who was big into football and she'd sign the form if we agreed to let this O'Connell girl play for us.'

'Why does that bother you? You're not saying girls can't play football,' Simone said darkly, challenging him to say the opposite.

'No, I'm not saying they can't play football, but I need people in the team who are good and she might not be good. I've never seen her play. She could be worse than Stevie.'

'None taken,' Stevie said.

Simone sighed. 'Look, you wanted to be in the tournament and now you are. That's the important thing.'

'I suppose you're right,' Noah said. 'Mrs Power rang Maggie O'Connell. The call woke her up even though it's a school morning, which means she's lazy, so that's not a good sign.

Anyway, Mrs Power asked her if she wanted to play in the tournament and now I have to meet this girl after school and talk to her. Apparently, *she* wants to see if *I'm* worth her time. Seems a bit cheeky to me.'

Simone suppressed a smile. She liked the sound of this Maggie O'Connell already.

'You ever heard of her, Stevie?' Noah asked.

'Afraid not. Under normal circumstances I'd see if I could find out any information on her playing ability, but we have more pressing concerns. I have to get the word out that we need to find twelve players by five o'clock tomorrow. I'll get some posters done up then I'll hit the social media.' He checked his watch. 'Oh no. It's almost ten to nine.'

'Don't worry, we'll probably still make it to school on time,' Noah said.

'Probably make it on time? Probably's not much good to me, Johnny Reckless. There's no way I'm losing my perfect record. See you later, Simone.'

He really does have a distinctive running style, Noah thought as Stevie raced down the corridor, his inhaler at the ready.

As the St Mary's girls began to arrive for another school day, several of them looked oddly at the St Killian's boy in their midst, but none more so than Jacinta Hegarty. It seemed as if she was on the verge of saying something nasty, but then appeared to reconsider, choosing instead to watch him closely with narrowed eyes.

*

The rain was holding off for now, but it looked as if it would be making its daily visit within the next hour. The school day had just ended and Noah and Stevie, only one of them carrying waterproofs for any future inclement conditions, were on the way to meet Maggie O'Connell in the town park. They passed by the supermarket and crossed the road, Noah holding up a hand to thank the driver of the car that had stopped to let them across.

'We need her on our side, so don't, you know, antagonize her,' Stevie said as he followed Noah. Keeping up with him wasn't easy.

'Antagonize her?'

'Make her angry.'

'I know what "antagonize" means,' Noah said, his hand tip-tapping along the railing that ran round the park's perimeter. He could hear the swollen river gushing past at the far end of the pitches. 'What makes you think I'd make her angry?'

'Oh, nothing, nothing at all. You're always a joy to be with. On a completely unrelated note, if she gets under your skin, don't react. Remember, without her there's no team and no team means no tournament.'

Noah stopped walking.

'What?' Stevie said.

'I'm not an idiot, you know. Sometimes you talk to me like I'm an idiot.'

He opened the squeaky iron gate and entered the park.

'There she is,' Stevie said.

The girl was sitting on a park bench. As soon as he saw

her, Noah knew that he'd met her before. It wasn't that he recognized *her*, more what she was wearing – an MLS jersey. Except this time it wasn't a Columbus Crew shirt as it had been when he'd seen her at the school gates. Now she was wearing the blue and flashes of red of the New England Revolution club. A zip-up backpack sat alongside her on the bench.

'Remember, be pleasant and listen to—' Stevie began.

'Don't worry, I kind of know her. It's going to be fine. I'll be charming,' Noah said, striding ahead.

'Charming? Like you were with Mr Hegarty and Brick? Remember how that worked out? Noah? *Noah?* Oh dear Lord, we're in trouble,' Stevie said, rushing after him.

'Hi, you must be Maggie,' Noah said when he reached the bench. He stuck his hand out for her to shake.

'Must I?' Maggie replied, keeping her hands firmly tucked into her pockets.

He looked at his outstretched hand, and then, not knowing what to do with it, ran it through his hair.

'You're only gorgeous,' Maggie said. 'You should do one of those L'Oréal ads.'

She was throwing him off his game. It wasn't so easy to be charming like he'd thought.

'Erm, we're here about the football. About the team. We've actually met before,' he said.

'I remember. You're the kid with the swollen face that waved at me like you were the Queen of England,' Maggie said.

'My face is better now.'

'The bruises have healed up, but I wouldn't say it's better.'

Stevie stifled a laugh.

Maggie got to her feet and looked Noah in the eye. He knew she wasn't checking to see if there were any traces of bruising left; she was testing him in some way. He stared right back at her. Her eyes were green. Very green. He didn't normally notice anyone's eye colour, but then he didn't normally stand this close to someone. It made him feel very uncomfortable and he wanted nothing more than to look away.

'I'm Stevie,' Stevie said, trying to break the building tension.

Maggie didn't acknowledge him so Stevie carried on the conversation by himself as if she had. 'Nice to meet you, Stevie,' he said. 'How are you today? Oh, I'm fine, Maggie, thanks for asking.'

The clouds above began to turn an ugly shade of grey.

'So you want to get a team together? Why would I want to be on your team?' she asked.

'Because we're going to win.'

'What are you going to win?'

'A tournament in Dublin. The winners get to represent Ireland in the Schools' World Cup. So we win in Dublin, then go to Paris and become world champions,' Noah said. 'Sounds good, right?'

'Sounds all right, I suppose,' Maggie said, her eyes still focused completely on Noah's. 'Why do you need me?'

He wasn't about to tell her the truth: he was being forced to include her in the team because her school principal wanted her to play. A lie was a better way to go, he decided.

'We need players and I heard you were good,' he said.

'I am. Put me on the pitch with ten other warm bodies and I'll win the match for you. I'm not talking about ten decent players either. When I say warm bodies, I mean anyone at all. A random collection of grannies on the way to collecting their pensions would do. Maybe some pre-school children. You could even put some scarecrows out there and if they're set up in any reasonable tactical formation, I'll win the match by myself.'

'You're not modest,' Noah said.

'Being modest is a waste of time and I don't like wasting my time. I don't boast – I tell the truth.'

Noah's eyes grew sore and before he knew it he'd blinked.

'Ha! I won,' Maggie said.

'Won what? We weren't playing anything,' Noah said, although he was annoyed with himself. He changed the subject quickly. 'If you're as good as you think, I suppose we'll be seeing you play for Arsenal Ladies or one of those teams in a few years, will we?'

'Nah, I'll be playing in the same teams as players like James Rodríguez and Neymar. Nothing's going to stop me.'

'But you're not a man.'

She gave him a withering look. 'Neither are you.'

'What? Ah, you know what I mean.'

'One hundred years ago women couldn't even vote, now we're presidents and prime ministers. You aim low, you never achieve anything.'

Noah was surprised and a little intimidated. This was the first person he'd met who'd had the same intensity as him when it came to making their way in the world of football.

Little Stevie stepped in between them. 'We don't have time for all this chit-chat. If we're going to enter the competition, we need names and we need them quick. We have a team to recruit. Maggie, are you interested in playing with us or not?'

'Depends.'

'On what?'

'I don't want to waste time playing for a rubbish team. Captain Blinky here—'

Noah turned to Stevie in protest. 'Captain Blinky? I only blinked because that's what human beings do. We weren't in a competition. I wasn't even trying.'

'– Captain Blinky here may not be up to my standard.'

'You're so wrong. I am up to your standard. In fact, I'm so far ahead of your standard that my standard is looking back at your standard and saying, where is it? The standard, I mean. It's like yours is in the distance and—'

'I have a lot of things to do today and waiting around for the end of that sentence isn't one of them, so let's forget the terrible trash talk and get down to business,' Maggie said. She unzipped her rucksack and took out a tennis ball. 'I carry one of these with me wherever I go. That way, if I get stuck anywhere I can practise. It's not as good as using a football, but it's easy to transport and helps the reflexes, concentration and coordination.'

Without warning, she dropped the ball and – *bang* – volleyed it high in the air.

Noah knew what she was doing. It was a test. A proper one

this time. This was the type of test he liked. He was in his own environment now.

The ball soared higher than Noah had anticipated. It turned out that Maggie O'Connell had the kick of a violently angry mule. That didn't mean she was a great player, but it was a good start, Noah thought.

The rest of the world faded away until all that remained was Noah and the tennis ball. His concentration was total. He tracked its fall and adjusted his position, moving a metre to his right to ensure it would drop slightly beyond him. He didn't want to be right underneath it. That'd make it too difficult to control.

He stuck his leg out, his knee bent at hip height. He caught the ball on his instep, lowering his foot towards the ground to cushion the impact.

'Not bad,' Maggie said, but she said it in a way that he knew she was impressed.

But Noah wasn't finished yet. He flicked the ball back up, let it bounce on his shoulder, then stooped beneath it in a flash, catching the ball on the back of his neck. He made it look as if it was the easiest thing in the world. The ball nestled there, perfectly balanced. He straightened up slowly and let it run down his back. He stuck out his heel and knocked it over his head before catching it on his instep again.

'I already said "not bad". No need to show off,' Maggie said.

Noah didn't reply. He began to tap the ball on the toe of his trainers, once, twice, three times, then volleyed it high in the air just like Maggie had done. Except he kicked it a little higher and a little bit further away. It sailed over her head and over the park bench.

She muttered darkly to herself, and then she reacted at speed. Turning and hopping on to the bench, she used the highest wooden slat as a lever to launch herself forward. She landed on the grass, skidding along on one knee, stretched out her left leg and intercepted the ball just before it hit the ground. There was no time to cushion it like Noah had. It popped up in the air. She clambered to her feet and took it on her thigh, then transferred it from her left leg to her right before bicycle-kicking it in Noah's direction at such a fierce pace that it fizzed past Stevie's ear.

'Hey,' he cried.

The pace didn't bother Noah, though. He jumped and controlled it on his chest before performing a series of flicks. He began to whistle jauntily, then side-heeled the ball into the air. Maggie was round the bench in a moment and controlled it quickly before doing a few flicks herself.

'Two show-offs doing tricks like a couple of performing seals seeking approval. We'll be here forever,' Stevie said to himself. 'Right, Noah and Maggie, you're both fantastic, but we have things to do so I'm putting an end to this.'

He strode purposefully into the space between the two of them, determined to intercept the ball. He missed, his fingers grasping fresh air as Maggie lazily looped the ball over his head. Noah tipped it back and Stevie jumped this time, just grazing the green fuzz, but not enough to knock it from its path.

'Hey, come on, I told you to stop,' he cried.

Before he knew it, he was the pig in a game of pig-in-the-middle. For the next minute Noah and Maggie teased him by knocking the ball over his head, under his legs, to his left, to his right, with a skill and precision that Stevie would have admired if he hadn't been on the receiving end of it. No matter what he did, the tennis ball was always just out of his reach. Eventually Noah felt sorry for him as his friend's cheeks began to turn red with exertion and his breathing became laboured. Noah trapped the ball under his foot.

'He's asthmatic,' he said by way of explanation, even though Stevie would have preferred it if he hadn't said anything.

'You two . . . are really . . . mean,' Stevie gasped.

'Mean, but talented,' Noah said.

'You're both great,' Stevie said wearily.

'Yeah, but I'm better,' Maggie said.

'Keep telling yourself that. It'll help your confidence,' Noah said.

'Right, this is like a really bad version of a WWE wind-up. Can we focus on what we need to do?' Stevie said. 'It's going to rain in a minute.'

'You know, my dad owns a company called OC Holdings so we're always moving around. I've lived in four different places in the last five years and I've never seen such miserable weather. Does it always rain here?' Maggie asked.

'Most of the time, yes. Anyway, I suggest that we go to Dee's Diner. We can get some seats there and sort out what needs to be done.'

CHAPTER ELEVEN

TWENTY-FOUR HOURS, FORTY-TWO MINUTES AND TEN SECONDS TO TOURNAMENT DEADLINE

' The FA have given me a pat on the back. I've taken violence off the terracing and on to the pitch '   Vinnie Jones

Dee's Diner was the only place in town that allowed crowds of young people to hang around all day long. To call Dee's a disgusting kip was to be unfair to disgusting kips. You couldn't slip on the grease on the floor there because the grease had been around for so long it had become a solid that obscured the original flooring. Young people ventured to Dee's because it was the only place in town where you could sit for hours unbothered by any of the staff as long as you bought a single item on the menu. And young people were the only ones who would risk their health by eating the food that was served. Young people and Dee's Diner had what could be called a symbiotic relationship.

It was half empty now and Jack, the owner, was behind the counter. He was an enormous man who looked like he'd spent the last thirty years eating nothing but his own burgers and battered fish. His red-and-white striped apron was stained with chip fat, pickle juice and flakes of cigarette ash. The rumours around town were that it hadn't been washed since the European Championships of 2004.

The decor was unpleasant – harsh lighting and an almost industrial quantity of plastic – but it was still the nicest thing about the place. Maggie ordered a burger while Stevie ordered a diet cola and Noah a bottle of water, the only thing on the menu he could afford until Simone got paid or his father sent on some more of his wages. The bottled water was cheap because Jack filled the bottles from his kitchen tap.

'Why aren't you two eating? Watching your figures?' Maggie asked.

'I don't like burgers,' Stevie said.

'They're not healthy,' Noah said.

'So?'

'If it's not good for the body, then it's not good for my game,' Noah replied, a little haughtily.

'Burgers are good. Eating them makes me happy. When I'm happy, I play well. When I play well, I'm one of the best players in the world.'

'Thanks for telling me. I'd forget you were one of the best players in the world if you didn't keep reminding me every ten minutes.'

Stevie tried to hide his grin by covering his mouth with his hand, but the glare Maggie gave him made him aware that he hadn't succeeded.

'Burger'll be another few seconds. Take a seat,' Jack drawled.

They settled on a spot near the back of the room, just a couple of tables up from the door. They sat down and made themselves as comfortable as possible on chairs that seemed to have been designed to produce the maximum amount of discomfort in the body of a human being. Noah decided it was time for a second attempt at being charming.

'Are you a Crew fan or a Revolution fan?' he asked.

'Neither. I don't support any team in general. I just like football,' Maggie said. 'My mom's American so half my family lives over there. My Uncle Scott travels around the States on business and every time he goes to a city with an MLS franchise he sends me home a jersey.'

'So how many jerseys have you got?'

'Ten, maybe twelve,' she said with a shrug.

'Sorry to interrupt,' Stevie said. 'But at present we only have two players for our team. We need twelve more and we need them by Friday evening, which is now approximately twenty-four and a half hours away.'

'Why do we need them so quickly?' Maggie asked.

'That's the tournament entry deadline.'

'Twenty-four and a half hours? To find twelve players? And we're sitting around here like saps talking about football shirts?'

They heard a *PING*.

'Microwave,' Stevie said. 'Your burger's done.'

Maggie chuckled for a moment, before stopping dead. 'You're joking, right? He doesn't cook them fresh?'

'Look around you, Maggie. Does this place look like it's one of those gourmet burger establishments?' Stevie said.

'Burger up,' Jack grunted from behind the counter.

Maggie began to rise from her seat.

'Stay where you are,' Noah said. 'The burger comes to you.'

Jack threw the burger, wrapped in white paper, across the chip shop. It was high and wide. It sailed over Maggie's head and outstretched arm. A hand flew out, reflexes like a rattlesnake, and caught it before it hit the ground.

'Great save,' Maggie said.

Noah and Stevie turned round and spotted the catcher. They looked at each other. They recognized the owner of that tough mug immediately.

'McCooley,' they said at the same moment.

'Throw it back to me,' Maggie said.

Kevin McCooley grunted. Jack's grunt was mellow, McCooley's was full of untamed menace. He was sitting by himself. There was no drink or food on the table in front of him. Slowly, with his eyes firmly locked on Maggie's, he unwrapped the burger and took a huge bite.

'Hey, that's mine!' she shouted.

A hush came over the other tables. There was a sharp intake of breath. Jack would have ducked behind the counter if it hadn't been too much of an effort. Instead, he decided to go to the back of the shop, suddenly intent on finding something in the stock room.

'What are you doing?' Stevie hissed at Maggie. 'That's Kevin McCooley.'

'He's eating my burger.'

'I'll buy you two burgers, three if you want them, if you just back down and say nothing. That's Kevin McCooley.'

'That's twice you've told me his name. I don't care what he's called. He stole my burger and he's not going to get away with it.'

She took a stride forward, but Stevie grabbed her arm. She stared down at his hand. Her eyes burned with the heat of a two-thousand-degree fire.

'Stevie, you shouldn't have grabbed her arm. That was a mistake,' Noah said.

'Yes, I realize that now,' Stevie squeaked, not daring to look up at Maggie.

'Then why are you still holding it?' Noah asked.

'I don't know.'

McCooley took another bite of the burger. He chewed slowly, extravagantly. He wasn't far off patting his belly and making *Mmmmmm* noises to show how delicious he found it. He was really rubbing it in.

'Listen, Maggie, I know you're new around here,' Noah

113

whispered, checking over his shoulder to make sure that McCooley didn't hear what he was saying. 'But that lad is tough. Not hard-but-fair tough, scary tough. He got bitten by a dog once, a Rottweiler. You know what he did? He bit the dog back.'

Maggie uncurled Stevie's fingers from her arm one by one. 'So what? I'm not afraid of him.'

She said it loudly, loudly enough for McCooley and the rest of the quivering population of Dee's Diner to hear.

'Then there's something seriously wrong with you. Because you should be. You should be very, very afraid.'

McCooley took the third and final bite of the burger. He chewed it up, then let out a belch of victory.

Maggie stormed forward. She slammed the palms of her hands on McCooley's table. There were several clicks and flashes as people from some of the other tables began to video and photograph the unfolding events.

McCooley looked up at Maggie. A slow grin spread across his flat face. Bits of mashed-up burger were stuck to his teeth. He took a bent and twisted paper clip from his pocket and picked at the bits of food.

'You're disgusting,' Maggie said.

Noah arrived at her shoulder. He balled his hands up into fists. Fists that were trembling more than he'd have liked, but fists nonetheless.

'Stop crowding me, Noah,' she said. 'Now you, Burger Boy. Why did you eat it?'

'Hungry.'

114

For the first time since he'd encountered McCooley six months earlier, Noah thought he saw a glimpse of something else beneath the terrifying mask.

'I don't care. Buy me another one,' Maggie said.

McCooley growled. It was a deep, low rumbling at the back of his throat. Little Stevie took a hit on his inhaler.

'This is bad, this is bad,' he wheezed.

Some of the other customers tried to shuffle their tables out of the way. They found to their dismay that they were bolted down. McCooley got to his feet, still growling.

'You don't intimidate me,' Maggie said.

McCooley lurched forward. 'Boo.'

Maggie and Noah jumped back as Little Stevie ducked beneath the table. McCooley chuckled to himself and turned and walked out of Dee's, pausing briefly to grab a handful of chips from another table. He stuffed them into his mouth before he swaggered out into the street.

'It's safe to come out now,' Maggie said.

Stevie peeped out from beneath the table. 'What? Heh, heh. You make it sound like I was hiding. Not at all. I just dropped a five-euro note and . . . here it is!'

He held up the note and waved it around. 'You know, why don't I get you another burger? Yes, that's what I'll do. Another burger on me.'

He hurried up to the counter as the sound of silence was replaced by the buzz of conversations in the diner. Jack emerged from his hiding place, looking mildly surprised that his property hadn't been reduced to rubble by McCooley.

'And you, what did you think you were doing?' Maggie asked Noah.

'What do you mean?' he asked. She sounded as if she was annoyed with him when McCooley was the one she should have been furious with.

'You thought I couldn't handle the situation?'

'That guy is dangerous. He'll punch anyone. Even girls. I was trying to back you up.'

'Oh, you thought I couldn't handle it because I'm a girl,' Maggie said.

'I don't care whether you're a girl or a boy,' Noah said. 'I – oh, forget it.'

He was exasperated. He'd known Maggie less than an hour and already she was in the top three of the most infuriating people he'd ever known. And she was rapidly heading for number one. He slumped down in his chair. Organizing a team was going to be a lot more troublesome than he ever would have imagined.

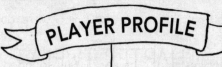

PLAYER PROFILE

Name: Hawk Willis

Nickname: None. Hawk's my real name, and no nickname could be better than that. It is too my real name and, no, I won't show you my birth cert to prove it. Get lost.

Age: 12 years, 10 months, 14 days old

Position: Winger. I'm the fastest thing on two legs. Just give me the ball and watch me go, man. You'll need a speed gun to track me – that's how swift I am.

Likes: Running. Talking. Music. Hanging out with my mates.

Dislikes: Sitting still. I'm always on the move, man.

Player you're most like: Arjen Robben. We could be twins, except I look a lot younger and I have way more hair. My hair is brilliant. Sometimes it takes nearly an hour to style it, but it's worth it because when I leave the house I look deadly.

Favourite player: Raheem Sterling. He burns up the pitch. He's small like me, but his legs are one big blur when he runs cos he moves so fast. It's like a cartoon or something. You have to see it to believe it.

Favourite goal: Suárez volley against Norwich from about one hundred metres out when he was playing for Liverpool. My old man was in tears saying it was the sweetest thing he'd ever seen in forty years of supporting Liverpool. Crying about a goal is weird, but it was genius.

Messi or Ronaldo: Ronaldo. He's fast. I'd love to race him.

CHAPTER TWELVE

'Please don't call me arrogant, but I'm a European champion and I think I'm a special one'   José Mourinho

Cornelius Figg, Ireland's richest man, was on the phone when his call was interrupted by the noise blaring from Barney's room. Cornelius strode down the enormous hallway, swung the door open and roared at his only child.

'Barney, turn that racket off. I can't hear myself think.'

Barney Figg, the sole heir to the enormous Figg fortune, was sitting on the smoked oak floor less than one metre from a seventy-four-inch plasma television screen filled with the animated characters of a football game that wouldn't be on sale to the general public for another six months. He had a narrow tanned face, spiky blond hair and ice-blue eyes. He wore a Real Madrid jersey with 'Figg 7' on the back.

'Shouldn't you be training?'

'I *am* training,' the boy scowled. 'I'm learning tactics.'

'Tactics,' Cornelius muttered to himself. 'Well, keep the noise down. I have business to attend to.'

He shut the door.

Cornelius Figg yelped at the sudden and unexpected

appearance of Plunkett Healy, his personal assistant. 'Healy, stop creeping up on me like that. You're going to give me a heart attack one of these days.'

'My apologies, sir.'

Plunkett was impeccably dressed in a tailored suit. He hadn't a hair out of place and his skin glowed the way it only can when a man eats nothing but fruit, vegetables and lean meat.

'How is young Mr Figg?'

'Good, he's, er, practising tactics. He's fantastic, isn't he?'

'He's a delight, sir. Your football players have arrived.'

'Excellent,' Figg said, rubbing his hands together. 'Sort out the legal mumbo jumbo and then send them down to the pitches and I'll meet them there. We'll see what they're made of, huh?'

He slapped his employee on the back, in what he imagined was a hearty fashion. Healy covered up his displeasure and discomfort with a tight smile.

'Certainly, Mr Figg.'

Healy walked down the long marble hallway towards one of the house's seven reception rooms. The four young men waiting in the poshest room in which they'd ever been were gripped by a sudden silence the moment Healy arrived. They were glad he'd turned up because they were so fidgety and full of nervous tension that three of them were certain they were going to break something that they couldn't afford to replace. Each had a kit bag by his side containing boots and shin pads, the tools of the footballer's trade.

'Are you ready, gentlemen?' Healy asked.

They nodded. Healy went to a desk, unlocked the drawer and took out four separate contracts, each one printed on Crane & Co. pearl-white paper. He checked the names then handed them in turn to the appropriate person. Three of the recipients looked at their contracts with a blank expression, as if they didn't know quite what to do with them. The fourth, thirteen-year-old William Sheehan, began to thumb through the pages. Healy placed a selection of ballpoint pens on the desk.

'Do we sign 'em?' one of the teenagers asked.

'Yes. Once you sign, the deal we made is legally binding,' Healy said.

'And we get the money you promised?'

'Yes, Mr McGuckian.'

The first three signed immediately. They couldn't wait. This opportunity was far too good to turn down. William Sheehan waited, though. It annoyed Healy slightly, but he didn't let it show.

'Is everything all right, Mr Sheehan?'

'Yeah, it's just . . . is this real?'

'I can assure you it is.'

William took another look around the room. Every single item in there looked as if it would cost more than his mother had earned in a year back when she was working.

'It just seems crazy,' he said. 'Five thousand euro to play in a few matches.'

'Mr Figg is a very generous man.'

'But why? Why does he need us to do this?'

Plunkett Healy had expected that William might be a problem. The others were like sheep – they'd do whatever they were told. But William was different. Smarter. If he'd had a choice, he'd have left him out completely, but Slugsley had been insistent. The boy was that good a player. It wasn't easy to find good footballers, especially ones who weren't well known and were willing to put themselves forward for a scheme that would require the utmost discretion and secrecy.

'Just one moment, Mr Sheehan.' He turned to the other three. 'Those of you who have signed the agreements, if you would like to cross the hall there's a welcome package waiting for you.'

'A welcome package?' McGuckian said.

'Yes, of course. We want to make your time with us as comfortable as possible. There's new training gear. Top of the range boots. Tracksuits. Dry-fit tees. A couple of footballs. Ahm, what else? Oh, yes, a new Xbox, an iPad, an android phone that hasn't been officially released yet, things like that.'

'Deadly.'

They didn't need to be asked twice. They were across the hallway like a shot. Their shrieks of excitement could be heard all around the east wing of the house.

'Now, we can talk,' Healy said.

He sat on the soft leather couch and signalled for William to sit in the armchair across from him.

'I'll be honest with you, William,' he began dishonestly.

'Ten thousand.'

'Pardon me?'

'I don't want five thousand euro. I want ten. And ten more if we win the tournament.'

'What? Why you greedy little—'

'Don't act like you're all upset, Mr Healy. You're not bothered. You're just pretending. It's not your money and Figg can afford it.'

'Yes, but the contracts will have to be redone and that would take too much time and—'

'I'm thirteen. You can't sign a contract until you're eighteen. You need a parent or guardian with you so anything I sign today is just for show.'

'You've surprised me,' Healy said. 'I thought footballers were supposed to be stupid.'

'People make that mistake all the time,' William replied.

'Are you sure you're only thirteen?'

'I'm sure. Now that we're being honest with each other, tell me why we're doing this.'

Healy sighed. He wasn't supposed to say anything. Not a single word. But if he didn't he had the sense that William Sheehan would make things more difficult somehow. He decided the best thing to do was to tell the truth.

'It's Barney Figg's greatest wish to have his football ability recognized by the world, and right now that involves winning a schools' tournament in Dublin and representing his country in the World Cup in Paris.'

'Is he good?'

'There have been dogs who have run on to the pitch during a match who have displayed more skill than he ever has. I'm not just saying that: he's really awful.'

'But he's trying to improve?'

'Oh no, he's completely self-delusional. He thinks he's fantastic already. In his own mind he's Pelé and Zinedine Zidane and Messi all rolled into one.'

'That makes no sense. How can he not know how bad he is?'

'He's been brought up to think he's brilliant at everything he's ever tried. His parents praise him excessively. If he scrapes by in an exam, they tell him he's Albert Einstein. He puts a plaster on a cut and he's Jonas Salk. He spots the moon in the night sky and he's the new Neil Armstrong.'

'I should have asked for twenty thousand,' Sheehan said. 'He thinks he can be a great footballer without working at it.'

'Quite simply, yes.'

'But—'

'I know.'

'It—'

'*I know.*'

'So what does he think is going on? Four new players on his school team all of a sudden? Where will he think they've come from?'

'He won't think about it. He doesn't care about anything but himself. It's all happening without Barney even noticing or caring. It's like this, Mr Sheehan: Barney goes to Pengardon Academy. Barney wants to win the tournament. The current

Pengardon football team is not good enough to win it, so our scouts have located some of the best underage players in the country. The headmaster has registered them as students in the school because Mr Figg makes large donations of cash to Pengardon and the headmaster wants that to continue. He has turned a blind eye to the ethical problems of the situation. So now the players are eligible to represent Pengardon. They, and by *they* I mean you too, are getting paid to play in the tournament as ringers – I believe that's the right term – so that Barney can win and revel in the glory of his tainted achievement.'

'All right, but what if he realizes his father's buying him the tournament?'

'I suspect he won't really pay it that much attention. He doesn't engage with that sort of thing. He's what you might call self-absorbed. Everything is about him.'

'And because his father's super-rich he gets what he wants.' William smiled, although it was rather a grim sort of smile. 'Here I am scrabbling around trying to make money for my family and Barney gets everything handed to him on a plate. I guess the world isn't fair.'

'No, it's not. Which is why we have to get to work now. By the way, with the contracts, you're right, your mother has to co-sign to make it appear to be legal, but Mr Figg will have her signature forged if necessary and if you break the contract, by which I mean breathe a single word about it to anyone, he'll have you sued. He'll drag the case out for years and your family will have to hire lawyers. Mr Figg's lawyers are the best in the business, so they'll bring things right up to the point of going to court, then withdraw it at the last minute. Your family will have to sell everything they own just to pay their legal fees. I don't mean to sound heavy-handed, William, but that's the kind of person that's employing us.'

'Best thing to do is keep my mouth shut, then.'

'That is indeed the best thing to do. Now, let's collect your colleagues and we'll go to the training pitch.'

Plunkett led them outside to the gravel-covered courtyard. Two white Range Rover Evoques were parked alongside each other, a chauffeur sitting behind the wheel of each one. William could see the town in the distance beyond the rolling hills.

'Everything you can see from here to the town is owned by Mr Figg,' Plunkett said.

William saw lush fields full of horses and, to his right, a huge stable yard. Further on there were houses, farms and perfectly manicured gardens stretching all the way down to a man-made lake. It was hard to believe that one person could own so much.

'All right, gentlemen. Into the cars, please.'

'Oh,' a tall boy said. 'I thought you said the pitches were on the estate.'

'They are. They're on the far side, behind the house,' Healy replied. 'But if we travelled by foot it would take us over forty minutes to reach them.'

'A forty-minute walk and we're still at his house? Damn, this man is *super*-rich,' McGuckian grinned, elbowing William in the side.

'Yeah,' William replied. 'He sure is.'

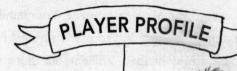

Name: Barney Figg

Nickname: The Man. Like, 'You're the man, Barney.'

Age: 13

Position: When you have my level of talent, you can play any position you like. I wouldn't play as a goalkeeper, though; you always put the worst player in goal.

Likes: Adam Sandler movies. Designer clothes and sunglasses – you have to look good to wear them, though, so most people shouldn't bother. Getting new gadgets and phones and all kinds of stuff ages before anyone else gets them.

Dislikes: Poverty. If you're poor, you don't have the money to buy cool stuff and you probably have to spend your time with all sorts of horrible people cos you can't afford to go anywhere. Sounds awful to me.

What you like about football: If you play for a top club, people worship you and you get to be famous and you can do whatever you want. Who wouldn't like that?

Player you're most like: I'm Paul Pogba and Alexis Sanchez and Kevin De Bruyne and Gareth Bale and Anthony Martial all rolled into one. Yeah, physical power and technique and pace and skill and vision. I've got it all!

Favourite player: Luis Suárez.

Favourite goal: I scored an amazing goal in a match last year – a diving header. People gasped when they saw how good it was.

Messi or Ronaldo: Ronaldo has his own clothing range, so definitely Ronaldo. Also, Messi's small and I don't like short people.

CHAPTER THIRTEEN

ONE HOUR, FOUR MINUTES AND FORTY-THREE SECONDS TO TOURNAMENT DEADLINE

' *Take a walk around my centre-half, gentlemen.*
He's a colossus '   Bill Shankly

'It's brilliant, Dave. Really, really great,' Noah said.

The big man grinned so widely that the edges of his beard tickled his ears. It was four o'clock on Friday afternoon and Noah was surveying one of the worst football pitches he'd ever seen. He didn't care how bad it looked. They could fix it up. What mattered was that they had somewhere to train and play practice matches.

All they needed now was a team.

The pitch was on the far side of the town at the back of a half-empty housing estate and it looked as if it hadn't been used in years. It was uneven and bumpy and strewn with rubbish. The grass was patchy, ragwort grew everywhere and the goalposts were in dire need of repair. But it was theirs for the next six weeks. Dave's boss owned the land, an area known locally as The Hatch, and had given Dave permission to use it in exchange for some free overtime.

'Here come the lads,' Dave said.

Tony, whom Dave called his little brother, even though he

was very far from little, was deep in conversation with Stevie. Tony looked like a thinner, ganglier version of Dave. A sun-dried version, Stevie had said. He didn't have a beard, but he did have the same huge mop of hair. His family called him by his nickname, Limbsy, and he asked the others to call him that too.

'Right, it's not much,' Dave said to Noah, 'but here it is.'

The outside of the wooden hut they'd be using as a dressing room was covered in fairly crude, and in most cases misspelled, graffiti. Dave unlocked the door. The smell of damp rushed out to meet them.

'Wow, it really stinks,' Dave said.

'It's perfect,' Noah replied, and he meant it.

The hut wasn't too big, just about large enough to accommodate a football team as long as they didn't all stand

up at the same time. A wooden bench ran along the edges of the walls. There weren't any windows. Dave switched on the only light source, a single bulb that hung from the ceiling. He seemed surprised that it was still working.

'Well, here's the key,' Dave said, handing it over to Noah. 'Word of warning – don't come here after dark. A lot of the town's most, y'know, unpleasant characters like hanging out here at night, but during the day you'll be fine. If there's any trouble, you can always give me a call.'

'I can't believe it's almost four o'clock and there are only two players here,' Stevie said.

'Don't worry about it – it'll be cool,' said Limbsy.

'I don't know if it will in fact *be cool*. We have to get these forms sorted and faxed through in less than an hour. Factoring in the time it takes me to get home, we're going to need to find a player once every three minutes and seventeen seconds,' Stevie said. He stepped into the dressing room and was nearly knocked over by the powerful smell. 'Whoa, that's not going to be good for my allergies.'

He pulled a cloth handkerchief from his pocket and used it to cover his nose and mouth.

'Don't worry, Stevie. I'm sure lots of players will turn up,' Dave said softly.

They'd worked hard, but finding players at such short notice had been a difficult task. Stevie had put the word out on Facebook and Twitter the previous night. He'd asked for anyone who was interested in playing to turn up at The Hatch at four o'clock after school on Friday evening. He said he'd had a good response, but Noah thought it was easy for people to say yes online; when they had to get out of their comfy chairs on a cold Friday afternoon, they might not be as enthusiastic.

Maggie had said she'd ask around too, but since she'd only moved to the town recently she didn't know that many people, and it turned out that most of those she did know, she hated. She said she'd ask her neighbours, a twin brother and sister, who often played football in their back garden, and seemed, in Maggie's words, relatively normal.

Stevie had printed up posters on his parents' computer, and Simone and Noah had walked all over town on Thursday night dropping them into shops and asking the owners to display them in their windows. Most had said no, but a few had agreed, including Jack in Dee's Diner.

The next day in school, Noah and Stevie had mentioned it to everyone in their classes and plenty of others they'd met in the corridors and in the yard at break-time. Word must have got back to Jim Reynolds because he ran up to Noah when he saw him heading back to class after lunch.

'I heard you're going to play for St Mary's. I know you always acted like one, Murphy, but I never knew you really were a little girl.'

'Good one, Jim,' Noah had said. 'Been thinking that one up since you saw the message online last night?'

The disappointed look on Reynolds's face told Noah he had been doing exactly that.

By the time the school bell rang at three o'clock and they were ready to make their way to The Hatch, Noah reckoned they'd made contact with everyone in town who'd ever kicked a ball. That was no guarantee anyone would turn up, of course. He hadn't been worried, not since his dad had sent him an encouraging email the previous night telling him that he was right to stand up to Hegarty. He was delighted his dad had said that – it gave him a boost. Noah hadn't told him why he was so eager to play in the tournament, though. He suspected his old man was just pleased that his son seemed to have fallen in love with football again. But, as the clock ticked past four, Noah had begun to fret a little. It was getting close to the deadline and they only had three definites – Noah himself, Maggie and Tony 'Limbsy' Donnelly. And Limbsy, as pleasant as he was, looked about as coordinated as a drunken spider on a wild night out. He'd managed to fall over twice already and they'd only met him twenty minutes earlier.

'People will turn up. It'll be fine,' Noah said to Stevie, not sure if he was trying to convince his friend or himself.

His stomach rumbled and reminded him that he hadn't eaten anything since the night before. All the running around was taking its toll. The rumble was drowned out by Stevie's phone ringing for the twentieth time that day – the ringtone was the 'Maradona es mi amigo' song.

'The Hatch. The Hatch. Behind the River Valley estate. Hurry up. We have forms to fill in and they need to be sent in –' he checked his watch – 'fifty-six minutes. Please hurry.' He hung up. 'Why anyone ever chooses to do a job that involves stress is beyond me.'

'How many players have you got locked in, little dudes?'

Dave asked, just ducking in time to prevent his head from hitting the light bulb.

'We've got between twenty and thirty who said they're interested, but that doesn't mean they're going to turn up. We'll just have to wait and see what happens,' Noah said.

Within five minutes they had their first arrivals. Maggie had brought along her neighbours just as she'd said she would. Frank Courtney was five feet seven and a half inches tall, quite big for a twelve-year-old, but his twin sister, Barbara, was five feet eleven. She hunched her shoulders as if she was trying to make herself smaller. Her clothes were black and shapeless and her fringe hung down over her eyes, like a curtain blocking out the world. Maggie had told Noah and Stevie that her neighbour was self-conscious about her height and warned them not to mention it. Standing beside those two, as well as Limbsy and Dave, Noah felt as if he'd been transported to a land of giants. He could only imagine how Stevie felt.

'Frank and Barbara live two doors down from me,' Maggie said by way of introduction.

'Hi, I'm Noah,' Noah said, with an awkward little wave that he immediately regretted. What is it with me and waving at people I've only just met? he wondered.

'Hi, I'm Frank, obviously. This is my sister, Barbara,' Frank smiled.

He had a relaxed, easy manner in contrast to his sister's self-consciousness. He seemed like the sort of person who hadn't a care in the world. Stevie didn't introduce himself. He didn't even notice Frank. He just stared at Barbara intently until

Maggie was on the verge of telling him to quit it.

'Wow,' he said. 'Look at how tall you are.'

Maggie swore under her breath and Barbara mumbled something incomprehensible.

'I'd love to be that tall,' he added. 'You're amazing.'

To everyone's surprise, she parted her curtain of hair so that enough of her face was visible to allow her smile to be seen.

'I'm Barbara,' she said shyly.

'OK,' Frank said. 'This is becoming weird and uncomfortable. We're here to join a football team.'

'Stevie, start filling in the forms,' Noah said. 'We're in a rush, remember.'

Snapping out of it, Stevie immediately set to work.

'I'll get out of your way. You have a lot to do,' Dave said, almost bent double to get through the doorway. 'Catch you later.'

When the familiar faces of Darren and Sunday arrived at the door five minutes later, Noah's nerves began to disappear. They were replaced by a feeling of excitement. It just might work. If the players that turned up were even half decent, then they had enough time to get them into some sort of shape. If they were smart and organized themselves well, they might have a slight chance. He could live with that. That was all he needed from the team if he was going to show off his talents and make an impression on the scouts at the tournament.

He introduced the newcomers to the rest.

'Nice to meet you,' Maggie said as she shook Darren's hand. 'In the future you'll remember this moment – the day you met the greatest player that ever lived. When I'm rich and famous and far too important to talk to the likes of you, you'll be telling all your friends that you once knew me.'

'Wow, just wow,' Darren said.

'She makes Cristiano Ronaldo look humble,' Sunday said.

The next person that arrived was someone Noah and Stevie recognized immediately. He was a boy who sat behind Noah in class. He was always on his own at lunchtime and didn't appear to have any friends. Everybody said he was weird. He didn't look as if he cared what anyone thought of him. He was comfortable in his own skin. He had mousy brown hair and a pale complexion. His name was Michael Griffin.

'Hey, Michael, isn't it?' Stevie said.

Michael Griffin nodded.

'You're here to join the team?' Noah asked.

Michael Griffin nodded again. This nod was less emphatic than the first, as if he regretted the extravagance of his opening nod. This one was more to his liking. It was barely perceptible.

'Well, it was great talking to you,' Noah said. 'If you want to grab a pen from Frank and fill out the pages. Just some information we need for the entry form.'

The next person through the door was someone Noah was delighted to see even though he'd never clapped eyes on him before. He was wearing a full goalkeeper's outfit. He had the big thick gloves, the long-sleeved jersey, and the baseball cap to protect his eyes from the sun, not that there was much sun out today. He was even wearing football boots, which meant he could be heard clip-clopping his way down the footpath before he was seen.

Noah grinned as he fist-bumped a gloved hand. 'I don't need to ask what position you play.'

'That is correct. I am a striker.'

Noah stared at the boy's extremely serious face. Suddenly the newcomer began to roar with laughter. He gave Noah a friendly thump on the shoulder, which was strong enough to knock him off balance.

'I am joking with you. I am the goalkeeper. I am Piotr.' He waved to the room. 'Hello, everyone!' he boomed.

He got a few hellos and waves in return. When Noah had finished introducing Piotr to the others, there was someone else waiting at the shed door.

'Hey, Hawk,' Stevie said, recognizing the boy from his class.

Hawk Willis, who was small and thin, regularly claimed he was faster than Usain Bolt was at his age. He looked around the room, taking in all the faces.

'Hey man, this is where the football's at, right?'

'That's right,' Noah said.

'What's with the girls? Are they here to look after our kit or something?'

Noah and Stevie exchanged worried glances. Luckily, Maggie and Barbara were deep in conversation and hadn't overheard Hawk, otherwise there would have been trouble.

'It's a mixed team, Hawk. You don't have a problem with that, do you?' Noah asked.

'Nope, it's all cool. Wait, why is it a mixed team? Nobody told me about that,' Hawk said, his face wrinkling up in confusion.

'It was on the Facebook page. It's on the posters in the shops. And it's on the leaflet I personally handed to you yesterday,' Stevie said. 'I think I even said the words "it's a mixed team".'

'Huh. First I've heard of it. So there are girls playing on our team?'

'Technically, we're on their team. We're playing for the girls' school.'

Hawk Willis's mouth opened and formed a perfect circle of surprise.

'We're playing for a girls' school? Do we have to pretend to be a girls' team?' he spluttered. 'We'll look like idiots. We'll have to wear dresses. I don't want to do that, man. I'm the coolest thing in town and wearing a dress would ruin my rep.'

'Girls' teams don't wear dresses, Hawk, they wear jerseys and shorts just like us,' Noah said.

'Are you sure?'

'I'm certain. And do you really want to miss out on the chance to play in a World Cup tournament just because you're worried about playing with gir—'

'WORLD CUP,' Piotr bellowed.

'No, no, no, I'll play, man. Just wanted to get it all clear in my head,' Hawk grinned. 'I'm not going to miss the World Cup for anything. I love the World Cup. I can't wait to mix it up with dudes like Pogba and Veratti. Hey, if we play Argentina I'll get Messi's autograph. I'll swap shirts with him after the match. I could have Lionel Messi's shirt!'

Noah sighed. 'I'm afraid Messi won't be there, Hawk.'

136

'Cos he's injured?'

Noah spoke slowly to make sure his new teammate got it.

'No, because he won't be playing. There won't be any professional footballers playing. They're all too old. It's a qualifying tournament for a schools' World Cup. *Schools*. That means people our age. The winners of the tournament get to play for Ireland in the Schools' World Cup in Paris. Do you understand?'

'Course I understand,' Hawk said. 'I'm not stupid.'

He took his place on the bench beside Piotr who high-fived him so hard that for a moment Noah thought Hawk's hand was broken.

'How many have we got now?' Noah asked over the noise of the conversations that were buzzing around the shed. People were chattering excitedly. The atmosphere was building and he found to his surprise that he liked it. It was far more pleasant than the atmosphere in the St Killian's dressing room with stupid Jim bossing everyone around.

Stevie counted them out. 'Ten.'

They were still four short of the fourteen they needed for a squad and there was only twenty minutes to go before they had to get to Stevie's house and send off the paperwork.

'OK, I have an idea. I know it's really stupid, but don't laugh. What if we put you down as a player?' Noah said.

'Me?' Stevie's eyes lit up with excitement.

'Yeah, I mean, you obviously wouldn't get a game or anything because you can't play football to save your life, but you'd get to dress up like a player and stand on the sidelines. I know we'd be in a tight spot if we got injuries, but if the worst came to the worst we could stick you up front or somewhere you wouldn't do much damage.'

'Oh. Yes, certainly. That sounds lovely,' Stevie said, a little deflated.

'Great,' Noah replied.

Barbara smiled sympathetically at Stevie. It didn't make things right, but it did make him feel a little better.

Five minutes later and they had two more players – Cormac McHugh, a dark-haired boy in a Liverpool jersey, was first in the door. 'Hey, guys,' he said to the gang as Noah welcomed him. He was followed by Adam O'Brien, another boy from Stevie's class. Adam had long, jet-black hair that reached halfway down his back. He wore a Metallica T-shirt with the sleeves cut off and his arms were covered in snake, skull and dagger tattoos. Noah presumed they were fake, but if they were they were extremely convincing fakes.

'Hello there. You must be Noah. I've seen you around the school,' Adam said chirpily. 'I'm Adam. I was wondering if I could join your football team, if it's not too much trouble.'

He's as polite as Stevie, Noah thought.

They'd almost reached the magic number. If they included Stevie, they were at thirteen, only one short. But there was barely any time left. Noah's mind was racing. He turned to the group.

'Hey, we're short a player for the squad and we have about five minutes to find someone. We have thirteen, we need fourteen,' Noah said. 'Anyone got any ideas?'

He struggled to be heard above all the voices.

'Be quiet,' he roared.

Silence descended immediately. A deep silence, as if someone had sucked all the energy and life from the room in a flash. Noah studied the faces of his new teammates. They were staring at him with, well, almost fear on their faces. They really respected him. That was exactly what he needed from them. It was a good feeling.

'Sorry for shouting, but –' he began.

Then he realized that they weren't actually looking at him after all. They were staring past him towards the shed door.

'You're looking for a fourteenth player. I'm that guy.'

Noah didn't need to turn round, although he did. He knew the owner of that voice immediately. Even the people who'd never encountered him before knew by his presence that he wasn't someone you messed with.

It was Kevin McCooley.

CHAPTER FOURTEEN

'*Individuals can and do make a difference, but it takes
a team to really mess things up*'   Anonymous

For a moment, Noah didn't know what to say. Then he did.

'Kevin.'

It was only a small step up from saying nothing. He had to
say something else, something that would let Kevin McCooley
know he wasn't wanted and hell would freeze over before he'd
get anywhere near Noah's team. The trick was he had to say it
in such a way that Kevin wouldn't take offence and show his
displeasure by rearranging Noah's features or, if he was really
angry, his limbs.

'It's great that you . . . ahem . . . turned up . . . didn't even
know you liked football . . .'

McCooley glowered at him.

'And we'd love to have you as a player . . . It's just that—'

'You have thirteen – you need fourteen. I heard you. I'm the
fourteenth.'

'No, you're the thirteenth,' Maggie said, getting to her feet.

Noah looked at Stevie. Had they got their maths wrong?
That was unlikely. Stevie never made mistakes like that.

140

'There's thirteen of us, Maggie. Even if we don't count Stevie—'

'No, thirteen. Because if that psycho burger thief plays, then I don't.'

She looked angry, unlike McCooley, who had that pre-anger calm. He delivered a sense of menace with the barest flicker of an eyebrow. A hint of a smile played on his lips. He reached into his pocket.

Stevie hit the ground, covering his head like a grenade was about to go off.

'He's got a weapon,' he squealed.

Nobody else acted as rashly as Stevie, but there were a few who looked as if they wanted to. Noah was one of them, but he forced himself to stand there. He was afraid, he knew McCooley knew he was afraid, but he wasn't going to show it, if that was possible. A bead of sweat trickled down the side of his head as McCooley took his hand out of his pocket. His fist was full of coins. One cent, two cent and five cent coins. He dropped them on the ground. They pinged off the surface, some spinning where they fell, some rolling across the wooden floor, others getting trapped between the rotting floorboards.

'There's enough there to buy as many burgers as you want, girl,' he said, smirking at Maggie.

She didn't flinch. 'You think that's all it takes after the way you behaved? I'm not playing on the same team as you unless you do two things.'

McCooley raised an eyebrow in approximation of a question.

'First of all, you're going to *hand* me the money you owe

me,' Maggie said.

'I ain't pickin' up nothin',' McCooley said.

Stevie, feeling a little foolish at his hasty dive for cover, stayed on his hands and knees and began to pick up some of the coins, hoping that people would think that was his intention all the time. Barbara joined him.

'Thanks, Barb.'

'She goes mad if I call her Barb,' Frank whispered to Michael Griffin who didn't consider the matter worthy of an acknowledging nod.

Sunday and Darren, sensing that if they didn't do something a massive row would break out and ruin their chances of playing in a proper football tournament, joined Stevie and Barbara in picking up the coins. Piotr tried to join in too, but he found it almost impossible to get a grip on the small pieces of metal with his thick goalkeeper's gloves.

'These things were not made for delicate work,' he bellowed.

Maggie and McCooley stood there, unmoving, while all the coins were collected. Stevie took a freezer bag from his folder and deposited the coins in there before zip-locking it. He held it out for Maggie.

'I want him to hand it to me,' she said, meaning McCooley.

'Maggie, we have no time left for this kind of game. You didn't have to pick up the coins, so please just take the bag,' Noah said.

To his surprise she did.

McCooley and Maggie continued their stand-off like two gunslingers in the old Wild West.

'You said: two things. What's the second one?' McCooley asked.

'I want you to say sorry.'

'I don't apologize for nothin'.' McCooley chuckled.

'What are you laughing at, you donkey?' Maggie said.

'Who are you calling a donkey?'

McCooley moved forward as Noah stepped between him and Maggie. Noah raised his arms in a gesture of surrender.

'Whoa, whoa,' he said.

Even if he'd seen the punch coming, he wouldn't have had time to react. It was that quick. It caught him plumb on the nose before he'd even realized it was on its way. His knees buckled, his head began to swim and the next thing he knew Maggie's hands were under his armpits as she stopped him from crashing to the floor.

He put his hand to his face. There was blood on his fingers. That was twice in a week that he'd been punched.

Once more and he'd have a hat-trick.

'Ow,' he said finally. It really stung. Far worse than Brick's seven punches had.

'Sorry, sorry,' McCooley said. 'Thought you was goin' to hit me.'

That was unexpected. Once McCooley'd arrived in the hut, there was always the possibility that someone was going to be on the receiving end of some random violence. That was the McCooley way. Apologizing was new.

'He said sorry,' Noah said, stumbling to his feet and drowning out the angry swell of voices that were gathering around him. Maggie was the only one trying to get to McCooley, though. Dazed as he was, Noah just about managed to hold her at bay. The others were happy to register their disapproval from a safe distance.

'Maggie, he said sorry. Is that good enough for you?' Noah said above the hubbub.

'But he wasn't apologizing to *me*.'

'The girl's right, I wasn't apologizin' to her.'

'She didn't ask you to apologize. She asked you to say sorry.' He turned to Maggie again. 'He said sorry. Now, it's over.'

Maybe it was the impact of the punch on his brain, but he suddenly felt like they were listening to him. Either that or they were mesmerized by the blood dripping from his nose.

'Did you hear me? It's over!'

'OK, OK,' Maggie said.

'Everyone heard you,' McCooley said. 'Stop goin' on about it.'

Noah looked at his watch, wiping a drop of blood away from its face. They had nine minutes left.

'Stevie, give Kevin one of the forms and help him fill it out.'

'I can fill out me own form. An' it's Mr McCooley to you.'

'Yes, Mr McCooley.'

'It's Mr McCooley to all of you, right?' He looked around the shed at the fearful faces.

They all nodded. A few of the braver ones murmured a yes.

'No problem, Kevin,' Maggie said.

McCooley ignored her.

When all the paperwork was finished, Noah and Stevie raced to Stevie's house. They scanned the forms and faxed them off to the schools' football association. As the PC beeped to confirm the fax had been sent and received the clock in the bottom right hand corner read 16.56. They'd made it with only four minutes to spare. They were in the tournament.

It was only when they were talking about it afterwards that the realization fully hit Noah.

'Did we just allow Kevin McCooley to join our football team?' he said.

'Yes, I was just thinking the same thing. It all happened so fast with the deadline and the need for players that we just seemed to get swept along with it. It was kind of bizarre and terrifying, wasn't it?' Stevie said.

'I hope we haven't just made the biggest mistake of our lives,' Noah said.

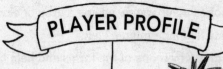

PLAYER PROFILE

Name: Kevin McCooley

Nickname: Some people call me Macker. They're idiots. Dead idiots if I catch up with them.

Age: Why do you care what age I am?

Position: Murphy says that I play as a defensive midfielder. I don't believe in proper positions and tactics and things like that. Football is simple: if you have the ball, you score a goal; if you don't have the ball, you kick someone until they give it to you and then you score a goal. There's no need to make it all complicated and stuff.

Likes: People who mind their own business and leave me alone.

Dislikes: People who don't mind their own business and get me to fill out stupid player profiles.

Player you're most like: Nigel de Jong. I love his tattoos and his attitude. No one messes with him. Our useless gaffer said I remind him of Vinnie Jones, but I never saw that Jones kid play.

Favourite player: I'm not a five-year-old girl. I don't have a favourite anything. Grow up.

Favourite goal: To hurt people who ask me lots of stupid questions.

Messi or Ronaldo: I hate both of them.

CHAPTER FIFTEEN

' *If you eat caviar every day, it's difficult to return
to sausages* '　　　　　　　　　Arsène Wenger

Even though they'd been training for three days straight, William
Sheehan still hadn't got used to how good the football facilities
were at the Figg estate. If he was dreaming, he didn't want to
wake up. There were three pitches alongside each other. One
was full-sized and the grass was as perfect and green as grass
could be. The playing surface was like a carpet. It had been cut
to give it that beautiful criss-crossed pattern that William loved.
The sun shone down and a light breeze rippled the thin cord
of the nets. The posts and crossbars were almost impossibly
white.

'It's the same proportions as the Santiago Bernabéu pitch in
Madrid,' Plunkett had told him. 'To the millimetre.'

The other two pitches were smaller. The second one was half
the size of the first and the goals were reduced proportionally.
The third had training gear littered all around: a plastic wall
shaped like four men for practising free kicks, two piles of
saucer-shaped markers, half-metre-high hurdles for dynamic
strength, cones for dribbling practice, elasticized leashes for

power sprinting and, of course, a big bag of fresh footballs. The best kind – footballs that hadn't been kicked yet.

'I think I've died and gone to heaven,' McGuckian had said.

William had picked up one of the footballs that first morning. It was the same type they used in the Premier League. He pressed it against his face. He loved the smell of a new football. He loved the way it felt in his hands.

When he was growing up in Droombeg Flats, he'd never had a proper football. Instead, he'd kick a cheap plastic ball up and down the hallway because it was too dangerous to go outside with some of the unsavoury characters that hung around the flats. The ball would ricochet off the windowsills and skirting boards and fly off at weird angles, but it all helped with his control. Once you'd done that a couple of thousand times, you got to know in which direction a ball was going to go in any situation. One thing he'd noticed in some of the kids with whom he used to play football was that when they found something too difficult they'd give up. Not William. If he found it tough, he'd just try harder. It gave him a huge advantage. People used to tell him he was lucky to be born with such a great talent. He'd smile and say thanks, but it drove him mad. Lucky? There was nothing lucky about it. It was hard work and lots of it. But that was a truth nobody wanted to hear.

Plunkett Healy arrived on the main pitch with Arthur Slugsley in tow. Slugsley ran the training sessions and to William's surprise and delight they were entertaining and inventive. Today was going to be a little different, though. Today was the first day they were going to train with Barney Figg. The team's captain had been in London for a film premiere so he hadn't been able to make it to training before now.

William got his first look at his new captain. He positively gleamed with good health. Healy had said he was a terrible footballer, but in his top-of-the-range designer tracksuit and with his perfectly styled hair Barney Figg looked every inch the professional. Cornelius was just behind his son, a mobile phone in each hand, the one in his left pressed to his ear.

'You do it because I said to do it. And if it's not finished by six o'clock tomorrow evening you'll be unemployed and your children will be begging on the streets,' Cornelius Figg said.

He finished the call and threw the phone to Plunkett Healy, who not being particularly athletic just about managed to catch it after a brief fumble. Off to the left stood the majority of Pengardon Academy's football team, but Barney was staring at the four new players. His ice-blue eyes narrowed.

'I don't recognize them. Who are they?' he asked.

'They're your new teammates,' his father replied.

'They'd better be good.'

Barney took a football from the bag and nudged it forward before unleashing a shot of tremendous power and terrible accuracy. It flew wide, closer to the corner flag than the goalposts and ended up startling a rabbit that had been happily minding its own business.

'Windy today,' Barney said, trying to excuse his failure. He turned and looked at William. 'You're one of the new ones.'

'Yep,' William said.

'You go to my school now? You don't look like Pengardon material. I've seen scarecrows with better hairstyles.' Barney grinned, showing off his row of straight, perfectly white teeth.

'I'm just here to play football. I don't care about fashion.'

'That's obvious,' Barney said. He addressed all the newcomers. 'You're going to have to learn my style of play very quickly if you want to make the team. Everything revolves around me. I'm the one who controls the game, so learn to fit in or get lost.'

'He's a born leader,' Cornelius Figg said.

'He's certainly a chip off the old block, sir.'

They began training by doing a few sprints. After the first few Barney decided that he'd had enough. Sprinting was too much like hard work.

'I'm going to make a call,' he said. 'Let me know when you've finished the boring workout stuff and you're ready for the actual practice game.'

'Right, lads, gather round,' Slugsley said when Barney disappeared inside and Cornelius was back to shouting at someone on the phone. The players old and new huddled around him. 'Now that His Nibs has gone, we'll get started. We all know what's going on here and for most of us it leaves a bad taste in our mouths, but we've made our decisions, so we're going to do what we have to do.'

He looked at each face in turn.

'You're all good players and you can adapt to anything. For the next hour we're going to practise situations in which we're a man short. All the best teams train with every eventuality in mind, including injuries and players being sent off. Well, in this tournament young Figg is going to be playing in the centre of the midfield, so every match is going to be like playing with a man sent off. Every match is ten against eleven. But we can do it. You're good lads and we'll prepare right.'

Within minutes, they were togged out and on the pitch, fizzing the ball around.

Noah and St Mary's were going to have their work cut out against this lot. Figg's teammates were good. They were very good indeed.

PLAYER PROFILE

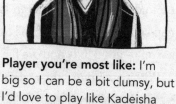

Name: Barbara Courtney

Nickname: Babs

Age: 12

Position: Centre-back is usually where I play, not that I've played many official games. None to be exact. I've always been a bit nervous of joining a proper team and just when I was thinking about it CC United, our local club, closed down. Most of the time I just kick a ball around the back garden with my brother, Frank.

Likes: I love any kind of music. I love swimming too, especially in the sea. I really want to try surfing as well, but I'm worried that I'll look stupid on the board, especially if I end up falling off loads of times. That'd be really embarrassing.

Dislikes: Public speaking. I prefer listening to talking. Cooking – my mam says I'd burn water. Making women play their World Cup on artificial turf. Real pitches, please.

Player you're most like: I'm big so I can be a bit clumsy, but I'd love to play like Kadeisha Buchanan. She's fantastic.

Favourite player: I don't just have one! Savannah McCarthy. The great Abby Wambach. Yoreli Rincón. Tang Jiali. Amandine Henry. Jade Moore. I could go on forever.

Favourite goal: Mizuho Sakaguchi's goal for Japan against Holland in the Women's World Cup. Stephanie Roche's goal for Peamount United. Lucy Bronze's goal against Norway.

Messi or Ronaldo: Why haven't you put a woman footballer in here as a choice? There's the Brazilian superstar Marta, or you could choose a goalkeeper for a change, like Nadine Angerer or Hope Solo.

CHAPTER SIXTEEN

*'I wouldn't say I was the best manager in the business,
but I was in the top one'*   Brian Clough

The man known as Dig Grimsby drew himself up to his full height of five feet six and a half inches. He didn't look like he'd once been a professional footballer, but he had, even if that time had been very long ago. Noah couldn't imagine him ever having been fit and healthy enough to run around a pitch.

It was Barbara and Frank's father who had suggested Grimsby as a coach. He worked with the man in the local plastics factory and had spent many tea breaks being bored by Grimsby's tales of his footballing life. Since nobody else could think of any other possible candidate they could find at such short notice, they had decided to meet him to see if he was the right fit for the St Mary of the Immaculate Conception School for Girls' football team.

Grimsby had thick black curly hair, a beetroot-red face and a perfectly round belly that made him look like someone who was shortly to become a mother for the first time. He let out a belch. Spotting the disapproving look on Stevie's face, he said, 'Better that it comes out this end than the other.'

He guffawed and thumped Noah on the back, as if he was part of the great joke.

The entire team was packed into the hut that was now the St Mary's headquarters. They were dressed in a variety of training kit: some in T-shirt and shorts like Noah, others, like Stevie, in a full tracksuit and baseball cap.

Noah was nervous. This was a big test. He'd spoken to his dad on Skype earlier, telling him about everything that had been happening and that had cheered him up for a while, but later when he remembered that he wouldn't see him in the flesh for another four long months the good feeling had worn off, and his determination to bring his father home had grown even stronger. It had been one thing assembling a team – that had been great – but now they were about to find out if the players they'd cobbled together were any good.

Grimsby pointed to the crest on his tracksuit, a tracksuit that was a little tighter on him than he would have liked.

'You lot see what's written there?' he asked.

The entire group leaned in closer to him. There were pictures of a bird and a steam train above the words that ran diagonally across the crest.

'*Swindon Town FC*,' Hawk Willis read aloud.

'Aye, lad. Swindon.

Great club. I made two League Cup appearances for them back in the late eighties. Over twenty-five years ago and I still fit into the same tracksuit I wore that day,' he said, patting his belly as the seams of the tracksuit strained to their limits. Grimsby spat on his hands and rubbed them together. 'Right, let's have a better look at this bunch of tulips.'

He lined them up by the bench that ran along the walls of the hut. They were like soldiers facing a parade inspection, although soldiers were rarely squashed together like they were.

'You, what's your name?' Grimsby asked, jabbing a finger into Darren Nolan's chest.

'Darren,' he replied. His accent stood out and Grimsby latched on to it immediately.

'You're from Dublin?'

'Yeah,' Darren said.

'Better hide my wallet so,' Grimsby chuckled. When he saw nobody else was joining in the laughter, he shook his head. 'No? Nothing? You're a dry lot.'

He moved along the line, shaking his head in disbelief at the state of the players in front of him. He stopped when he reached Maggie O'Connell. He stared at her for a moment and his face scrunched up, either in confusion or as a result of the previous night's curry.

'You're a good-looking lad, but pretty boys don't make great footballers.'

Maggie scowled. 'I'm a girl.'

'You're a *girl*?'

'Yeah, I'm a girl. Have you got a problem with that?'

155

Noah placed a comforting hand on her arm. The last thing he needed was her kicking off.

'Don't get me wrong,' Grimsby said. 'I have no problem with a girl playing football as long as she plays with other girls, but this is a different level. Men are stronger and faster than women, love. That's not my decision – that's nature's. But if these guys want you playing on their team then I'm not going to argue, and you can always tidy up the dressing room after we've finished.' He chuckled.

Maggie shook off Noah's hand.

'I'm going to smash—'

Frank and Cormac managed to grab her just before she launched herself at Grimsby. He seemed unperturbed by her attempt to attack him.

'Sparky. I like that attitude. Keep that anger going. It'll help you on the pitch.' Adam O'Brien was the next in line. Grimsby glanced at Adam's tattoos and long black hair, then shook his head sadly before turning to Barbara. 'You're a tall one. What's your name, lad?'

'Barbara.'

'That's a girl's name.'

'I *am* a girl.'

'At least you're smart enough to disguise it, huh? You'd easily pass for a bloke in that baggy old tracksuit. Fair play to you.'

Stevie's cheeks reddened up, but he didn't say anything. He just squeaked a little, which made him sound like a disgruntled mouse.

'Who made that noise?' Grimsby asked. He looked around for a moment before finally looking down. 'Oh, it's you. I hardly saw you all the way down there. Nobody told me we were remaking *The Hobbit*.' He grabbed Stevie under the arms and lifted him into the air. 'There, that's better. Now we can look each other in the eye. I hope you're not a player, son. You're not much bigger than Yoda.'

'I'm not a player. I'm an analyst,' Stevie said defiantly.

'An analyst? What's that supposed to mean?'

'If you put me down, I'll be happy to show you.'

Grimsby lowered him to the bench and Stevie grabbed his bag, unzipped it and handed over a black plastic folder.

'It's an analysis of all the players: their strengths and weaknesses. Also, everything I could find out about some of the teams we might be playing in the tournament. Plus foods we should be eating, suggested individual training programmes, things like that,' Stevie said proudly.

Grimsby flicked through the folder. Everything was neatly typed, several pages had diagrams and pictures, and each sheet was in an individual plastic sleeve. It was an impressive dossier. He studied it for a few moments before closing the folder and holding it above his head for the others to see.

'There's been an awful lot of work put into this,' he said.

Stevie beamed.

'But it's been a complete waste of time. Like my old ma said – better to be a smart dosser than a busy fool.'

Stevie's face changed immediately. Now he appeared to be on the verge of tears.

Grimsby threw the folder to the ground. 'When I train a team, I build it in my own image. I don't have folders or smart computers or any of that nonsense. I know what's right and wrong because I feel it in my gut, not because I look at some statistics compiled by a nerd in his underground cave. I live and breathe the game and no one here knows more than me, so I expect complete acceptance of what I say. It's my way or it's the wrong way.'

He looked around, then pointed at Michael Griffin.

'Have you ever played football for a living?'

Michael shook his head.

'You?' he asked Sunday.

'No, I never have.'

'Deliverance, what about you?'

McCooley refused to respond. He just stared at the coach.

'I'll take that as a no. So, it looks like I'm in a field of one. That makes me a specialist. An expert. The only way this is going to work is if you accept my methods. If you do, I'll make you the best you can be. But I'm not going to do it unless you sign your lives over to me. I have a hectic schedule and I'm not going to waste my valuable time unless you're willing to give it a hundred and ten per cent.'

Little Stevie coughed. 'Ahm . . .'

'What is it, squirtleberry? Spit it out.'

'Well, it's just that, you know, you can't actually give more than one hundred per cent. It's impossible.'

'That's the kind of attitude that mashes my potatoes. Nothing is impossible. If my manager at Swindon asked me to run through a brick wall, I'd do it for him and then I'd eat the bricks. I want you lot to be the same way.'

'You want me to run through a brick wall then I will do it,' Piotr said enthusiastically.

'Good man! That's what I'm talking about. Now, I'm going to step outside for a smoke and you lot can have a girly chat. I'll give you five minutes. When I come back in, you're going to tell me if you're up for it or not.'

He stuck a cigarette in his mouth and headed outside. He popped his head back inside for a moment.

'Sorry about that,' he said.

'Sorry about what?' Noah asked.

'You'll find out soon enough.'

Stevie, being the lowest to the ground, smelled it first. 'Oh no, he's let one go.'

'That's vile.'

'Oh, dear God, my nostrils are burning.'

'Somebody punch me in the face so that I'm distracted from the smell.'

They wasted two of the five minutes Grimsby had allotted them recovering from the noxious gas attack.

'OK,' Noah said as the air finally cleared. 'What do you think?'

'I think he needs to see a doctor. Nobody should be able to produce an odour like that,' Sunday said.

'All right, all right, he's horrible, but this is serious. What about having him as a coach?'

'I think he's a fool,' Maggie said. 'A fool and a Neanderthal.'

'You think everyone's a fool,' Noah replied.

'No, just him,' she said. 'And you.'

'He might be a fool, but he knows football, right. I mean, you don't get to play for Swindon if you can't play, do ya?' Darren said.

'It's Swindon, though, not Milan. And he only played twice,' Adam O'Brien said.

'Twice more than anyone we know,' Cormac McHugh replied.

'He was mean to Stevie,' Barbara said.

'I don't mind,' Stevie replied cheerfully.

'Right,' Noah said. 'On the one hand he's a mean, gas-producing idiot who doesn't think women are good at football. On the other, he's played the professional game, so he knows how things are done.'

'He's not right for us,' Maggie said.

'Maybe not, but what other choice do we have? Who else are we going to find to coach us with only six weeks until the tournament? None of our parents want to get involved. So, it's either train ourselves or go with Dig Grimsby.'

Noah looked around the room. He wasn't feeling it. There was no enthusiasm for Grimsby, but he also knew there were no other options. There were some strong personalities in the squad, and if they tried training themselves every session would end in chaos and most probably a fight. Anyway, Grimsby might talk a load of rubbish, but he'd once been fit and skilful, so he had to have a trick or two up his sleeve. To become a professional he probably had to be the best in his local club team, then good enough to get spotted by a scout from England and invited for a trial. That was impressive enough, but after that he'd have had to have been one of the best players in the trials or else he wouldn't have been offered a contract. Lots of people wanted to be professional footballers – very, very few made it. There had to be some talent in there that their team could put to use.

'Let's vote on it. Show of hands. Who wants Grimsby to be our coach?'

It was easier to count the people who kept their hands down. It was just the two girls and Michael Griffin. Everyone else had their hands stuck high in the air.

'Grimsby it is,' Frank said.

Noah opened the door. 'Mr Grimsby, we've made our decision.'

'The right one.' Grimsby grinned. 'No need to look so surprised. I was eavesdropping. All right, ladies and germs, outside and we'll get this party started.'

They filed out into the fresh gale-force wind. For once Noah was glad of the gusty air. Anything was better than the confined space of the mouldy hut.

'OK,' Grimsby said. 'I'm not going to be able to remember all your names, so I'm going to call you whatever comes to mind when I see you.'

He pointed at Darren. 'You're from Dublin, so you're Jackeen. And you're Tweenchy McSmall,' he said, nodding at Stevie.

'Harsh, but fair,' Stevie said, accepting the insult.

And on and on it went. Dave's brother Tony was the Octopus. Sunday was the Kenyan, because he resembled a Kenyan runner. Despite Sunday protesting that his background was Nigerian, Grimsby refused to change his mind. Only Hawk Willis retained his name because, as Grimsby said, only an idiot would forget the name of a person called Hawk.

'Right, one final thing. My name is Dig Grimsby. I will not answer to Dig. I will not answer to Grimsby. Try me.'

'What?'

'Say my name.'

'Dig?'

Grimsby turned away, pretending not to hear. 'See, no response. From now until we win this tournament, you will call me Gaffer.'

'Mr Gaffer?' Hawk Willis asked.

'No, just Gaffer.'

'I don't get it.'

'I don't get you. Have I given you a name yet?'

'No, you said Hawk was too cool a name to forget.'

'Right, well I've changed my mind: from now on you're Pain in the Ass. Now, listen up all of you. From this moment on you will be in agony. You will pull muscles with names you can't pronounce. You will never suffer as much in your lives as you will in the next six weeks. You will envy the dead. Some of you will weep. Others will beg for their mammies. You will hate football by the time I've finished with you, but you will be winners. Winners play through the pain and you will be in as much pain as any ten-year-old has ever been.'

'We're all over ten,' Noah said. 'Some of us are nearly thirteen.'

'Are you? Great, I can make training even harder so.'

McCooley thumped his captain between the shoulder blades. 'Nice one, Murphy.'

Noah didn't respond to the instant pain or the shuddering sound that rang through his ears. He knew it was for the best. It was taking time to get used to the idea of being in the same team as Kevin McCooley. Sometimes he'd forget about it and think he was dealing with a normal person, but random acts of violence like that sudden thump on the back concentrated his mind wonderfully. As far as he could tell, the others seemed to be reasonably comfortable in McCooley's presence. As long as they didn't annoy him or speak to him or make any sort of eye contact, everything was fine. Only Maggie seemed intent on antagonizing him.

'The reason you're going through all this is for one purpose and one purpose only: to win this tournament,' Dig Grimsby said. 'We are going to win. We have to win. Do you know who doesn't win?'

'Us?'

'No, Octopus, not us. We're going to win because we're winners. The ones that don't win are losers. I am a winner and the team I lead will win. First is first. Second is nowhere.'

'What about third?' Hawk Willis asked.

'That's nowhere too, Pain in the Ass. Now, we've talked enough. It's time to start training.'

CHAPTER SEVENTEEN

'Well, Clive, it's all about the two Ms – movement and positioning'   Ron Atkinson

'Did anyone bring a ball?' someone asked.

'A ball?' Grimsby spluttered. 'It'll be a long time before any of you lot will be kicking a ball. You have to earn the right to kick a football. You have to prove you're hungry enough for it.'

'Excuse me, Gaffer,' Stevie said politely. 'Studies have shown that most football training works best when you actually use a ball. On his podcast Ken Early said—'

'Who does Ken Early play for? Who does he manage?'

'He's a journalist, but he knows a lot about football. I think he had trials for Marseille.'

'Trials, me backside. I had trials for the *X-Factor* years ago. Sang a Glenn Medeiros song. Doesn't make me a bloody pop star. Now, you lot listen to me and listen to me good: thinking is the enemy of football,' he bellowed.

'You're wrong—' Frank Courtney began.

'Right, that's it,' Grimsby snapped. His cheeks puffed out, even redder with sudden rage. 'Drop to the ground and give me twenty.'

'Are you joking?'

'If I'd made a joke, you'd be laughing right now. Make it thirty. And count them out for me.'

Frank dropped to the ground and started his press-ups. He'd never done more than ten before and his arms wobbled like strawberry jelly. 'Two,' he huffed. 'Three. Four.'

'Let that be a lesson to you. No talking back. Anyone else got anything they'd like to say? Anything they want to get off their chest?'

Thirteen heads shook left to right and back to left in unison. Noah frowned. This wasn't the start he'd been hoping for. With so little time before the tournament he'd thought Dig would begin assessing the players immediately. Once he'd found out their strengths and weaknesses he'd find their best positions and focus on improving them as much as possible. Noah looked over at Stevie, who gave a little shrug.

'Five,' Frank spluttered. The tip of his nose touched the ground.

'Is that the best you can do? When I was your age, I could do fifty using only my right arm, forty with my left and fifty-six with my old man standing on my back.'

Noah wondered why Dig Grimsby needed to have his father stand on his back when he was doing press-ups, but he wasn't about to ask.

'Oh, for pity's sake,' Grimsby said, wiping away a sheen of sweat with the sleeve of his nylon-polyester mix tracksuit. 'I can see we're going to have to get a lot fitter.'

Darren began to chuckle. Grimsby spun round. Maggie was

doing press-ups. Smoothly, easily. Her form was perfect.

'Twenty-eight, twenty-nine, thirty,' she said, not even breathing heavily.

'What are you doing?' Grimsby asked, more than a little confused.

Maggie hopped to her feet and broke into a grin. 'Just getting them out of the way early. We both know I'm going to say or do something to annoy you at some point, so I thought I'd get a head start on the punishment.'

'You and me are going to have a falling out, girl,' he said.

'The name's Pretty Boy,' Maggie replied.

'Right, drop to the ground and give me thir—'

Dig Grimsby caught himself just in time. He walked round the back of the shed muttering to himself and returned with an old fire-engine-red racing bike that had seen better days. It had a very thin frame and looked far too light to accommodate Grimsby's bulky mass, but surprisingly it didn't buckle when he climbed aboard.

'Same kind of bike as Stephen Roche won the Tour de France with,' he said.

'Are we going cycling, Gaffer?' Adam O'Brien asked.

'*I'm* cycling. You lot are going to jog.'

There were more than a few groans.

'Off you go, two abreast. Past the edge of the pitch, then straight on. I'll let you know if you're going in the wrong direction.'

He took a whistle from his pocket. Two loud shrills pierced the air.

'One peep means go right, two means left. I know that's far too complicated for most of you, but you'll get the hang of it.'

This is just an exercise in team building, Noah told himself. If every player hates the coach, then we'll bond as a group and that'll help us. Yes, the man was allowing himself to be hated just to help the team. Grimsby was a psychological genius.

Grimsby wasn't a psychological genius, he realized half a kilometre later.

'Technically, I'm not even part of the team,' Stevie gasped as he struggled along.

'Quit your guff,' Grimsby said as he conducted the impressive feat of lighting a cigarette while cycling his bike.

Stevie huffed and puffed along the footpath.

'What's wrong with you, lad? You must be the most unfit young fella I've ever met.'

'Cigarette smoke . . . not good for asthma . . . and pollen count high today.'

'What's that got to do with anything?' Grimsby asked.

'He's got allergies,' Noah said. He was breathing easily. Running had never been a chore for him.

It wasn't a chore for Maggie either. She was striding ahead, showing off. Occasionally, she'd drop back, run a couple of rings round McCooley, duck out of reach of the flailing arm he'd swing in her direction and sprint to the head of the group again.

'Allergies? Don't believe in them,' Grimsby said, sucking deeply on his cigarette.

'But science . . . has—'

'The power of the mind overcomes everything,' Grimsby said, tapping the side of his head with his finger and inadvertently singeing his eyebrows by bringing the lit cigarette too close to them. Thankfully, the odour of burning hair was quickly lost in the wind. 'When I was young, there was no such thing as allergies and we all got along fine. If we didn't like what our mothers put on the table and refused to eat it, then we went hungry. You couldn't afford to be allergic to anything back then. Now, enough chatting. You'd better speed up if you're going to keep up with me because in the words of Mr Christopher Cross, I'm going to ride like the wind.'

When they'd lapped the nearby housing estate, where their only audience was mothers pushing babies in buggies, and a few sullen teenagers hanging around with nothing to do, they headed towards the town centre with its busy traffic and shoppers. People stopped what they were doing to watch as the motley crew huffed and puffed by, jogging two abreast on the footpath, led by an overweight cigarette-smoking cyclist in a too-tight tracksuit.

'This is mortifying,' Barbara said to herself.

They reached the top of the town and looped round the statue of the town's least corrupt mayor.

'Water,' someone gasped.

'Water is for winners,' Grimsby said, slamming his hand on the roof of a car that had dared to get too close.

When the group returned to The Hatch, their earlier vim and vigour had been replaced by plodding and panting. They collapsed on the pitch in a messy heap, their lungs gasping for air, their cheeks flushed pink, their muscles aching and quivering.

'You're a disgrace,' Grimsby called out as he cycled around them. 'You're young, in the prime of life, and look at the state of you. And here's an old lad like me and I'm hardly out of breath.'

'In fairness, you are on a bike, Gaffer,' Cormac McHugh cried out in an agonized voice.

'Excuses, excuses. Meet me here tomorrow and we'll see what you're like as footballers.'

'We've earned the right to use the ball?'

'Not even close, buddy boy,' Grimsby said. 'Power lifting and drills. Lots and lots of drills.'

'Please, no more, man,' Hawk Willis whispered. 'Shoot me now. Put me out of my misery or else I'm just going to lie here and wait for the sweet kiss of death.'

'How far do you think we've run?' Noah asked. He wasn't feeling bad at all, but he didn't want to act like he was fine when the others were in bits.

'Forty kilometres,' Hawk Willis said.

'Three,' Stevie wheezed. He rolled up his tracksuit sleeve to reveal the running watch strapped to his arm. 'This records heart rate, distance, all . . . those kinds of things. According to the stats . . . I'm no longer alive.'

Michael Griffin was the first to get back to his feet.

'You OK, Michael?' Noah asked, hopping up.

Michael shrugged his shoulders.

'We'll recover. That was just Mr Grimsby throwing his weight about, showing us who's boss. Tomorrow will be easier,' Noah said.

Tomorrow was twice as hard.

Name: Frank Courtney

Nickname: Courts. The Judge. My nicknames are so uncool it's unreal.

Age: 12

Position: I'll play anywhere. Often at centre-back because I'm fairly tall although you wouldn't think that if you saw me standing beside my sister. She's a giant, a gentle giant – until she starts playing.

Likes: Hanging out with my friends and having a laugh. Someone's always saying something stupid and it's really, really funny.

Dislikes: Going to bed early. What's the point of that? Since humans learned to control electricity we don't have to sleep just cos it's dark outside so why do people still think it's great to go to bed early? Can't understand it.

Player you're most like: Per Mertesacker. I'm fairly decent, but I don't have much pace. Being slow means you have to read the game better, though. Xabi Alonso said that tackling isn't a great quality, that it's kind of a last resort and I think the same way. If you're in the right place at the right time, you'll intercept the ball and there's no need to risk a tackle. Most of the people I've played with disagree with me. They love a sliding tackle more than anything.

Favourite player: Zlatan Ibrahimović

Favourite goal: That goal against England. You know the one, the overhead kick. Wow. Zlatan's a monster.

Messi or Ronaldo: Ronaldo for me.

CHAPTER EIGHTEEN

‘ *Fail to prepare, prepare to fail* ’
Roy Keane

‘I don't know,’ Stevie said. ‘I like the ones with the stripes. What about you?’

‘I hate stripes. I'm not a zebra,’ Maggie said.

‘Pick whichever one you want, man. I look good in anything,’ Hawk Willis said, running his fingers through his thick head of hair.

Stevie and Barbara were flicking through a sportswear catalogue. Big Dave had got one from his friend Elaine, just as he'd promised Noah he would. There were pages and pages of football kits available in all sorts of colours and sizes, more combinations than Noah could have ever imagined existed. Elaine had been kind enough to give them a large discount and Mrs Power had agreed to pay fifty per cent of the costs; it was up to Simone to organize the rest of the payment. But getting his teammates to agree on what shirt and shorts combo they were going to wear in the tournament wasn't easy. Everyone had very different taste and everyone thought their taste was good.

Slightly more than half of the team were in the makeshift clubhouse and dressing room at The Hatch waiting for their next training session. They were huddled into the shed, which was in semi-darkness even with the light provided by the solitary sixty-watt light bulb. The wind howled outside, rattling the door. It was almost gloomy enough to start telling ghost stories.

'What do you think, Noah?' Stevie asked. 'Which shirt do you like best?'

Noah gave a mental sigh, but smiled encouragingly at his friend. He couldn't care less about the jerseys. They could be any colour as far as he was concerned; he had far more important things to worry about. As long as they didn't choose a pink shirt he was fine with their choice – he didn't like pink at all. Yellow as well – he wasn't a fan of yellow. Far too bright for his liking. And orange wouldn't be great either, come to think of it.

'What about black jerseys? We'd be like a team of Darth Vaders. That'd be awesome,' Cormac McHugh said, pointing a slim finger at a picture on page twenty-eight.

Adam O'Brien, who was in the process of tying his long hair into a ponytail for training, nodded in agreement. He loved black too. All his clothes were black, even his pyjamas.

'That jersey is cool,' Barbara said. Her cheeks flushed and she lowered her chin when she realized everyone was listening to her.

'I don't know,' Limbsy said. 'My mother makes my dad wear black shirts all the time to try to hide his belly. She says black is slimming. If I slim down any more, I'll disappear.'

'Can I have a look?' Noah said.

Stevie handed him the catalogue. Noah knew the moment he saw the jersey it was the one for him. It was as black as a starless night. The v-neck collar had a strip of white and two white stripes ran across the shoulders and down to the tips of the sleeves. It looked . . . perfect. He didn't have a phone, but he'd borrow the catalogue and ask Simone to take a picture of the jersey and text it to their dad.

'You're right, Barbara,' he said. 'It is cool. Let's go for it.'

'You can't make that decision without consulting me,' Maggie said, leaning over his shoulder to take a look. But she must have liked it too because she made a noise that signalled approval. 'I'll wear number nine. And make sure you get O'CONNELL printed on the back.'

'It's not the Premier League. We don't get our names on the jerseys.'

'Then how will people know it's me?'

'Don't worry, Maggie, I'm sure you'll find a way of letting people know who you are,' Noah said.

She grinned and gave him a friendly shove. 'Right, but we're wearing white shorts, OK?'

'We will be black and white like the penguins or the nuns,' Piotr yelled.

Noah couldn't believe they'd actually come to an agreement. It seemed far too easy for this bunch of players. Maybe it didn't always have to end up with shouting and threats, he thought.

'They're late,' Stevie said, referring to the rest of the team as he checked his watch.

'So's the gaffer, man,' Hawk Willis said.

Noah counted the heads in the room. Including himself, there were only nine there, eight if you didn't count Stevie who wasn't even a player. There was no sign of Darren, McCooley, Sunday, Frank or Michael Griffin. Five of them late for training, and they'd only been under the supervision of Dig Grimsby for a week. That wasn't good at all. He found it hard to blame them, though. Stevie's posters and online messages had promised them football and fun, and what had they got instead? A week of misery. The training had been extremely tough and about as much fun as an ice-cold shower on a winter's morning. With each passing day, the team's enthusiasm had faded and Noah knew that he was going to have to do something drastic or half of them were going to quit on him. And if they quit then his

175

chances of being spotted by a scout and recruited by a football club were over. He wouldn't be able to bring his father home. After his struggle to get into the tournament, he wasn't about to let everything fall apart that easily. His own doubts about Grimsby's so-called expertise had multiplied and Maggie had been quick to say *I told you so*. It was time for a conversation with the gaffer. He wasn't looking forward to it. Grimsby was far from being a reasonable man.

His thoughts were interrupted by the commotion outside. A moment later, Darren and Sunday staggered through the door. Sunday had blood dripping from his nose and his T-shirt was torn at the shoulder. Darren looked even worse. His lip was cut and he was missing a clump of hair, as well as a shoe. That wasn't the odd thing, though. The odd thing was that they were both laughing.

'What's going on?' Noah asked. 'Are you OK?'

'Never better,' Sunday said, wiping his nose.

Barbara jumped up and guided Darren and Sunday over to the bench. She made them sit down even though they protested that they were fine.

'What happened to you?' Limbsy asked.

Darren and Sunday looked at each other and grinned.

'Whacker Ryan,' they said in unison.

'Who's Whacker Ryan?' Maggie asked.

Noah remembered now that Darren and Sunday had told him that Whacker Ryan had been after them because they'd helped out some young boy on their estate. He must have finally caught up with them. That explained the cuts and bruises. It didn't explain the laughing and joking, though, not unless they'd both gone insane.

'Where is he? Is he outside?' Noah asked.

'Whacker's gone. We won't have to deal with him again,' Sunday said.

'Why?'

'Because he made a terrible mistake. Whacker and his friends attacked us on the way to training, but it turned out that one of our teammates wasn't too far behind us,' Sunday said. 'He made sure that Whacker won't even dare to look at us from now on.'

'There he is. There's the man,' Darren said, getting to his feet as Kevin McCooley arrived in the shed.

He tried to wrap an arm round McCooley's shoulders, but McCooley quickly shrugged him off.

'This guy saved our lives,' Darren said.

'Nice one, Mr McCooley,' Stevie said.

Barbara and Limbsy began to applaud, but when McCooley's eyes narrowed they reconsidered and stopped mid-clap.

'Why do you lot have to be so annoyin'? Everythin' that happens doesn't have to be a big deal. It's over, so just shut up about it, all right?'

It may have been over, Noah thought, but he could see that Darren and Sunday weren't going to forget it any time soon and neither were the others the way they were gathering around McCooley, much to his annoyance. Noah noticed that everyone was in better humour now than they had been after an entire week of training. His mind was made up. He was going to do things differently from now on. He was going to make sure they had fun. And if they had fun they might play well and then he'd have a chance in the tournament. He was going to fire Dig Grimsby as their manager. After all, this was supposed to be about football and they hadn't even played a practice match yet and it was the eighth of May; the tournament was only just over a month away.

'Afternoon, ladies and germs,' Grimsby said, arriving at the door just at the moment Noah was thinking about him. He smelled of beer and stale cigarettes. He was still wearing the same tracksuit he'd had on for every training session so far. It had become so worn it was shiny.

'Hey, Gaffer, I need to have a word with you,' Noah said.

'No time for a word now, Moses. We've got a match to play.'

CHAPTER NINETEEN

‘*Newcastle, of course, unbeaten in their last five wins*’   Brian Moore

When Grimsby had told them a few minutes earlier that he'd organized a match, the St Mary's team had been delighted and Noah had wondered if he'd misjudged the man after all. But when he saw the opposition waiting on The Hatch's pitch, he knew he hadn't. Noah had expected them to be tough, but he hadn't expected them to be grown men.

Not a single one of them was under thirty and two of them looked as if it had been at least a couple of years since they'd seen their sixtieth birthdays. The rest of the St Mary's team stared open-mouthed at the big bruisers trotting around the pitch battering the ball back and forth to each other as they warmed up.

'All right, lads,' Dig Grimsby said. 'I see you're acquainting yourself with the opposition. A few of the lads from work. They'll give you a right old game.'

Ten minutes later, after much grumbling from Noah's teammates, they were ready to play. Only ten of the St Mary's squad were getting a game even though it was an

179

eleven-a-side match. Dig Grimsby had decided that he would be better able to assess the quality of his players if he was right in the middle of the action, so he was playing in the match himself. He was going to be a striker. To their consternation, Maggie and Barbara were stuck shivering on the sideline.

'All right, lads, gather round,' Grimsby said.

They formed a huddle around him just on the edge of their eighteen-yard line. Since they hadn't got their own kit yet, most of the St Mary's team wore replica football jerseys. Darren may have been missing a shoe, but at least he had a pair of boots with him. Michael Griffin wore a full Dukla Prague away kit that had belonged to his father. Cormac McHugh was in a red Liverpool shirt just as he always was, while Sunday was dressed in the green of Nigeria.

McCooley wasn't wearing a football jersey at all. Instead, he wore a ripped T-shirt that depicted a horde of zombies feasting on a screaming victim. His boots had holes all over them and they were held together by duct tape.

'Right, this lot aren't great skillwise, but they are tough. They're not going to want to be shown up by a bunch of kids, so if you manage to get past them they'll probably kick you up and down the pitch until your legs are hanging on to your knees by a strip of tendon. Now, remember, it's a man's game. If they hit you, get back up immediately and act like you're fine. I don't want you lot embarrassing me, so no whingeing or cry-baby stuff. We need real men like my old pal, Seamus Barry. He got hit so hard once he dislodged his own Adam's apple. Played on till the end of the match before driving himself to hospital.

So badly injured he never spoke again, but we won the match 2–1, so the sacrifice was worth it. *That's* what I want from you today.'

'You want us to permanently disfigure ourselves?' Darren Nolan said.

'They can kick my head off if they want but there is no way they are scoring a goal,' Piotr shouted. He jumped up and down and slapped his gloved hands together.

'Aren't you going to discuss tactics?'

'Who said that?' Grimsby peered over the huddle and spotted Stevie. 'Ah, it's my old friend, R2D2. Beep-beep-boop. Always chattering away. You spend too much time thinking. I've warned you about that. The tactic is: give me the ball and I'll score a goal.'

The opposition's captain and his fellow midfielder, a steely-eyed man in a Pearl Jam T-shirt, stood in the centre circle, ready to start. The wind swirled around, blowing a plastic coffee cup and a discarded red *Grudz* packet across the pitch.

There was a sound like thundering hooves on the turf as the captain passed the ball to the Pearl Jam fan. Noah glanced round to see McCooley racing forward. He was a blur of motion. A squat, barrel-chested blur of motion. As soon as the Pearl Jam fan received the ball, McCooley went through him. It was a matter of conjecture as to whether he got the ball or the player first. To Noah, it looked as if he got them both at the same time. Mr Pearl Jam and the ball went flying through the air.

'Wow, that kid's mental,' Grimsby purred. He turned to Noah. 'You see that? That's *exactly* the kind of passion and unthinking behaviour I want from each and every one of you.'

The opposition were gobsmacked. They knew they were in a game now and the centre-back and the goalkeeper acknowledged the fact by extinguishing their cigarettes. The opposition's captain looked beseechingly at Grimsby, who was also acting as referee.

'Not even close to being a foul. Play on,' Grimsby shouted as McCooley took the ball under control on the second bounce and passed it to within a couple of metres of Noah.

It wasn't a good pass, but the other team were slow to react and Noah was on the move, floating past one, two players in a heartbeat. Hawk Willis flew down the wing. The left midfielder turned and tried to go with him, but he was forty-five years old and hadn't been fully fit since the spring of 1998. Willis was too fast and, more importantly, too far ahead to be fouled.

Noah, using his foot like a wedged golf club, lofted a long pass into the corner, into the space behind the left-back. To Noah's surprise, and to Hawk Willis's too, the young flyer managed to control the ball in one movement, before whipping in a cross to the edge of the area. McCooley had continued his run and met the cross first time with a ferocious volley.

Noah had never seen a football struck so powerfully. He had never seen one struck so inaccurately either. It pinged at least six metres above the crossbar, sailing high over a fence and into the wasteland behind the pitch.

It took them ten minutes to find the ball and get the match restarted.

It was competitive, but no one put in any hard tackles on the younger team. It wasn't out of respect or because they didn't want to hurt a group of youngsters. It was fear, pure and simple. They were too afraid of what McCooley might do to them. By half-time it was still 0–0 and the older men looked exhausted and drained. Most of them weren't used to regular exercise and it was just the captain and one of the midfielders holding things together.

Stevie made notes on a spiralbound pad, furiously scribbling down every thought that passed through his mind.

'What do you make of it?' Maggie asked him.

'Better than I thought. It's disjointed, but that's partly down to quality of the pitch and partly because Mr Grimsby is playing players in the wrong positions. Mr McCooley's possibly the hardest worker I've ever seen, but he can't pass the ball to save his life. And that tackle in the first minute?'

'I know, right. Wasn't that the most awesome thing you've ever seen?'

'If by awesome you mean terrifying, then yes. I think a couple of the poor man's teeth landed near me,' he said.

Maggie smiled. 'What else?'

'Well, if Limbsy relaxed he could be a real handful. Hawk is lightning fast, but he doesn't always make the right choices. Piotr hasn't had much to do, but he looks confident and capable. Michael Griffin and Darren Nolan are obviously full-backs, so I don't know why they're playing in the centre. And as for Mr Grimsby, well, he shouts very well and he managed to kick Hawk a couple of times, but it's almost impossible to believe he's ever played professional football.'

'Good analysis,' Maggie said.

She winked at Stevie before jumping up and down and waving her arms to attract Grimsby's attention. 'Hey, Gaffer. It's time to put me on. Pretty Boy needs some game time.'

'You'll get your chance when I say so,' Grimsby said, much to her frustration.

Noah saw Maggie throw her shin pads on the ground in anger. He looked at their middle-aged manager huffing and puffing as he practised juggling the ball when he should have been giving his half-time team talk. It was ridiculous. Noah felt the anger beginning to well up inside him.

St Mary's began the second half well, but their good form faded quickly and they were soon under pressure. The opposition, realizing belatedly that they had a height advantage, pushed their forwards further up the field and began to launch the ball high and long into the box.

A couple of minutes later and Noah's team was 1–0 down. A belter from twenty-five metres was finger-tipped on to the post by Piotr. The captain was on the rebound in a flash. He had one arm in the air celebrating before he realized Piotr had somehow managed to scramble across the goal and get his hand to it again. The goalkeeper wasn't able to stop the third shot, though. The grown men leaped about manically in celebration as Piotr thumped the ground in frustration.

'What kind of defending was that? If Robbie Savage saw that, he'd poke his own eyes out,' Dig Grimsby shouted, pulling at his hair and jumping up and down. 'My old mother could have done a better job and she has varicose veins and an inability to turn left. I've seen better defending from school kids.'

'We *are* school kids, Gaffer,' Darren Nolan said.

'You think you're so smart, don't you? Twenty press-ups, Jackeen.'

That's it, Noah thought, he's lost the plot. Even the opposition were staring at Grimsby as his red face turned purple. None of them had ever seen a man in his forties throw a tantrum like a two-year-old in a supermarket before. It seemed as if it was only a matter of time before he burst into tears.

'Can we stop all the messing, lads? We have to kick off,' Frank said, rubbing his ankle. He'd gone over on it as he tried to tackle the goal scorer. Darren dropped to the ground and began doing press-ups as Hawk tapped the ball to Adam O'Brien who raced off with it, his ponytail flying out behind him, his tattoos an inky-blue blur.

Noah had finally had enough. He'd reached breaking point. This was all wrong. Not a single person on his team was enjoying themselves, except Piotr maybe – that guy seemed to make the best of everything.

'That's it,' he said. 'Darren, stop doing press-ups.'

'I give the orders around here, Moses,' Grimsby said. He was practically spitting with fury. 'Drop and give me twenty.'

'No,' Noah said. 'I'm not doing things your way any longer.'

'O-ho, boyo. You need to learn a lesson. Make it thirty press-ups, so. Keep pushing me. I can count past a hundred.'

'Mr Grimsby, I've had enough. We've all had enough. You're a joke. You're fired.'

Grimsby began to splutter with fury. He couldn't believe his ears. 'Fired? Fired? *You're* firing *me*? You can't fire me, you little shih-tzu.'

'Then how come I just did?'

'Hey, Noah,' Frank called. 'Sorry to interrupt, but we've just let in another goal.'

With Noah and Dig Grimsby arguing, and Darren still paused in the press-up position, the team was outnumbered and the older men had muscled their way through to blast the ball past Piotr. It was 2–0. Kevin McCooley let out a roar of anguish.

'Now look what you did,' Grimsby shouted. 'You take charge for one second and we let in a goal. This team doesn't need you – it needs me. I played for Swindon Town.'

'In the League Cup,' Sunday said. 'Nearly thirty years ago.'

'It still counts,' Grimsby roared. He puffed out his chest. 'I'm not going and there's nothing you can do about it.'

'Don't make us do this the hard way, Mr Grimsby.'

'I dare you to try,' Grimsby said.

'Mr McCooley,' Noah said. He waved at McCooley to attract

his attention. 'Can you escort our former gaffer off the pitch, please.'

'Ha, you don't scare me. I played against the likes of Danny "Leg Chomper" McDougal so a ten-year-old kid doesn't frighten me,' Grimsby harrumphed.

But as Kevin McCooley took a couple of steps towards him the older man swiftly reconsidered. He scampered off the pitch.

'Aw, are you going, Mr Grimsby? We're really going to miss you,' Maggie said as her now former manager hopped on his bike.

Grimsby ignored her.

'One week and half a match. That's how long you gave me to work my magic,' he roared at his former players. 'Even Chelsea Football Club gives managers longer than that. You don't deserve my expertise, you bunch of ungrateful, moaning, girly little whingers.'

He reached inside his tracksuit top and produced a short silver tube. He held it up for them all to see.

'This is a Cuban cigar. Cohiba Esplendidos. It cost me over fifty euro. I've been saving it for a special occasion. Well, I've just decided when that occasion is – the day you lot of snot-kickers get knocked out of the tournament. That'll be one sweet moment.'

He kissed the cigar tube before pocketing it, then lit a cigarette, waved goodbye using only two of the available fingers on his right hand and cycled away, shouting something about how cheeky young people were these days. Nobody was sorry to see him leave.

'I was really warming to that man,' Piotr said.

Well, almost nobody.

'Can you give us a minute?' Noah said to the other team's captain.

'No problem.'

Noah gathered the team around him. The day's first drops of rain began to fall.

'OK, we have about ten minutes left. Forget the score, let's just do what we can.'

Maggie appeared beside them. Her brand new San Jose Earthquakes jersey was spotlessly clean. 'Who's coming off so I can go on?'

'My ankle took a battering and it could do with a rest,' Frank said.

'I'm not playing at the back,' Maggie said. 'I'm a creator not a destroyer.'

'All right,' Noah said. 'Barbara, you're on for your brother.'

Barbara's face was emotionless, but her fingers trembled as she struggled to unzip her tracksuit top.

'They're bringing on a girl. Now we're really in trouble,' someone shouted.

A trademark McCooley glare shut him up.

'Who is that kid?' one of the opposition whispered to a teammate.

'I think he's a McCooley,' was the hushed reply.

'That explains *a lot.*'

It was Kevin McCooley who went off the pitch to be replaced

by Maggie. He didn't say anything to anyone – he just walked off.

'Thanks, Kevin,' Maggie said with a smile, before turning to the others. 'Right, let's show this lot how to play the game. None of this long ball stuff or just panicking and getting rid of it.'

'Wait, I'm the captain. I'm the one who should be talking about tactics,' Noah said.

'Who died and made you Queen of Everything?' Maggie asked.

'We don't have a manager, so the captain's next in line. Now let's—'

'We need a manager, man,' Hawk Willis said. 'I don't work well in an unstructured environment.'

Michael Griffin nodded solemnly.

'I know,' Noah said, 'but we don't have one and—'

'Stevie should be manager,' Barbara said.

Thirteen faces turned in her direction and she reddened up immediately.

'What?' Noah began to laugh, but then the laugh caught in his throat. 'Are you being serious?'

'That's actually a good idea, Barbara,' Darren said.

'Yeah, I agree. Stevie's always analysing stuff. He knows everything there is to know about us. It makes sense,' Sunday said. 'He's the one who spotted the loophole that allowed us into the tournament as well. And he can't be any worse than Grimsby.'

Noah thought the idea was ridiculous. Stevie wouldn't do it – he couldn't handle the pressure.

'Ahm, yeah, well, actually,' Stevie began. 'I wouldn't . . . you know . . . mind giving it a go. If it's not putting anybody out or causing any trouble,' he said.

'Right, show of hands. Who wants Stevie as manager?' Maggie asked.

Everyone raised their hands – everyone except Noah, that is. He was still in shock. Little Stevie Treacy a manager? He didn't like being the centre of attention. Yet there he was, beaming with delight.

'OK, much as you all want to sit around braiding each other's hair and telling each other how great you are, we have a match to win. What are we going to do, boss?' Maggie said.

Stevie steadied himself and took a deep breath.

'Just keep it simple. You're good players and you're faster than they are, but, other than Mr McCooley, they're stronger, so you basically want to use your pace and avoid any confrontations,' he said, his voice trembling. 'Find some space, get the ball, pass it quickly and move into more space. They won't be able to keep up. Some of them turn as slowly as an articulated lorry. Don't just belt the ball away. That's playing into their hands. Pass. Move. Pass. No battles. No long balls. Is that OK?'

There were a few cheers. They finally had some clear instructions that involved playing football, not just resorting to violence and the possible sacrifice of body parts. Barbara gave Stevie a high-five as the new manager took his place on the sidelines.

Their form began to improve almost immediately. Noah was instrumental in everything and took control of the midfield, playing little one-twos and spinning around to ease the ball forward, but their first goal came from an unexpected source.

Noah played a one-two with Sunday and clipped the ball forward into the space between the left-back and the centre-back. Limbsy Donnelly ran on to it, confusing the defenders with his leggy physics-defying movements. He tried to knock the ball forward towards Maggie who was roaring for a pass, but managed to play it off his own leg instead. It looped in the air and over the keeper before hitting the crossbar and bouncing off the back of the keeper's head and into the net. The team was too stunned to celebrate. Even Limbsy himself was gobsmacked.

Maggie got a second goal a couple of minutes later, a beautifully controlled volley from just inside the area.

The opposition's centre-half clapped his hands in appreciation. 'Great finish, kid.'

'I've scored better,' she said with a shrug.

They still had time to hit the bar with a ferocious Cormac McHugh shot before Stevie's iPhone beeped to signal the end of the match with the score still at 2–2. Half the older team collapsed to the ground afterwards, more exhausted than they had been since U2 were in their prime. The captain shook Noah's hand.

'Unusual tactic, firing your manager during the match, but you did the right thing. Dig's one of those lads who gets worse the more you get to know him. You were much better in the ten minutes without him than you were in the forty minutes with him.'

'Thanks,' Noah said as the team trooped off.

He felt a bit guilty about getting rid of Grimsby the way he had, but he knew if he was going to succeed it had to be done. He'd given the ex-gaffer enough chances to prove himself.

Noah had wondered what kind of squad he had and now he had the answer – not a bad one at all. There were plenty of good players and those that weren't good tried really hard. They showed promise.

Everyone was in high spirits and they crowded around Stevie patting him on the back and showering him with praise. Noah felt a strange pang in his chest. It took him quite some time to recognize that the feeling was jealousy. He was considering whether or not he should talk to Stevie about what had happened when the empty *Grudz* packet blew right into his face.

The only person he'd ever seen eating *Grudz* sweets was Mr Hegarty. But why would he have been hanging around The Hatch? Apart from kicking Noah off the team, Hegarty had never shown the slightest interest in football and he was surely unlikely to start now. It must just be a coincidence.

It wasn't.

PLAYER PROFILE

Name: Tony Donnelly

Nickname: Limbsy. I'm kinda tall and gangly. I think that's why I got the nickname. Don't mind it, though. It's all for a laugh, isn't it?

Age: 12

Position: Forward, but I'm happy to play anywhere really. I just love playing football. The best day I ever had was during the last summer holidays when me and a bunch of lads from the estate played a game on the green for about four hours. In the end, there were dads coming home from work and joining in and we ended up with about twenty-five players on each side. We couldn't keep track of the scores and there were loads of arguments. It was epic.

Likes: Sherlock; I love all those mystery stories. I'm good with bikes too. My dad has an old motorbike he's always fixing up in our back garden – Mam goes mad because of all the bits and pieces lying around – and I help him with it.

Dislikes: Being stuck on a bus with a smelly guy in the next seat. It happened to me once and I kept gagging for hours afterwards. Other than that I kinda like most things, but nothing more than football. Football rocks.

Player you're most like: People say I'm like Peter Crouch cos I'm tall and skinny. I can see what they mean :) but I think I'm more like Shane Long.

Favourite player: Wayne Rooney. What a player.

Favourite goal: His bicycle kick against Man City a few years ago. I have never seen a better goal in my whole life.

Messi or Ronaldo: Messi

CHAPTER TWENTY

'Football is a simple game: twenty-two men chase a ball for ninety minutes and in the end, the Germans win' Gary Lineker

The weeks began to fly by and soon May was coming to an end and the summer holidays were almost upon them, which meant that everyone was in good form. There was even a rumour that Kevin McCooley had been seen smiling, but no one could confirm it. With Stevie in charge of training, the team had improved immeasurably in a short space of time. And what was even better was that they had improved while enjoying the sessions. Noah had been playing organized football for almost seven years and he had never enjoyed training as much as he had done in those few weeks. He didn't tell Stevie that, though.

'How do you do it, Stevie, man?' Hawk Willis asked at the end of one session. 'I've never had so much fun in my life.'

'Oh, it's just basic science and a touch of psychology,' Stevie said. 'In the past, teams trained collectively, the way Mr Grimsby trained us. That means if you had fast-twitch or slow-twitch muscles, if you were skinny or stocky, you were trained the same way. There are certain general training methods that work for all of us, but to maximise a player's potential you have to give them individual training programmes too. For example,

Hawk, you have a lot of fast-twitch muscles like most sprinters so getting you to pound out the miles is counter-productive. You need to protect your hamstrings yet enhance your speed—'

'Thanks for that, Stevie. Now I've never been so bored in my life. Next time I show any interest in anything you do, shoot me immediately,' Hawk said.

'I think it's impressive, Stevie. You're like a walking, talking Google,' Frank said.

'He sure is,' Barbara agreed.

Most of the training was done with a ball at their feet just as Stevie had told Grimsby it should be. Stevie would walk up and down observing everything, always making notes on his clipboard, as they played mini-games and did their passing drills.

Occasionally he'd film sections of the training on his phone and review them later. He filmed them dribbling through cones. There were always wildly varying results: Noah and Maggie were usually perfect, some of the players were average, but no matter what day of the week it was or what the conditions were Kevin McCooley was terrible. Unremittingly awful. The ball and McCooley's right foot repelled each other as much as a couple of magnets with the same polarity and he never managed to wriggle through without knocking over at least one of the cones.

'Keep going, Kevin, you're doing great work,' Stevie would shout every time.

And every time that part of the session would end with McCooley angrily booting one of the orange cones as far as he could. Once he managed to get one to land on the roof of the hut and he took a bow when everyone applauded. As far as Noah could tell, the squad had begun to accept him as a teammate, especially Sunday and Darren. That wasn't to say that the squad weren't still wary of him. They always knew that he could go berserk at any time. It was a little like dealing with a dog you can't quite trust, but as long as they didn't aggravate him he left them alone.

Some players blossomed under Stevie's guidance, especially the quieter ones, as he never roared at them or criticized them in any way. He only encouraged them and everything he said was positive, which meant their confidence improved. When the ball came to them, instead of kicking it as far away as possible, like it was a grenade about to explode, they tried their best to control it and look for the best pass. They learned that it was OK to take risks and it wasn't the end of the world if their pass went astray or the ball bounced away as they tried to trap it. If they made a mistake, they learned from it and if the risk worked out they felt good about themselves. He gave them the freedom to express themselves on the pitch and they learned when to try something wildly unpredictable and when to play it safe. They didn't just play football – they loved it.

Stevie was a little different when it came to Maggie and Piotr, the two most over-confident players in the team, possibly in the northern hemisphere. He had to remind them that, as good as they were, they still needed to keep their focus if they weren't going to become sloppy. To Noah's surprise, Maggie actually listened to what Stevie said and, despite all her bluster, she trained exceptionally hard, always giving it everything in her desire to improve. Everyone seemed to take Stevie's words on board and the only person he didn't offer any advice to was Noah.

To stop little groups or cliques forming, Stevie mixed the teams up constantly so that everybody got used to each other and never became too comfortable.

Of course, as the players improved and their confidence grew, Maggie started to show off.

'Oh, I hope that wasn't too embarrassing for you,' she'd say as she nutmegged Darren, or, 'Thank goodness you're smart, Sunday, cos you're not much of a footballer,' as she rainbow-flicked the ball over his head.

The rest of the team was really progressing well too, Noah noted. Piotr was an excellent keeper, sometimes a little too eager to race out of his goal – and to run his mouth off – but he gave the defence confidence and organized them well.

Frank and Barbara were great in the air, solid on the ground and never switched off their focus for one second. Noah had heard that some twins have a telepathic link. It seemed that Frank and Barbara certainly did when it came to football.

The full-backs were Darren Nolan on the right and Michael Griffin on the left. Darren was fast and a good worker and listened to the commands of his centre-backs, but Michael Griffin was a revelation. He wasn't particularly speedy and he didn't have outrageous skill, but he read the game better than anyone Noah had ever played with or against. He seemed to know what was going to happen three or four passes before it did. He hardly had to make a tackle because he was always in the right place at the right time. Noah couldn't believe he'd never even had a trial for the school team.

Noah himself was in the centre of midfield with Kevin McCooley. Poor Kevin wasn't a great communicator and he was slow over a few metres, but he could run all day long and once he wound himself up and got going there was no stopping him. His skill was winning the ball and making a simple pass. And he ran just as hard at the end of a session as he had at the beginning. On the left, Sunday was a winger with a nice range of skills, but he wasn't very fast. The other wing had a different problem – Hawk Willis was lightning quick, but brainless. One minute he'd look like the greatest player that had ever lived, the next as if he'd never seen a football before.

Noah thought his own game was improving too, especially with Maggie playing between the midfield and Limbsy up front. She always made intelligent runs, which made Noah's eye of the needle passes look even better and if she was a little less selfish she'd have been a brilliant team player, but then she wouldn't have been as spectacularly good.

Adam O'Brien and Cormac McHugh gave it their all. They turned up early for every training session, listened to every instruction and piece of advice and spent a lot of their free time practising new skills. Nobody worked harder than them, but despite all their effort they looked increasingly like squad players rather than starters. If they minded, they didn't show it. They made a pact with each other not to sit sulking on the sidelines. Instead, they were going to do some extra training and try to prove they were good enough to make the first eleven.

They knew that their new manager was fair and that they'd get plenty of game time even if they didn't always start. And when they got their chance they were going to do their best to take it.

Stevie got all the players to practise shooting early before the goalkeeper or defenders were set in their best positions and told them that they should shoot low whenever possible as it meant the keeper had further to travel to save the shot. He got them to play in every position on the field at various times so that they'd understand what their teammates were doing and learn something about how to outfox their opponents. Every day they learned something new.

After every training session they'd go to Dee's Diner. It was here that they really got to know each other. They helped each other out and mocked each other mercilessly. It was where they became a team.

In the last days before the holidays, a couple of weeks before the tournament was due to begin, they played two practice matches. It hadn't been easy to find opponents to play them. A few teams considered them a joke for playing for a girls' school, others were terrified of playing against a McCooley, and Noah suspected that some of the teams had been threatened or put off by Hegarty and Noah's old team captain Jim Reynolds. Stevie was like a terrier, though, and didn't give up until he'd managed to sort out some games.

They played the first one on one of the town pitches, which made a nice change from The Hatch. Their official jerseys still weren't ready so they wore white T-shirts and a variety of different coloured shorts.

Within minutes the team realized how good Stevie's training had been. They were several classes above the opposition who ran around like headless chickens while Noah's team passed the ball crisply and efficiently around them. Maggie was breathtakingly good and scored a magnificent bicycle kick in the fifth minute. They scored three more goals before half-time and by the final whistle they were 7–0 up.

The second match two days later was even better. Noah scored four goals from midfield, Maggie got a hat-trick, Limbsy got two and Darren Nolan and Hawk Willis both scored a goal

each. Hawk's was an over-hit cross that deceived the keeper, but he claimed that he meant it and nobody could persuade him otherwise.

Nobody noticed Mr Hegarty watching the match from the discomfort of his slightly-too-small car. He was parked in the supermarket car park across the busy road and was able to remain out of sight while keeping an eye on things. As Frank scored a header from a corner in the last minute, Hegarty dialled a number on his mobile phone. A moment later he heard Arthur Slugsley pick up.

'Noah Murphy is playing for another team,' Hegarty said.

'You told me this already,' Slugsley said. 'Some ex-pro called Grimsby was putting them through the paces. I heard his methods were from the Stone Age.'

'Yes, but things have changed. They've got a new trainer and they actually look good.'

'How good?'

'Good enough for you to be worried.'

'OK,' Slugsley said. 'I'll get someone on it.'

The match finished and Noah and his team shook hands with their exhausted opponents. Hegarty put his phone away and smiled to himself.

Name: Piotr Zajac

Nickname: The Cat because I have got great reflexes. It is my own nickname. Other people call me Super Boom because I talk very loudly.

Age: 12 $^7/_{12}$

Position: Goalkeeper. It is only the best position on the whole of the pitch. You have to dive, jump around and be the most athletic and flexible of all of the players. Nothing is better than a fingertip save, a small touch that sends the ball on to the post and then it breaks the striker's heart. Amazing!

Likes: Playing on the PlayStation. Teasing my brother. He is so serious all of the time and when I play tricks on him he gets very angry at me and says he is going to hit me with a hammer. It is the funniest thing I have ever seen.

Dislikes: School. Who wants to sit around all day listening to someone talking and talking and talking? It is boring. There is too much else to do in life.

Player you're most like: David de Gea, but I do not have a little beard. Ha, ha.

Favourite player: Thibaut Courtois. He is the greatest goalkeeper in the world. My favourite outfield player is a Belgian too: Eden Hazard.

Favourite goal: I prefer saves to goals. Anyone can score a fluke of a goal – my brother once scored a volley from 30m and he is a terrible footballer – but an amazing save – that is never a fluke. Did you see that one Jerzy Dudek made against Andriy Shevchenko when Liverpool won the Champions' League in 2005? Un-bel-iev-able. I have watched it a million times on YouTube. Dudek is Polish, like me.

Messi or Ronaldo: Messi is a genius. Ronaldo is the best athlete ever to be on a pitch. I like Lewandowski too, but people always talk too much about goal scorers. If a goalie keeps a clean sheet all of the time, then the team cannot ever lose a match. Think about that.

CHAPTER TWENTY-ONE

*'Playing with wingers is more effective against
European sides like Brazil than English sides
like Wales'*   Ron Greenwood

It was early in the afternoon and Noah was at home alone,
since Simone was working a shift in the cafe. He was doing
the washing-up, a job he hated and had been putting off all
afternoon. The sink was full to the brim with dirty dishes.
Noah squeezed in plenty of washing-up liquid and turned on
the hot water full blast. It splashed straight over the plates and
cups, over the side of the sink and on to the floor. He sighed
and turned off the tap. Now he was going to have to wash the
dishes *and* mop the floor. He decided that he'd definitely buy a
dishwasher just as soon as he earned some money.

As he scrubbed away at a greasy saucepan, his mind drifted
to football, as it almost always did. There were only six days left
until the tournament now. *Six days*. He could hardly believe how
quickly the last few weeks had gone by. One minute, he'd been
sitting in Hegarty's office being told he was off the team and
now, what seemed like five minutes later, the summer holidays
were here and they were about to play some of the best schools
in the country. His dad appeared to be as excited about the

tournament as Noah. When he'd first gone to Boondoggle Bend, they'd spent a lot of their time on Skype talking about mining and wildlife and all things Australian, but for the last little while they'd spoken about nothing but football when they had their weekly chats. It was almost like the old days again. But almost wasn't good enough. It was one thing talking to Dad through a webcam, it was another to be in the same room with him, and unless Noah was successful they'd only be in the same room again a couple of times in the next year.

Noah's thoughts turned back to football again. And from there to his teammates and manager. Stevie the manager. He still wasn't used to it. But he had to admit that Stevie was excellent, far better than he'd ever expected. Not that he'd told him that. Things felt a bit weird with Stevie these days. They still talked, but usually only at training. Of course, things were different in other ways too. Before, it had been just Stevie and Noah hanging out, but now there was another group of . . . well, friends, Noah supposed.

His thoughts were interrupted when the doorbell rang. He wasn't expecting anyone, but the days of him being surprised by someone calling at the door were long gone. There was a constant stream of visitors to the house these days: Dave, Maggie, Limbsy, most of the team had been there at one time or another, everyone except McCooley and Michael Griffin. On this occasion, the visitor was his manager.

'Stevie? Why didn't you come round the back?'

'Last time I tried that it didn't work out too well,' Stevie said. 'Can I come in?'

He looked anxious and not like himself at all, Noah thought. His eyes were red and watery and he was tugging and scratching at his arms and belly as if he had an itch that wouldn't quit.

'Are you OK?' Noah asked as he led Stevie into the kitchen.

'Not really. I'm not very good at all.'

Stevie sat down and began drumming his fingers on the tabletop.

'More allergies?' Noah asked.

'Hives, Noah. I'm covered in hives.'

'Hives are a pain,' Noah said sympathetically.

'A pain?' Stevie laughed a hollow laugh. 'That's the understatement of the year. I can't sleep a wink. I'm driven to distraction by the itching. I try not to scratch because I don't want to make things worse, though how they could be worse I don't know.'

'That's rough,' Noah said.

'Oh, I'm not finished yet. I'm also covered neck to toe in my mother's homemade hive lotion. My mother is a lot of things, but a good lotion maker is not one of them. It stinks, Noah. I mean yesterday when I was out for a walk Matt Lawlee's dog came over to me, took one whiff and ran off whimpering.'

Noah did his best to suppress a smile. 'Why don't you go to the doctor?'

'Because I know what's causing it. It's not an allergic reaction – it's stress. Horrible, horrible stress.'

'From the pressure of being a manager? Or are you worried about Hegarty?' Noah asked.

Stevie looked his best friend in the eye. 'It's you, Noah.'

'Me?'

'Yes, you. You're stressing me out.'

Noah was incredulous. 'But I haven't done anything.'

'Exactly.'

'Huh?'

'You're my best friend and when I got the job of manager you didn't even congratulate me. You never said a word. All the years we've spent talking about football, all the analysis over the last six months, all the work I've done, and then I get my dream job on the team and there's not a peep out of you.'

Noah knew he hadn't exactly been over-exuberant about Stevie taking the job, but he didn't think he'd made it obvious.

'Are you sure? I thought I did say something, but, even if I didn't, why would that cause you to break out in hives? I don't get it.'

'It's not just that. You never even say whether you like the training sessions or not.'

'Everyone's always going on about how much they like your sessions. They're always saying how great they are, how much fun they're having.'

'Everyone except you.'

'What difference does that make?' Noah asked. He was beginning to feel uncomfortable. Part of him wanted to get up and walk out of the room. He really didn't like talking about things like this. All these emotions and stuff? What good could come of it?

'Because I want to know if the sessions I designed to get the most out of everyone are actually working for our best player.'

'You think I'm the best player?'

Stevie threw his hands in the air, a gesture of exasperation. 'Of course you're the best player. You stand out a mile. Don't get me wrong – the others are very good, even Mr McCooley has his strengths, but you're extra-special. You don't do flicks and tricks all the time, but you see everything that's happening. Sometimes I think you see what's happening eight moves ahead of everyone else. You *understand* football. You know when to move, when to pass the ball. You control the tempo of the game. Just because you don't always come up with a Hollywood pass doesn't mean anything.'

'Thanks, Stevie.'

It was nice to hear that. Sometimes he wondered if people ever really saw what he brought to the teams he played for. Jim and most of the Killian's crowd didn't seem to appreciate it. Most people only noticed the showy stuff – the highlights reel, as his dad used to call it – but there was much more to football than that.

Stevie was looking at Noah with an expectant expression on his face.

'Oh, your sessions are excellent, Stevie,' Noah said finally.

Stevie breathed out in relief. 'You're not just saying that, are you? I mean, you do like them?'

Noah found himself staring at his feet. He noticed every scuff mark on his trainers, every scratch and small tear. 'I do. Your sessions . . . all the training . . . it's . . . well, it's the most fun I've had since I was the Mighty Dynamo.'

'The Mighty Dynamo? What's that?' Stevie asked.

A hot flush of embarrassment spread over Noah's cheeks. He'd said too much. 'Nothing. Forget about it,' he said.

Stevie was on his feet. 'No, this is exactly what I'm talking about. You're always holding something back. You wouldn't have told me about breaking into the school if you hadn't needed to borrow my phone. You never tell me anything any more. You haven't told me anything since –'

He stopped himself before he said the words, but they both knew what he was talking about. *He means since Mam died*, Noah thought. He shifted uncomfortably in his seat. Why did Stevie want to talk about all this stuff anyway? And why now?

Neither of them spoke for almost a minute. Noah could hear his neighbour pottering around his garden. The man was singing to himself. He didn't have a good voice.

'By the way, I got my tablet back from Mr Hegarty on the last day of school,' Stevie said, breaking the silence. 'Five weeks after he said he'd give it back. And it's not even my tablet. Well, he *says* it's mine, but there's nothing on it, nothing at all. And the serial number is completely different. It's lucky that I'd backed up my school project or else I'd have lost months of work. I think he gave me a brand-new model and he swapped it with my old one for some reason. He claims the hard drive got wiped because he left it beside a magnet, but there's no magnet in the school powerful enough to do that so I don't know what he's playing at.'

Noah knew that Stevie had sensed his embarrassment and was trying to change the subject. He really was lucky to have a friend like him. An annoying friend – a very annoying friend – but one who had always looked out for him.

'I—' Noah began.

'What is it?'

'Nothing. Forget it.'

'No, go on. Please, Noah.'

'Well, it's just . . . you complain about your parents all the time, but at least they're around. My dad's in Australia. I mean, who loses their job and then can only find one in Australia? And now we're playing in the greatest competition any of us will ever play in and he can't even afford to fly home cos he needs to save the money for the stupid mortgage.'

'You miss your dad.'

'Of course I miss him!'

'You never said.'

'Why would I say it? Isn't it obvious?' Noah snapped.

Stevie didn't reply. He just sat there, patiently waiting for Noah to continue.

'Saying it won't make any difference, will it?' Noah said, a little more softly. 'It's not going to bring him home. He's still in the middle of nowhere. And Mam is still –'

He couldn't bring himself to finish the sentence.

'She was here and then she was gone. People talked and talked. It didn't matter what they said. Nothing changed. And nothing's going to change if I talk about my dad.'

They sat in silence again listening to Noah's neighbour singing an awful version of 'Dancing Queen'.

'I don't like saying anything bad about people, but that man is a terrible singer,' Stevie said.

Noah almost raised a smile. He found himself warming to his old friend again. He placed his hands on the kitchen table and took a deep breath.

'Do you remember when Mam was here? What she spent all her free time doing?'

'Yes, of course – reading. She had the best library I've ever seen.'

'Exactly. This must be one of the smallest houses in town, but there wasn't anybody who had more books than us back then. They were stacked floor to ceiling in every room.'

'And the hallway. Remember when I was going up the stairs and that huge pile of books on the landing toppled over?'

Noah started laughing. 'That's right. You must have been only six or seven and loads of them—'

'An avalanche of books cascading down towards me. I thought I was going to die. I've still got a red mark the shape of Italy behind my ear from where her hardback copy of *War and Peace* hit me. So, what have the books got to do with anything?'

'Well, I don't like books the way Mam did, the way Simone does. It was always just football for me. The team I was really into back then was Dynamo Kiev. Must have seen them play on television or something. When I used to kick the ball around the back garden, I was always commenting on my own matches. You know – *and now Noah Murphy has the ball. He gets past one, and another and . . . what a shot from Murphy! That's the hat-trick!* – that kind of stuff.'

Stevie knew. He'd often done the same kind of thing himself.

'I'd be the star of the team,' Noah continued. 'But it wasn't just me. I imagined teammates as well. I made up names for them. I've forgotten most of them, but I still remember there were three Davies brothers – Jack, Mike and Peter. Mike was the goalie. Anyway, my mam used to watch me out of the back window all the time. She'd hear me commentating so when I'd come in she'd ask me what happened in the match and we'd sit by the fire and draw pictures of the action and we'd make up little stories together. She used to call me the Mighty Dynamo after Dynamo Kiev—'

Without warning, Stevie jumped out of his chair. 'We're the Mighty Dynamo!'

'What?'

'Don't you see? Barbara and Maggie and Mr McCooley and Piotr and all the lads. We're the players now. We're mighty. Mighty Dynamo Football Club. We're the friends that you never had. But we're not imaginary – we're real.'

'Er . . .' Noah said.

'Too cheesy and sentimental?' Stevie said.

'Far too cheesy and sentimental. I think I'm going to be sick.'

'You know, I sensed it was too much as soon as I said it. I'm sorry. I got carried away. I just like the excitement and the camaraderie and . . . oh, well, everything. Being the manager of a football team is the closest I've ever been to *being cool*,' Stevie said, using air quotes to emphasise *being cool*. 'I was even thinking about putting a rip in a pair of jeans. Me. With ripped jeans. Can you believe it?'

'But you didn't actually rip them, did you?'

'Goodness, no. It'd be a terrible waste. They're still quite new and if I'm being honest I'd be terrified of what my mother would say if she saw them.'

'I don't know much about being cool, Stevie, but I think if

you use air quotes and you're terrified of your own mother, you don't really qualify,' Noah said.

'Perhaps you're right,' Stevie said. He saw the look on Noah's face. 'There's more, isn't there?'

Noah nodded. It took him a couple of minutes to gather himself. His neighbour was in the middle of murdering 'Bohemian Rhapsody' when Noah spoke again.

'It's . . .' He stared at his trainers again. 'I haven't been the best teammate.'

He couldn't stop himself talking now. It was as if someone had flipped on a switch. It didn't feel quite as terrible as he'd imagined, but it wasn't easy either. A trip to a cruel dentist would have been more fun. He hoped all the talking was a passing phase. He couldn't imagine being like this all the time.

'What do you mean?' Stevie asked. 'You've been a great teammate.'

'No, I haven't.' Noah sighed. 'We're supposed to be a team, but I've been doing this for myself.'

And then he told Stevie the truth. He told him why he had spent the last six months working so hard, far harder than he ever had in the past. He told him everything.

'Let me get this clear,' Stevie said. 'You want to become a professional footballer so that you can earn enough money to pay off your dad's debts and bring him back home from Australia?'

'Yes,' Noah said.

'What's wrong with that? I know the odds are against you, but I don't understand why it makes you a bad teammate.'

'Well, because I wasn't honest. I tricked you into organizing things and then I got all the players rounded up and they're all doing this thinking it's because I want to win the tournament and play in the World Cup just like them, but it's—'

'OK, that's it. I've had enough. I know you're trying to be nice, but it doesn't suit you. It makes you kind of creepy, if I'm being honest. Answer a question: do you want to win the tournament?'

'Yes, but—'

'No buts. And do you want to play in the World Cup?'

'Yes.'

'Well, there you go. That's it. What difference does the rest of it make? You've pulled the wool over my eyes a little with all the analysis and everything, but you never twisted my arm. I loved doing it and I wouldn't have done it if I didn't want to. As for the others, they're not doing it for you – they're doing it for themselves. Maggie wants to win to show the world how great she is. Barbara is delighted to finally get a chance to play a proper football match. Frank loves all the messing. Mr McCooley never had friends before, but he likes being part of a team even if he'd rather chew off all his fingers than admit it. We all have our own reasons for doing this, Noah.'

The way Stevie explained it, it seemed plausible. Maybe Noah hadn't done anything wrong after all. Just a bit of deception. That was normal enough, wasn't it? He'd never wanted to be a goody two-shoes anyway.

'Are you sure?'

'I'm sure. I can't believe you even thought about it.'

'I didn't until I started enjoying training,' Noah said. 'Thanks.'

'So, all we've got to do is win the tournament and make sure you get spotted by a scout from one of the top football clubs. Easy peasy.'

'Sounds great,' Noah smiled.

'Are we OK now?' Stevie asked. He looked a little worried. 'I didn't mean to offend you when I came in all guns blazing.'

'Of course we're OK. And, Stevie, you're the least offensive human being, like, ever.'

'Well, that's not quite what I'd like on my tombstone, but I'll take it. So, should we hug this out?' Stevie asked.

'Nope. Definitely not,' Noah said.

'You footballers jump all over each other and kiss each other when you score goals, but you can't hug a friend?'

'That's different. Anyway, you have hives. Aren't they contagious? Don't want to get sick before the tournament.'

'OK, OK, I get it.' Stevie grinned, then his face changed. It was his turn to look serious. Noah had told him a lot of private things, now it was time for Stevie to tell his friend the truth – that he wanted to get on the pitch in the tournament. He wanted to play, even if it was only for a minute, even if he'd only get to make one pass or take one shot. He wanted it more than anything.

'You look like you've got something to say,' Noah said.

Stevie hoped Noah wouldn't laugh at him. He didn't mind people making fun of him, but that was about other things. This was different.

Just as he was about to speak, the doorbell rang. Then it

rang again. When it still hadn't stopped nine seconds later, Noah ran down the hall and pulled the door open impatiently.

'What?' he shouted.

Mrs Power was the last person he expected to find standing there.

'Now, is that any way for the captain of St Mary of the Immaculate Conception School for Girls to address his principal?'

'No, ma'am.'

'Ma'am? I may be old, but I wasn't born in the nineteenth century, Noah. Mrs Power will suffice.'

'Sorry. Um, Simone's not here.'

'I know. I just spoke to her. She told me you'd be here and it's you I need to talk to. Who's your friend?'

'Steven Treacy, pleasure to meet you. I've heard a lot about you,' Stevie said, pushing himself forward and shaking Mrs Power's hand.

'Ah, the brains of the operation. Well, boys, we appear to have hit a little snag.'

'What do you mean?'

'They're trying to kick you out of the competition.'

PLAYER PROFILE

Name: Michael Griffin

Nickname: Michael Griffin

Age: 12

Position: Left-back

Player you're most like: Lahm

Favourite player: Lahm

Favourite goal: Lahm

Likes: Films

Dislikes: Meeting people

What you like about football:
Playing it

Messi or Ronaldo: Lahm

CHAPTER TWENTY-TWO

' Sporting Lisbon in their green and white hoops, looking like a team of zebras '

Peter Jones

The next hour and six minutes was a very unpleasant experience for Noah as Mrs Power swung her car round each bend at an inventive new angle. His head bounced off the window as Stevie, who was beside him in the back seat, slammed into him before rebounding when his seatbelt pulled him back.

'Ow,' Stevie cried.

'Ow? You've been too mollycoddled, young man. You need to get used to a bit of rough and tumble.'

'Sorry, you're right. My parents have been a little bit overprotective by shielding me from certain death,' Stevie said as the countryside whizzed past them, a blur of green and brown. 'You get quite a bit more speed out of a Fiat 500 than I would have suspected.'

Once they'd raced through the town, jumping a couple of lights along the way – 'They're not red. They're just a very dark shade of orange' – Mrs Power explained the situation to them.

There had been a last minute objection to their participation in the tournament and the person who was going to decide whether or not St Mary's should take part, a man by the name of Mr McGlinnigle, was making his decision within the hour. He was a member of the national schools' football committee and one of the chief organizers of the Dublin tournament. As the closest committee member to the town of Carraig Cruach – only 123 km away – he had been delegated as the person to deal with the anonymous complaint made against the St Mary's team.

Due to a misplaced letter, which she darkly suspected was the interfering work of Jacinta Hegarty, Mrs Power had only found out about the meeting at the last minute, which is why she was driving at top speed now. If they missed the appointment, she told the two boys in the back seat, McGlinnigle would almost certainly find against them and they'd be out of the competition. They had a lot of road to cover and very little time in which to do it.

She crunched through the gears and overtook a motorbike that happened to be in the middle of overtaking a car.

'We're on the wrong side of the road, Noah. We're on the wrong side of the road,' Stevie squealed.

'What's her problem?' Mrs Power shouted moments later as she blasted the horn at an elderly lady driver who had the temerity to follow the rules of the road by staying on her own side in between the yellow and white lines.

'To be fair, I think she was in mortal terror. We were only inches away from her.'

'An inch is as good as a mile.'

'Then, if it's not too much trouble, could you stick with

the mile in future, Mrs Power?'

Stevie turned to Noah. 'You know, when I rang my parents to ask permission to go on this trip, they said I'd be safe with a school principal. I'd be safer if they tried to send me to Mr McGlinnigle's office by attaching a rocket to my bum and lighting the fuse.'

After a few minutes had passed in silence and with only an additional two terrifying incidents, Noah remembered something. 'Hey, Stevie, back at the house, before Mrs P called, you were going to say—'

'What? Oh, that. It was nothing. Forget about it,' Stevie said.

By the time they'd pranged the front bumper by parking a little too vigorously, Stevie was greener than a slimed Hulk.

'You OK?' Noah asked.

'Am I still alive?' Stevie replied.

'Yes.'

'That'll do for now.'

As it turned out, Mr McGlinnigle had gone for a late lunch so in the end they were waiting for almost half an hour before he turned up. His office was quite small, as was the man himself. Even though he was a solicitor he had a kindly face. He reminded Noah of his late grandfather. If he had believed in signs he might have taken that as a good one, but he didn't so it was nothing more than a pleasant coincidence.

McGlinnigle adjusted his tie, rummaged through a file and then looked at the three people sitting across the desk from him.

'Now then,' he said, his false teeth rattling slightly.

'We appear to have a wee dilemma.'

'It would appear so,' Mrs Power said. Her lips grew thinner. 'Before you say anything else, Mr McGlinnigle, let me state for the record that no law has been broken, that we have followed all the procedures laid down by your football association's governing body and we are outraged at this last-minute attempt to derail all the good done by our poor pupils.'

'Really?' Mr McGlinnigle said, peering at Mrs Power over his glasses. 'Is that how you wish to proceed – by faking outrage? No, Mrs Power, technically your school has not broken any rules, but you know full well that the rules were not intended to be interpreted in this way.'

'I—'

'Let me finish, Mrs Power.'

To Noah's surprise, she shut her mouth immediately.

'Thank you. You have broken the spirit of the law. Now, you can call me old-fashioned, but the spirit of the law is important to me. Some people take football very seriously indeed. I don't. I know what football is: it's a wonderful distraction from real life, a place where the best of human nature can be seen. Sportsmanship, athleticism, team spirit, joy – these are the things I hold dear. A football pitch is a place where it doesn't matter if you're rich or poor, pretty or ugly, a saint or a sinner. Once you cross that white line, you're all equal and all woes are forgotten. Now that may be idealistic, but that's what I believe and with your shenanigans you've gone against what schools' football is all about and I'm afraid I can't allow it.'

Noah felt a familiar feeling of disappointment creep up on

him. No matter how often he tried, everything seemed to be conspiring to stop him playing in this tournament. He tried to think of something to say, but his mind drew a blank.

The intercom on Mr McGlinnigle's desk buzzed. He leaned forward and pressed a button to allow his personal assistant to speak.

'I'm sorry. I couldn't stop them,' the voice crackled.

'Stop them?' McGlinnigle said, a little confused. 'Stop who?'

Noah thought his eyes were deceiving him. The office door swung open and there was Piotr, larger than life.

'Hello, my friends,' he roared. 'Sorry I am late.'

'How did—?' Noah began.

'Stevie texted us,' Maggie said, bundling in the door behind the goalkeeper. 'My mam gave a few of us a lift. Piotr's dad has a minibus and he took everyone else. Luckily, most of them were in Dee's Diner.'

'No rules of the road were left unbroken,' Piotr bellowed.

'Shhh, he's a solicitor,' Barbara said.

'And a barrister, but I'm not a policeman,' McGlinnigle said. 'Now, what is the meaning of this?'

He was normally an extremely calm man, at ease in almost any situation, but as more and more of the St Mary's

221

team barrelled into the room he began to feel increasingly uncomfortable.

'You can't stop us playing,' Maggie said.

'We were hoping for a more subtle approach, Miss O'Connell,' Mrs Power said.

'Er, who are you exactly?' McGlinnigle asked.

'Oh, hey there, Mrs Power,' Maggie said, before turning her attention back to McGlinnigle. 'We're the team you're trying to ban from the tournament. Don't stop us playing.'

'As I was explaining to your . . . Ahm, could you ask that boy not to stare at me so intently?' McGlinnigle said.

'He means you, doofus,' Maggie said, shoving Kevin McCooley in the back.

'Ahem, yes, now where was I? Oh yes, my problem, the committee's problem, doesn't lie with the *players*, rather the *underhand methods* you've used to gain entry to the competition.'

Noah was amazed. Within thirty seconds all the players on the team had managed to squash themselves into the office. They were followed by McGlinnigle's extremely harassed-looking personal assistant.

'If it wasn't for these so-called "underhand methods" then we wouldn't have been able to play,' Darren Nolan said. 'I don't stand a chance of playing on my own school team yet I want to play in this tournament more than anything.'

'Well, the nature of sport is competition and if you couldn't make the team then—'

'I could make the team,' Maggie said. 'If St Mary's entered a team, I'd have made it, but there weren't enough girls interested.

222

And I wouldn't have been interested in playing for a girls' team anyway.'

'I don't follow.'

'I want to be the best footballer in the world. Not the best *woman* footballer, the best footballer. I can't do that if I only play against the girls,' Maggie said.

'Yes, well—'

'Ever heard of Bobbi Gibb?' Maggie asked.

'The runner?'

'Yes, she was the first woman to run the Boston marathon back when women were told they wouldn't physically be able to run twenty-six miles. She didn't let that stop her and you don't want to be the person who tries to stop me.'

'Well, as beautifully threatening as that is—' McGlinnigle began.

'The school's insurance policy covers them. I've checked it out. Just in case you're worried about that,' Mrs Power said.

'I'm sure it does, but if you wouldn't mind letting me finish . . . You, boy, could you not eat that burger in my office? You're dripping pickle juice on the carpet.'

'Sorry about that, man. I'm starvin' like Marvin,' Hawk Willis said.

'The actor Lee Marvin?'

'It's rhyming slang for hungry,' Mrs Power said.

Everyone began to speak at once, all putting forward their case for remaining in the tournament in a terrible cacophony. There were so many competing voices that nobody could be heard clearly.

'Oh, now . . . please all of you . . . be quiet,' Mr McGlinnigle said.

Beads of sweat had begun to form on his brow and on the back of his neck. There were far too many people in his office. Three was quite a lot and made the place seem a little cramped, but there had to be nearly fifteen here now. He was growing increasingly exasperated.

'Could someone open a window, please?' he asked. 'I need some air.'

'I got it,' Limbsy said. His gangling limbs knocked over a glass trophy. It bounced off the windowsill and crashed on to the tarmac outside. 'I'm so sorry about that. I'm sure I can repair it –'

As he reached out, he knocked McGlinnigle's framed degree off the wall. It hit the floor and the glass in the frame shattered into hundreds of pieces. Limbsy leaned down and began to pick up the pieces of glass.

'Just leave it,' McGlinnigle said. 'Please just—'

'Yowsers. I cut my finger.'

Cormac McHugh was on his mobile. He waved frantically until he caught the solicitor's attention. 'What's the address here?'

'Fourteen Greville Place. Why?'

'I'm ordering in a few pizzas. Half of us left our lunch behind in Dee's Diner and it's a long journey back.'

'Anyone got a plaster?' Limbsy asked. 'And a cloth to clean the carpet. I'm pumping blood everywhere.'

'Right, that's it,' McGlinnigle said, getting to his feet. 'All of you, please listen to me. SHUT UP!'

It took some time for his words to have an impact, but in the end they hushed each other until finally there was silence.

'Thank you. Now, what happens if I refuse to allow you to play in the tournament?'

'Nothing,' Frank said. 'We'll keep trying to persuade you until the very last minute.'

'So, I'll have nearly another week of this,' McGlinnigle said, more to himself than to anyone else. He turned to Noah. 'Now that I've met your team, I can see that, despite being the most infuriating bunch of people I've ever had the misfortune to meet, they don't seem to be as unsporting or devious as I first suspected. If I allow you to play, will you give me an undertaking that you will play in the spirit I outlined to your principal earlier?'

Noah smiled broadly. 'Definitely.'

'And one final stipulation – I will never see or hear from any of you ever again. Is that clear?'

Fifteen heads nodded in agreement.

'Mr Lenihan, can you type up a letter to that effect?'

'I'm already on it,' his assistant said, scurrying into the outer office.

As cheers rang out around the room Mr McGlinnigle buried his face in his hands. He'd got into schools' football for all the right reasons, but sometimes he really, really hated young people.

CHAPTER TWENTY-THREE

'If that had gone in, it would have been a goal'   David Coleman

After they'd driven back from Mr McGlinnigle's office, and Mrs Power had said her goodbyes, the group gathered in Dee's Diner, much to the owner Jack's delight.

'You kids are my best customers by far,' he said as they squashed themselves around a couple of the immovable tables.

'That doesn't reflect well on us as human beings,' Frank Courtney muttered.

They ordered some food, mostly burgers and chips.

'Let's get down to business,' Maggie said. 'What was all that about?'

'The meeting with McGlinnigle?' Limbsy asked.

'No, Cormac's weird new haircut. Yes, of course, the meeting. It's serious, right?'

'My haircut's not weird. I like it,' Cormac said. He'd modelled it on Neymar Junior's and he was proud of it.

'It's very nice, Cormac,' Barbara said.

'The whole McGlinnigle thing happened because someone objected to us being in the tournament,' Noah said.

'Yeah, but who?'

'I think it's my school principal.'

The St Mary's team knew that Noah had been banned from playing, but they weren't aware that Hegarty might go that far.

'Mr Hegarty? Why would he object? He got rid of you from the St Killian's team because he thought you started some fight. Why would he care about anything else you got up to?'

'I'm not sure,' Noah said.

'He might think you're trying to circumvent his authority,' Stevie said.

Noah stared at his friend blankly.

'Dumb it down a little, man,' Hawk Willis said, expressing exactly what Noah was thinking.

'His punishment was to stop you from playing football, but then you go ahead and play football anyway. He might think you're being cheeky or rebellious or something and making him look bad at the same time,' Stevie said.

'Or maybe he really did recognize us that time I tried to break into the school and he's paying me back.'

'No, he'd have probably tried to kick all four of us out of school if he'd really seen us that night. And he'd definitely have brought our parents in for a meeting,' Sunday said.

It was the first time Kevin McCooley had heard about the attempted break-in.

'Whoa, back up there a second, Murphy. You tried to break into the school? When?'

As the smell of microwaved burgers wafted across the diner, Noah explained the events of that night again, even though

227

most of those gathered at the tables already knew the story inside out.

'Wow, I'm impressed. You're not as much of a wimp as I thought,' McCooley said when Noah had finished the story.

'I get that he might hate *you*, but Stevie's the best student in school and he can't have anything against Darren, Sunday, Cormac or Adam,' Maggie said.

'Or me,' Hawk Willis said.

'Well, let's not go that far,' Maggie said.

'She zinged you there, my friend,' Piotr yelled.

Maggie turned to Michael Griffin. 'Hegarty doesn't have anything against you, does he?'

Michael shrugged his shoulders.

'And he doesn't know me. There's no reason for him to be against St Mary's, so his problem must be with Noah and nobody else. Did you do something to annoy him?' she asked.

'Like what?' Noah wondered.

'I don't know – date his daughter, let the air out of his tyres, toilet-roll his house?'

'No, nothing like that. He never even noticed I existed until a couple of months ago.'

'You should do them things. It'd really get under his skin,' McCooley said.

'If he's so determined to stop you succeeding at the tournament, then maybe he's willing to go further than getting in touch with McGlinnigle,' Frank said.

Stevie exchanged glances with Barbara, as if they'd both been thinking the exact same thing.

'Like what?' asked Noah again.

'He could poison you,' Hawk Willis said.

Sunday threw his eyes up to heaven.

'No, nobody's poisoning Noah. What I mean is,' Frank continued, 'he could bribe the referees so results go against us or, I don't know, lots of things.'

'We need to figure out what he's doing. If we're one step ahead of him rather than one step behind, then we'll be all right,' Noah said, even though he wasn't sure if that was true.

'If he was lying about the fight or just using it as an excuse, then what other reasons could he have for banning you?' Sunday asked.

'Because Noah's the best player in town,' Darren said.

Maggie laughed out loud, but then she realized Darren wasn't joking. 'Wait, are your eyes not working properly? You've seen me play. My skills are far better than his.'

'It's not all about skills,' Sunday said.

'You're just jealous of me. You're going to have to settle for a boring life cos you're not going to make it as a professional footballer.'

'I don't want to be a professional footballer,' he replied.

Maggie's jaw dropped open, as if she couldn't contemplate anyone who loved the game actually uttering that sentence. 'You don't want to be a . . . Why not?'

'I'm going to be an engineer. An aerospace engineer. Football's fun, but I don't want to spend my whole life kicking a ball around.'

'You're a weird kid, Sunday.'

'No, he's not. I love football too, but I don't want to be like those old lads on the television who spend the rest of their lives talking about matches they played when they were in their twenties. I'm going to be a businessman. I've even set up my own online company,' Frank said.

'Really? Doing what?' Darren asked.

'Selling anything I find interesting. I've bought stuff in car boot sales and sold it for twice the price online. I've even sold some of Barbara's paintings.'

'You draw, Barbara? Are you any good?' Adam O'Brien asked.

'I'm OK.'

'OK? She's like Vincent van Gogh, except she's a girl and she's got two ears,' Stevie said.

'I'd love to have my own business,' Adam said. 'Selling metalhead T-shirts. I can't draw to save my life, but I've got all these great ideas. If you could design them, I could sell them.'

'Call round to my house later and I'll show you what I've done. If you're interested, we can—'

Kevin McCooley slammed his fist down on the table. Everyone jumped even though they should have grown used to his ways by now. 'Stop yammerin' away like a bunch of old women. We have to fix this Hegarty problem before it gets worse,' he said.

'Well said, Kevin,' Maggie agreed. 'We have to do something.'

'Have to do something about what?' Hawk Willis wondered.

'You know, Hawk,' Maggie said with a sigh, 'my mom

says that there's always an idiot in the room and that if you don't know who it is then it's you.'

'There's an idiot in the room?' Hawk Willis said. 'Who is it?'

'Burger's up,' Jack shouted.

Piotr was on his feet in a flash as the burgers zipped across the room. He stretched out his long arms and caught them all, one after the other. He didn't even fumble once.

'The Cat is the king,' he said with a huge grin on his face.

'I didn't order a burger,' Kevin said as Piotr placed one in front of him. He was feeling the pinch and had less than twenty cents in his pocket.

'I got it for you,' Maggie said. 'You ate one of my burgers, but you gave me enough money for two that time back in The Hatch. Now we're evens, chump.'

McCooley tried his best to stop himself from smiling, but he failed miserably. Noah, who was on his usual bottle of water, smiled too as McCooley swiftly got back to the point while the rest of the group stuffed their faces.

'So what are we going to do about Hegarty? Break into his house and look for, I dunno, clues or somethin'?' McCooley said, chomping into a burger as if he hadn't eaten in a month.

'We can't break into his house,' Noah said.

'Why not? You broke into the school.'

'No, I didn't. That's the whole point of it. Darren and Sunday stopped me.'

McCooley shrugged. 'We can't just do nothin'.'

'I agree, Mr McCooley, but we need to come up with a detailed, well-thought-out plan,' Stevie said.

'Hey, Gaffer,' Cormac McHugh said, tugging at Stevie's shirtsleeve.

'We have to figure out what he's up to,' Stevie continued. 'I can't imagine he'd be stupid enough to write down anything important so there'll be no notes for us to find. I mean, he even wiped my tablet clean.'

'Why?'

'I'm speculating that it was to delete any evidence of the fight just in case Noah found a loophole and managed to wriggle his way back into the tournament.'

'Wait, what about that Slugsley fella you mentioned? You said you've got his car reg and stuff. Can't we get something from that?' Limbsy said.

McHugh continued trying to attract Stevie's attention, without any success.

'I've already thought of that, Limbsy. I tried some of the car-check websites, but they won't give us any of the owner's details like—'

'Stevie, will you please talk to me?'

'Sorry, Cormac, what is it?'

He nodded discreetly in the direction of the huge plate glass window at the front of Dee's Diner. 'Don't all look at the same time,' he whispered.

Of course, they all did look at once. Thirteen heads swivelled in that direction until they were staring out on to the traffic-choked streets. Noah saw what Cormac was referring to at once – Mr Hegarty was across the street, standing by his parked car, talking on his phone.

Hegarty finished his call, took a couple of large empty shopping bags from the car and disappeared into the supermarket.

McCooley turned to the group. 'Any one of you lot want to give me a hand?'

'Doing what?'

'No time to explain.'

'I'll help you,' Noah said.

'Not you. He's got it in for you, so he'll be watchin' and be all suspicious and stuff. We need someone else.'

'Me then,' Maggie said.

She polished off the last of her burger and got to her feet.

Before anyone else had the chance to ask what they were up to, they were out of the door. Maggie and McCooley crossed the road and followed Hegarty into the supermarket. Noah watched anxiously, unsure of what they were doing, but suspecting the worst. The minutes ticked by agonizingly slowly. Every moment felt like an hour.

'They're not going to do something stupid, are they?' Stevie asked.

'It's McCooley and Maggie. On their own they're dangerous, but when you put the two of them together anything could happen. If the supermarket explodes in the next ten seconds, I wouldn't be surprised,' Darren said.

But it didn't explode and less than a minute later Maggie left the shop, then sprinted across the street between cars that were only inching forward, with Kevin McCooley just behind her. She arrived into Dee's pink-cheeked and laughing.

'That was a rush,' she said.

'What happened?' Noah asked.

'No time to explain,' Maggie said.

Kevin reached inside his jacket pocket and pulled out a mobile phone. To Noah's eyes it looked remarkably like the mobile Hegarty had been using only five minutes earlier. Stevie seemed to have arrived at the same conclusion.

'You stole his phone,' he practically shouted.

'Keep yer voice down. And I didn't steal it. I just borrowed it. It's the same as if I took yer car from outside yer house without tellin' you, but then I dropped it back a couple of hours later without you noticin' it had been gone. That's not really stealin'.'

'Taking something that doesn't belong to you without getting the owner's permission – that's practically the dictionary definition of stealing,' Stevie cried in exasperation.

Barbara patted his arm in an attempt to calm him down, but for once it didn't work.

'We'll agree to disagree,' Maggie said as Adam O'Brien slid his finger across the screen and unlocked the phone. 'Check the contacts and do it quickly. We have to get it back to him before he notices it's gone.'

'This is wrong, very wrong,' Stevie said. 'And it's not doing my hives any good.'

'Yeah, and what Hegarty did to Murphy was wrong too,' McCooley said. 'Remember the old saying – two wrongs make a right. He did wrong and now we've done it too.'

Noah thought Stevie was going to explode. 'That's not the

saying at all. It's two wrongs *don't* make a right. Oh, I, I . . . give up.'

'Got it,' Adam said. He'd scrolled through all the numbers until he'd found the one they were looking for. 'Arthur Slugsley.'

He borrowed a pen from Barbara and wrote down the number on the diner's cleanest napkin.

'OK, let's go,' McCooley said to Maggie. He grabbed the phone from Adam and rushed out of the door, Maggie just behind him. They disappeared into the supermarket. They were gone for less than half the time they had been earlier.

'Maggie dropped it into his shoppin' basket and he didn't even notice it. She'd make a great CIA agent. He'll see it when he goes to pay for his stuff and think he dropped it in there himself,' McCooley said when they returned. 'And this has nothin' to do with anythin', but that man buys far too many sweets.'

'I'm not sure about this,' Dave said later that evening in the kitchen of Noah's house.

Potatoes were boiling in a saucepan of water on the gas ring, the steam fogging up the windows. Simone was upstairs. They could hear her walking around the room above from the sounds coming through the ceiling.

Most of the St Mary's team had gone home directly from Dee's Diner leaving Noah and Maggie to put the finishing touches to the plan, not that it was much of a plan.

'Quickly, Dave, before she gets back downstairs,' Maggie said.

'If you don't want Simone to know what you're up to, then it can't be right.'

'First Stevie, then you. If I'd known this town was full of goody two-shoes I'd have begged my dad not to move here. Just read it out, Dave,' Maggie said.

'I think it might be illegal,' Dave replied, picking up the A4 sheet that was filled with Frank's writing.

'It's not illegal. It's illegal to impersonate a cop, but you're not doing that. You're not even impersonating a real human being.'

Dave was still wavering. Before he decided to take a stand and give them a definite no, Maggie took the phone from his hand, and keyed in the number that they'd taken from Hegarty's phone.

'Remind me why I'm doing this again,' Dave said. 'Being an actor isn't really my forte, y'know.'

'You're doing it because you're the only one of us who

sounds like a man,' Maggie said.

'And because, you know, you're really nice,' Noah added.

'I'm a fool, little dude, that's what I am.'

As the dialling tone kicked in, Maggie pressed the speaker icon so that they'd all be able to hear the conversation.

A man's voice answered the call. 'Hello.'

Maggie nudged Dave. Noah smiled in what he hoped was a supportive and encouraging manner. His mouth was dry and he felt nervous too, even though he wasn't going to have to do anything.

When Dave spoke, he didn't sound like himself any longer. He might have said acting wasn't his strong point, but he was well able to do voices. Noah thought he sounded exactly like one of those annoyingly chirpy DJs you hear on morning radio.

'Hellooooo, Mr Arthur Slugsley. This is Bobby Bob Robson from KCLMR, the station that rocks, rolls and gathers no moss and we're live on ninety-seven point seven FM. I'm calling with some fantastic news – you're a wiiiinnnnnner.'

'I am?' Slugsley sounded more downbeat than elated. 'What have I won?'

'We'll get to that in a moment, but first we have to have a little chat and then we'll ask you the big question for an enormous cash prize. What do you do for a living, Mr Slugsley, or can I call you Slugger?'

'Please don't. I'm a PE teacher and I coach schools' football.'

'So you're not a football scout?'

'No, what made you think—'

'Wonderful. Who doesn't love PE?' Dave asked.

'Lots of people, actually. Many detest it with a passio—'

'So, Mr S, what's the name of the school you teach at?'

Slugsley suddenly sounded suspicious. 'I'm not telling you that. How did you get my phone number, young man? I don't remember entering any radio competition.'

Dave ran his fingers through his mop of curly hair. 'Er, no, we actually choose our winners at random, Arthurio. It's a unique competition. You don't contact us – we find you. We're the seekers of the airwaves. And *we* found *you* because of that wonderful car you drive.'

'My Fiesta?'

'Yes, we love, love, love cars here at KCLMR and our favourite ever car is a, erm, red Ford Fiesta. One of our spotters saw you cruising around town, thought you looked as cool as an ice cube. We looked up the registration and there you were – our winner. Ha, ha.'

'That's not my car – that belongs to Figg's company– . . . wait a second, if you took my car registration and then tried to find me that's illegal. It breaches the Data Protection Act and has all sorts of privacy issues.'

Dave was visibly wilting now. The pressure was getting to him. Noah motioned for him to end the conversation as quickly as possible.

'No, we just, oh . . .' He began to hiss into the phone. 'Looks like the line's . . . breaking . . . up.'

'No, it's not. That's just you making random noises. Who is this and what kind of game are you—'

Noah leaned across the table and ended the call.

'Thanks for that, little dude. I was going into a spiral of doom there. And not the good kind. I'm glad you had the foresight to block our number so he can't try to find us.'

'So we know he's a football coach, not a scout, and it sounds like the car he drives is owned by a Mr Figg,' Maggie said.

'That doesn't really help us, does it? There's probably loads of Figgs in the country,' Noah said.

Maggie was already on her phone, googling the name. 'There might be, but one stands out.'

She handed Noah the phone. The tanned and slightly pudgy features of Cornelius Figg filled the screen.

'Who's that?'

'You've never heard of Ireland's richest man?'

PLAYER PROFILE

Name: Cormac McHugh

Nickname: Don't have one. My aunt used to call me Hugsy. I think she's a bit soft in the head.

Age: 12

Position: I'm versatile, which means I can play in any position, but I'm tall enough so I usually go in goal or play as a centre-back or centre-forward. A lot of guys don't like playing in goal, but I don't mind it. There's not too much running around.

Likes: I pretend to like Derby County because my uncles are fans, but I really like Liverpool. I love playing chess too.

Dislikes: Horror films. Just not my thing.

Player you're most like: Thomas Müller. But I wish I was like Riyad Mahrez. He's brilliant.

Favourite player: Neymar. All the skill in the world and he's skinny like me. My hairstyle is almost exactly the same as his. My mam hates it.

Favourite goal: When Philippe Coutinho scored the winning goal against Manchester City in the 2013/2014 season. I was sure Liverpool were going to win the league after that match.

Messi or Ronaldo: Ronaaaalllllllldoooooooooooo!

CHAPTER TWENTY-FOUR

'I'm as happy as I can be, but I have been happier'   Ugo Ehiogu

Noah found out a lot about Mr Cornelius Figg the next day, but none of it was very useful. He learned about the businesses he owned, how much money he supposedly had – more than any one human being should have, Noah thought – but he didn't find out anything that would connect him to Mr Hegarty or even to Arthur Slugsley. And as the days passed by and Hegarty didn't try anything else to stop the team from getting to the competition his interest in investigating began to wane. There was so much else that needed to be done that there just wasn't time to be a sleuth.

Noah unzipped his kit bag. The tournament was less than twenty-four hours away now and he was giddy with excitement. In a couple of hours, Piotr's father would collect him and the rest of the team in his battered old minibus and they'd be on their way to Dublin. The only thing dampening his enthusiasm was that his dad wouldn't be there to see him play. He'd have loved that. Still, it wasn't going to do him any good to dwell on it. He had to focus on the games ahead. He sat down on his bed, moving the bag to one side. He knew they only had a very slight chance of winning, but if all of them kept their heads and gave it everything, that was all he could ask from them. He looked at the black jersey Dave had given him the night before. It looked exactly like it had in the brochure. It was jet black with two white stripes on the shoulders, a St Mary's badge sewn on to the left breast and the number seven on the back. He loved it. Seven was the number he'd always wanted to wear. He was usually an eleven or a five when he played for St Killian's, but neither of them had ever felt right. He wasn't superstitious and he knew that having a favourite number on your shirt was just a bit of a quirk, but it was important to him, like wearing your jersey loose outside your shorts instead of tucked in. It was just one of those things.

There was a knock on the bedroom door, interrupting his thoughts.

'Come in,' he said.

It was Simone and Dave. It took Noah a moment before he noticed that there was something different about his sister.

'Your hair,' he said finally.

She'd dyed it black and white with a stripe of red just behind her left ear. St Mary's new colours – black jersey, white shorts with a red stripe.

'What do you think?' she asked.

'It's brilliant,' Noah said with a laugh. Trust his sister to make her own kind of statement.

'It sure is,' Dave agreed.

'Thanks again for getting the jerseys and shorts, Dave. You've done a great job.'

Dave bowed extravagantly and clumsily.

'Thank you kindly, little dude,' he said, righting a football trophy he'd knocked with his elbow. 'Shame we couldn't get socks as well.'

'How's Limbsy doing?' Noah asked.

'He's bouncing off the walls with the excitement. My dad was thinking of asking the vet for one of those animal tranquillizer darts to shoot at him and calm him down. He's freaky deaky happy. You and Stevie did a good thing getting this team together,' Dave said.

'OK, everybody's great,' Simone said with a smile. 'Are you almost ready? The bus will be here soon.'

She pressed a twenty-euro note into Noah's hand.

'I know it's not much, but it'll get you through a couple of days. And I get paid tomorrow so I'll bring some more up with me on Friday.'

'Thanks, Sim,' Noah said.

'And here,' she said, handing him a card. 'This arrived yesterday, but I thought now was the right time to give it to you.'

It had 'GOOD LUCK' written across the front. He opened it up. It read:

Best of luck in the competition. The Mighty Dynamo forever!
Xxx Dad

For a moment Noah thought he was going to cry, but he managed to blink back the tears.

'All the way from Australia,' Dave said, in his best Aussie

243

accent. 'Throw another tinnie on the barbie, mate.'

'It's shrimp, Dave. You throw shrimp on the barbie,' Simone said. She turned to her brother. 'Don't forget to ring me and let me know you got to the hostel safely.'

'Will do.'

They'd managed to find some cheap accommodation in Dublin in a hostel run by a woman called Bitsy. She was the sister of Jack from Dee's Diner. In fact, the hostel should have been closed a month earlier following a Department of the Environment inspection, but a clerical error meant that the date of closure was recorded as July rather than June so Bitsy's had been given a month's reprieve. Since she was in the process of closing down and wasn't taking any other guests, she was able to give them an excellent room rate.

After Simone and Dave had gone back downstairs Noah folded his kit neatly and put it in his bag. He'd left his boots until last. He'd spent an hour cleaning them the night before, scrubbing around the studs and in the grooves with an old toothbrush before greasing the studs with Vaseline and rubbing the outside of the boots with leather oil to keep them soft. They weren't top-of-the-range football boots like a lot of players had – Hawk Willis had bought a brand-new white pair with his name emblazoned on the side in glittering gold specially for the tournament – but they had been good to him. They were comfortable and although they'd got a little tight in the last while as his feet had grown he knew he'd get another couple of months out of them. Better than Kevin McCooley's boots anyway; they were held together by so much duct tape that Noah figured there had to be more tape than leather at this stage.

Stevie was dropped at the door by his father. They'd arranged with Piotr that the minibus would collect the team's manager and captain from Noah's house. Stevie's dad shoved a piece of paper into his son's hand before kissing him goodbye. It was a long list of dos and don'ts for Stevie's trip to Dublin. There were a lot more don'ts than dos.

'Thank goodness the tournament starts on a Thursday or else they'd be wrapping me up in cotton wool and carrying me all the way to the capital,' Stevie said. 'The only thing either of them hate more than me taking a risk is missing a day's work.'

'They'll be there on Saturday if we get through the first round,' Noah said.

'*When* we get through the first round,' Stevie corrected him. 'Mrs Power is so confident we'll make it to the final she's not even going to travel until Sunday morning.'

While they waited for the bus they checked their kit bags one last time. Stevie looked at his watch.

'Five minutes and Piotr's dad should be here,' he said. 'This is it.'

'Any word on the groups yet?' Noah asked.

Stevie furrowed his brow and shook his head. There were eighty teams in the boys' competition, which was broken down into sixteen groups of five teams. Stevie didn't know who was in their group yet as the organizers were waiting until the last moment to reveal that information, but what they did know was that they were going to play each team in their group once, so no matter what happened they'd play four matches – two on

Thursday and two on Friday. Hawk Willis had got very angry when he'd first heard this.

'My hamstrings are as highly strung as a couple of thoroughbred racehorses, man. They won't last if we have to play two ninety-minute matches a day,' he'd said.

Stevie had patiently pointed out that the matches were actually only forty minutes long, two twenty-minute halves with a short break in between, and that had calmed Hawk down.

The worry Noah had was that only the group winners got through to the round of sixteen, which meant they couldn't afford to make too many mistakes. If they didn't win the group, they were out; if they made it through then it was a knockout competition all the way to the final. Then it'd come down to one match and the winners of that final would represent Ireland in the World Cup tournament in Paris in October.

'I wish they'd let us know who is in our group,' Stevie said.

'It's much more difficult to prepare for a match when you don't know what the opposition's like.'

'That might be the way they want it. McGlinnigle likes football to be fun. It's going to be more fun when we don't know what we're up against,' Noah replied.

The minibus arrived at Noah's door a few minutes later. Piotr's dad, who was as exuberant as his son, blew the horn over and over again until Noah and Stevie were standing on the footpath, bags in hand. One of Noah's neighbours leaned out of his window, shaking a fist and shouting a variety of complaints about the noise, but Piotr's dad dismissed the man's concerns with a cheery wave.

The atmosphere was electric on board the bus. Everyone was in exceptionally good form. Maggie was laughing and joking with Barbara and Frank, Piotr was playing drums on his legs and Kevin McCooley even came close to smiling before he lay down across the four seats at the back of the bus and went to sleep. Michael Griffin sat between his parents. His mother was as silent as her son, but his father was talking so fast it was almost impossible to decipher what he was saying.

Piotr's father had decked the bus out in black and white balloons – the St Mary's colours for the tournament – and he and Piotr's mother were wearing matching black-and-white scarves. He beeped the horn three more times for fun. Hawk Willis began to sing a song with which nobody joined in; Darren and Sunday cheered; Piotr yelled out, 'World Cup!'; and with Simone and Dave waving them goodbye from the front door they set off for Dublin.

CHAPTER TWENTY-FIVE

*'I always used to put my right boot on first, and
then obviously my right sock'* Barry Venison

Bitsy's Hostel wasn't as bad as Dee's Diner – it was far, far
worse.

'Who'd have thought that Jack would have been the hygienic
one in the family,' Darren said, surveying the dorm room that
would be their home for at least the next two nights.

'If my mother saw the state of this place, she'd drag me
home by the ear straight away,' Stevie said.

'Stop whingeing, lads. I think it's all right,' Noah said.

That was a blatant lie. Noah couldn't imagine how anyone
had ever paid to stay there. He wouldn't have even given
Monopoly money for a night's stay if he'd had a choice. Even
if you were looking at the hostel through rose-tinted glasses it
was pretty terrible. The beds were lopsided bunks that teetered
on the verge of collapse. The mattresses were thinner than a
spendthrift's wallet, yet they'd still provide more comfort than
the threadbare grey blankets would. Paint peeled from the walls
and the windows were grimy enough to block out any sunlight.
If you didn't know the time and had to guess whether it was day

or night, the chances of guessing correctly were only fifty-fifty.

'This place makes The Hatch look like a palace,' Cormac McHugh muttered. If they managed to make it to the round of sixteen, Noah could imagine Stevie's parents' reaction when they came to inspect the hostel on Saturday. They'd probably have heart attacks.

'Quiet, McHugh. Noah's right. We shouldn't whinge about some mattresses. We've trained hard – we're a tough team now. We're hewn from rock,' Sunday said.

He leaped on to the lower bunk of the nearest bed and let out a yelp of pain.

'I guess that rock you're hewn from is kind of porous,' Darren said.

'The mattress is all pointy springs. It's like jumping on a

bed of daggers,' Sunday said as he got to his feet, rubbing his backside to relieve the pain.

'You bunch of babies make me sick,' McCooley said. 'I'll show you how it's done.'

He threw his kit bag under the bed that Sunday had just abandoned and then jumped on the mattress himself. As soon as he landed, his body spasmed with excruciating pain. He tried to keep his face from showing any of his agony, but he was only partially successful. His bottom lip quivered uncontrollably.

'Comfortable, Mr McCooley?' Stevie asked.

'Yup,' McCooley said through clenched teeth, his eyes watering. 'It's too soft if anythin'.'

Maggie and Barbara arrived in the room.

'Whoa,' Maggie said. 'I was going to complain about the state of our place, but this is far worse. Boys can be such pigs.'

'Wait a second. We only just got here. We didn't wreck the place,' Noah said.

'Stop making excuses, Noah. It makes you sound weak. I'm starving. Piotr's dad said he'd do a chip run.'

'We're not eating chips the night before a match,' Noah said.

Stevie the manager nodded his agreement.

'You're not, but I am. I need a decent meal to give me energy,' Maggie said. 'Anyone else want some?'

There were a few who did, but others who didn't, like Stevie, who seemed a little upset. They split up into two camps after they unpacked their bags. Stevie refused to unpack his, deeming it safer to leave his gear zipped up in his holdall.

'Less chance of any rats climbing into it during the night,' he said.

His comment was overheard by Bitsy, Jack's sister, who had materialized at the door.

'We don't have any rats here,' she said.

'Sorry, Bitsy. I didn't mean to imply—'

'It's a common misunderstanding. They're just very, very large mice.'

'OK, that's it. I'm taking a top bunk,' Stevie said.

Bitsy chuckled. 'What? You think mice can't climb? Thought you'd know they were experts at it, you being a country boy.'

Michael Griffin's father, along with Piotr's parents, had gone to complain to her about the state of their rooms, but their complaints fell on deaf ears. If they wanted to leave Bitsy's Hostel, she said, they could – it wasn't like they were prisoners. The only problem was they had nowhere to go. There was plenty of accommodation in Dublin, but nothing as cheap as Bitsy's and, unless somebody managed to come up with the best part of a thousand euros, they were stuck there. That didn't stop the parents from giving Bitsy hell, but all she did was shrug.

Later that evening, while Piotr's father drove some of them to the chip shop, the others, shepherded by Michael Griffin's father, got some salads and chicken from the local Spar, which was only a short walk away. To his dismay, Noah noticed that he'd used up nearly half the money Simone had given him already. Things were a lot more expensive in Dublin than they were at home.

During the meal, Stevie's phone beeped with an incoming text.

'It's the groups,' he said. 'I created a text alert for when they were released.'

'Who are we with?' Noah asked.

The other players crowded around Stevie, trying to read the phone's screen. They jostled him about and he had difficulty focusing. Adam's long hair fell forward, covering the screen. Barbara leaned over and gently took the phone from Stevie's hand.

'Back off, please,' she said.

Her voice was so calm and reasonable that the jostling stopped immediately. She handed the phone back to Stevie.

'Here you go, Gaffer,' she said. She glared at the others. 'It's rude to read somebody else's texts without their permission, you know.'

The rest of the team mumbled their apologies as Stevie cleared his throat and began to read.

'We're up against St Killian's,' he said.

'No way,' Noah yelled.

He punched the air in delight. He was playing against his own school. He'd be up against Jim Reynolds, Declan Merlehan and all the lads. It'd be like playing in a local derby. He couldn't have imagined a better draw.

Darren and Sunday exchanged high-fives. Cormac and Hawk bumped fists.

'Back of the net,' Cormac yelled.

'We can beat them,' Barbara and Frank said at the same time.

'I don't see why that makes you so happy, Noah. It's only going to cause trouble for us,' Stevie said. 'If they win, we'll never hear the end of it. If we win, then we'll be known as the guys who betrayed our own school.'

'You think way too much, Stevie,' Limbsy said.

'Thank you,' Noah said. 'I'm always telling him that.'

'None of you seemed to mind when his thinking got you into the competition,' Barbara said.

Stevie took a puff from his inhaler.

'Heeee, that's better . . . I've just . . . thought of something else. Mr Hegarty . . . will have it in for us if . . . we win.'

'Don't worry about Mr Hegarty, Stevie. It'll be fine,' Noah said, while thinking the opposite. 'Who else did we get?'

Stevie checked his phone again. 'Drumlock Grammar School. Pengardon Academy. Park Community School.'

He began googling all the names to see if there was anything that stood out, if there was any information or slight advantage he could gain. There wasn't too much out there. There weren't many football websites dedicated to schools' fourteen-and-under matches. In fact, there was only one. It was run by the schools' football association itself and it contained the name of each player in every squad in the competition.

'Hey, Noah, come here and look at this,' Stevie said as the others began to get back to what they'd being doing before the text arrived.

He handed over his phone. Noah stared at the list of names on the screen.

'What am I supposed to be looking for?' he asked.

253

'Look at the names of Pengardon squad.'

Noah read through them. McGuckian. Sheehan. Nash. Maher. Shanahan. Cooney. Loughnane. Tansey . . . Figg.

Figg? He knew that name.

'Is that—'

'I think so,' Stevie said. After a moment he managed to google a picture of the Figgs together. 'Barney Figg is Cornelius Figg's son. I'll have to check it out in more detail, but things are becoming a little clearer. Did you see the coach's name?'

Noah scanned the screen until he did.

'Arthur Slugsley. Their coach is Arthur Slugsley.'

'There's something seriously wrong here, Noah. We both know it.'

Noah thought about it for a moment. 'Leave it for now, Stevie.'

'But this could be the link we've been looking for – Barney to Cornelius to Slugsley to Hegarty. We might be able to uncover why our principal has it in for you and what's been going on. This is a schools' tournament, but it's looking like it's as corrupt as a bingo game run by the Mafia. We have to find out why.'

'Nobody wants to know that more than me, Stevie. And I will find out, but not yet. Hegarty didn't want me playing here for a reason. The one thing I can do is give it my best tomorrow and mess up his plans. After the matches are over, we'll look into it.'

'If that's what you want,' Stevie said a little glumly.

It wasn't what Noah wanted, not really. He wanted to uncover Hegarty's plot whatever it might be, but he needed to focus on playing. That was the one thing he *could* do. If Hegarty didn't want him to play, then the very best thing he could do to thwart him was play better than he ever had before.

Once the meals were over and they'd all met up again, they had a very light kickabout on a green behind the hostel. It backed on to the largest housing estate that Noah had ever seen. Houses coupled together like Lego bricks, rows and rows of them that rippled out to the mountains at the edge of the city.

Stevie talked them through the tactics for their first game in the morning against Drumlock. He told them that he didn't know that much about the opposition, but from his web search he'd found out that this was their first time entering a football tournament. They were mainly a rugby-playing school. He gave the team little pieces of advice and had words in different players' ears to boost their confidence before he asked them to do a few stretching exercises.

They were strolling around just kicking a ball and chatting, killing time before they had to go to sleep, when a couple of local lads around their own age crossed the green, one of them with a ball tucked under his arm.

'Fancy a game, bud?' the taller one asked.

Noah would have liked to play, but he knew they couldn't risk any injuries this close to the tournament, so he had to decline.

'Suit yerself,' the teenager replied.

They began to kick the ball around and within five minutes a few more of the guys from the estate had ambled over and joined in. They started up a game, marking out a couple of sets of goals with sticks they'd broken from the branches of a nearby tree. The sun's fading light gave the impromptu match a beautiful, almost haunting, quality.

Most of the players were excellent. Their first touch and close control was top notch. It had to be. By the time Noah and the rest of the St Mary's squad were getting ready to leave the number of players on each side had risen to over twenty. No player was given much time on the ball so every pass had to be quick and precise. There were cheers when someone produced a move of quality, jeers if someone just booted the ball away. They weren't afraid of contact either – the tackles flew in, but nobody complained, or if they did it was half-hearted grumbling. Noah would have given anything to be out there, testing himself against them.

Later on, when the St Mary's squad had settled down as well as they could in their broken-down beds, Noah sensed the mood had changed in the camp. Seeing those street footballers play their intricate, high-speed game had made the team nervous, as if they were realizing what they were up against for the first time. It was one thing playing practice matches against local teams that weren't very skilful or organized, but tomorrow was going to be different. Very different.

It was eleven o'clock when the lights in the dorm were switched off, but half an hour later every single player was still awake, lying in silence in the darkness. Noah knew they weren't asleep. He sensed it. Finally, Limbsy broke the silence.

'They were good, weren't they, those lads on the green?' he said.

'Yeah,' a couple of voices agreed.

'Lollipop was brilliant,' Adam O'Brien said.

'Lollipop?'

'The guy with the large head and skinny body. It made him look like a lollipop.'

'Oh yeah, he was fantastic. His head was huge all right, as big as one of those statues, you know the ones . . .' Cormac McHugh began.

'Easter Island,' Stevie said.

'Yeah, Easter Island.'

'And what about the blond guy? He was outstanding.' Darren said. 'The only difference between him and Zinedine Zidane was about three stone and a French accent.'

'Who's Zinedine Zidane? Does he play for Paris Saint-Germain?' Hawk Willis asked.

Frank was astonished. 'You've never heard of Zidane? He was one of the greatest players of all time. Don't you know anything about the history of football?'

'History is about stuff that happened. It's over. What's the point of the past? I don't think about the burger I had yesterday, man. I look forward to the burger I'm going to eat tomorrow.'

'Hawk, do you know how I know you're an idiot?'

'How?'

'You look like one.'

Hawk Willis chuckled good-naturedly.

'They were decent enough players, but that was street football. We're playing a different game and we're just as good as them,' Noah said.

Nobody backed him up, not even Stevie.

'I do not know,' Piotr said. 'They were very, very good.'

It was the first time Noah had heard Piotr sound doubtful about things. He didn't like it. Piotr was one of their most confident players and he needed him to keep that enthusiasm.

'Listen, Piotr,' Noah began, but Frank interrupted him.

'And they're not even playing in the tournament. If they're not playing, then you can only imagine the quality of the ones we'll be up against,' he said.

'I never thought of it like that,' Hawk Willis said. He belched. 'My burps taste weird. Like a bad curry. That can't be a good sign.'

'That's just nerves. It's normal to have some pre-match nerves. I hope you've all read the document I gave you on relaxation tech—' Stevie began.

'If you lot don't stop yer yammerin' and let me get some sleep, I'm going to personally shut every single one of your mouths. The next person who speaks is dead, right?' McCooley said out of the darkness.

There was immediate silence. A tense silence, but silence nonetheless.

'No more talking, then. Goodnight, Mr McCooley,' Adam O'Brien said. 'Goodnight, everyone.'

Noah heard bare feet slapping against the cool of the lino as Kevin McCooley slipped out of his bed. It was followed by a sudden thump.

'*Yow*,' Adam yelped.

'That's yer final warnin', Tattoo Boy,' McCooley said.

'Anyone else got somethin' to say?'

It turned out that nobody had. Everyone stayed silent, just lying there letting their nerves about tomorrow's tournament build in their minds until the thoughts of playing were almost overwhelming.

Everyone except Noah. He was visualizing playing in the opening match. At first he spent time thinking about how the grass would smell, the feeling of a breeze on his face, the buzz of the crowd as they gathered on the sidelines. Then he was imagining the ball being passed to him and how he might react in the different situations in which he'd find himself. He visualized himself jinking past opponents, playing the perfect through ball, executing a Cruyff turn. He went through every scenario until he drifted off into a dreamless sleep.

In the girls' room Barbara was wide awake. She couldn't switch off and relax no matter how many sheep she counted or how many breathing exercises she tried. She was overcome with nerves. Even if she had been calm enough to nod off she'd have found sleep difficult to come by as Maggie's snores rumbled throughout the dorm room.

PLAYER PROFILE

Name: Adam O'Brien

Nickname: Eve of Destruction

Age: 13

Position: Central midfielder, but I'd prefer to be a forward. Who doesn't want to score loads of goals?

Likes: PlayStation and Xbox action games. I can get to the end of nearly any game out there. Mad into heavy-metal bands too. The louder the better. And I love eating jelly snakes, wine gums, anything like that. I eat them until I feel sick, which I know is kind of stupid, but I just can't stop myself.

Dislikes: Cheese and people who don't like gaming. Gaming improves your hand-eye coordination and reflexes, and gets your brain processing stuff really quickly – try explaining that to my mother. My dad doesn't help – he's always pressing the wrong button. Once, in Tiger Ranger, he got himself killed in training mode. That's supposed to be impossible! I know he's nearly forty-two, but come on, Dad.

Player you're most like: Sergio Ramos. I'm not as good a player, but we've both got lots of tattoos. (OK, mine aren't real, but that'll change when I'm older.)

Favourite player: Arturo Vidal, the coolest man in the world.

Favourite goal: Papiss Cissé got one for Newcastle United against Chelsea once, a volley from a mad angle with the outside of his boot. I keep trying to score one like that, but I haven't managed it yet.

Messi or Ronaldo: Messi is by far the best. He's in another universe.

CHAPTER TWENTY-SIX

'When you are 4–0 up, you should never lose 7–1'   Lawrie McMenemy

After breakfast the next morning, it was a subdued and somewhat grumpy St Mary's that prepared to set off for the tournament's sports fields. There was no sign of any World Cup excitement. Stevie checked that everyone had their jerseys and boots and then continued checking every five minutes until he was on the receiving end of some rude words from Maggie who was finding his obsessive behaviour unbelievably annoying.

'Sleep all right?' Noah asked as the team began to climb aboard the minibus in dribs and drabs.

Nobody answered. Everyone was too tense.

Hawk was at the back of the line.

'There are going to be lots of people watching us, aren't there?' he asked.

'Plenty of them. We'll get a great crowd,' Noah said with a grin.

'I think I'm going to be sick,' Hawk said, rushing back to the hostel to use the bathroom.

'Nice one,' Maggie said.

'What did I say? Hawk loves showing off in front of people. He wants them to think he's the fastest thing on two legs. I thought that would encourage him.'

'You thought wrong. That's why Stevie's the manager, not you. He wouldn't have made a mistake like that. He always says the right thing,' Maggie said, even though she'd been complaining about Stevie herself only moments earlier.

'Why are you so crabby?' said Noah. 'I didn't think you'd be worried about playing in front of loads of people.'

'I'm not crabby,' Maggie said crabbily.

'Loads? Did you say loads? How many is loads of people?' Piotr asked.

'I have no idea,' Noah admitted.

Piotr grabbed him by the lapels of his jacket, his goalkeeper's gloves tickling Noah's nose, and lifted him into the air. He was much stronger than Noah would have guessed.

'I asked you how many? Ten? A hundred? I've never played in front of a crowd before. What if I make a mistake? What if I drop the ball into my own net? What if everyone laughs at me?'

'You'll be fine,' Noah said.

'That is it? You'll be fine. They are your words of wisdom? You are a fool, Noah Murphy.'

'Calm down, Piotr. Let me hear some of that Zajac enthusiasm we all know and love.'

'World Cup,' Piotr whimpered, as he gently lowered Noah to the ground.

'People are just a bit rattled. Playing at home is one thing, playing in a tournament is something else,' Stevie said to Noah quietly. 'Most of them have never played on a real team before and seeing how good those guys on the green were last night really brought it home to them.'

'I know, Stevie, but we really don't have time for this,' Noah said.

Barbara, not very confident in her own abilities at the best of times, rushed past, moving quicker than she ever had on the football pitch, her hand clamped over her mouth. In the end it became like a relay race – as soon as one emerged from the hostel's bathroom another would take their place.

Kevin McCooley didn't look nervous, but he *did* look exhausted, as if he hadn't had a wink of sleep. His eyes were red-rimmed and he had a hollow-cheeked look about him. When Frank sat beside him on the bus, Kevin's eye twitched and he growled.

'Think I'll stand for a while,' Frank said.

It had been Kevin's first growl for quite some time and Frank wasn't about to take any chances.

The bus finally got going at 9.53 a.m. and there was never a more silent bunch of passengers on any form of transport. The morning was bright and sunny, but the mood on the bus was as dark as an Arctic winter.

'What do you think?' Stevie whispered to Noah as the bus rattled its way to the sports field.

'They'll be fine. Any time I get nervous I forget about it the moment I start playing.'

'Won't they be weak and dehydrated from all their, erm, bathroom visits?'

'No, everything will be all right,' Noah said, not quite sure if he was saying it to convince Stevie or himself.

Luckily, traffic was light and they made good time. By 10.36, they were driving through the large stone gates that led to the sports fields. Those who had been nervous before found a reason to be even more nervous now. The event was enormous. Far larger than they'd imagined. This wasn't a kickabout at The Hatch. This was the big time.

Men in yellow fluorescent jackets directed buses and cars to three different temporary car parks set up especially for the tournament. There were marquees for refreshments and pop-up shops all in a row. Some of the shops had replica jerseys from all around the world on display, club jerseys of teams even Noah hadn't heard of before. Others sold the latest football boots and sports gear of all kinds. There were programme sellers and buskers. Multicoloured flags fluttered in the breeze.

And, of course, there were people who had come to watch the matches. Lots and lots of people. Children, parents and grandparents headed for the sidelines to catch the games. It made Noah miss his dad even more, seeing them all cheering their teams on and celebrating or commiserating with them afterwards. Simone had promised to come when she could get off work, so that was something, but it was still hard not having someone here rooting for him.

The officials and scouts made their last-minute preparations as the first of the matches kicked off. Players yet to play wandered around in matching tracksuits, some warming up, some taking in the sights. Unlike the other teams, St Mary's tracksuits weren't exactly coordinated. They consisted of whatever each player had in his or her wardrobe at home, which in Noah's case meant a patched-up sweatshirt and some bottoms that didn't quite reach his ankles.

'I think I'm going to be sick again,' Barbara said.

'Noah, man, you never told us it was going to be *this* big,' Hawk Willis said as he surveyed the madness, his eyes opening wide.

'I told you it was a qualifying tournament for the Schools' World Cup,' Noah said.

'I know, but how big could a World Cup be?'

Maggie was looking out of the window at the crowds as well. Her attitude was different to that of the others.

'I was born to do this,' she said to herself.

Piotr's father parked up and they disembarked, spilling into the swollen crowds. They had to push their way through the throngs of people. It was exciting and frightening all at once. Noah had never felt more alive. After all the time he'd spent practising and kicking the ball against the wall in the back garden, after all the early starts and late nights, he was here. This was the chance he'd been waiting for. If he played to the best of his ability, the scouts would recognize his talent and life would finally be better.

'Over here, boys and girls. Don't wander off and get lost.'

Michael Griffin's father was waving his hands frantically. When he'd got their attention, he pointed to a yellow information kiosk manned by a bored, gum-chewing teenage girl.

'Now, I know you're all practically grown up, but there is a very large crowd here today, so we don't want anyone getting lost now, do we?'

'I wish you'd get lost,' Noah overheard Mrs Griffin say.

'If anyone gets split up from their little friends, and they can't find them after ten minutes of looking, then we meet here at this information thingy,' he said.

'All they have to do is look for my giant head. I tower over everyone in this place,' Limbsy said.

'Right, that's it,' Cormac said. 'Anyone gets lost, then keep an eye out for Limbsy.'

'Yellow kiosk, not Limbsy,' Mr Griffin screeched, but no one was paying attention any longer.

Noah checked his watch. Only thirty-five minutes to kick-off. They were running a bit behind Stevie's schedule, but they should be OK. Piotr's parents went to the organizers' tent and signed the team in as Noah led the players through a stretching routine.

'Hey, Noah, can we have a couple of minutes to ourselves? You know, just to get into the right frame of mind,' Frank said when they finished up.

'Yeah, I need to go to the bog,' Hawk Willis said.

'Again? What's wrong with you, Willis?' Sunday asked.

'I need to grab some water,' Darren Nolan said.

'All right, but don't go far. We miss the kick-off and we forfeit the match. Ten minutes, then we all meet up back here,' Noah said.

He didn't like them splitting up, but he knew that Frank was doing it for Barbara's sake. He wanted to take his sister

266

aside and have a quiet word. He hoped the others would shake themselves out of their funk too.

He took a stroll himself, soaking up the atmosphere. He heard cheers as a goal was scored in one of the first matches of the day. Normally, he'd have wandered over to have a look, but he wanted to stay focused on his own game now. He took a quick look around the crowds on the edges of the pitches. Plenty of mums and dads, but no one who stood out as being a football scout. He supposed that made sense. They weren't going to advertise it by wearing a jacket with the letters SCOUT stencilled on the back.

He retied his laces, then popped his small shin pads into his socks. He taped the socks just above the ankle to stop the pads slipping down, then glanced around. Nobody was paying any attention to him. He unzipped the pocket on his tracksuit legs and took out a piece of paper wrapped in a small plastic zip-lock bag. It was a page torn from his mother's notebook, the little sketch with the words '*My Mighty Dynamo*' written on it. He folded it in half and slid it down the inside of his left sock, far enough down so there was no chance of it falling out, before finally tying the socks just below the knee with a strip of bandage Simone had given him.

He breathed in the smell of freshly cut grass. He reached down and let his fingers run over it. It was soft and slightly damp. It had either rained overnight or they'd watered the surface.

Two guys stopped in front of him. They were dressed in matching tracksuits and smelled of washing powder. They were

267

big. Uruk-hai big. One of them was reading from a bunch of A4 sheets, a printout of the day's group matches.

'This must be a misprint,' the more handsome of the two said. He looked like a movie star or a minor god. Noah felt small and weedy and very, very pale next to him.

'It says here that our group are playing a team called St Mary of the Immaculate Conception School for Girls.'

'May I have a look, please?'

May I have a look, please? These guys sure are polite, Noah thought. Our team would just have grabbed it, probably tearing it in half as they did so.

'Hey, doofus.'

It was Maggie. Her voice was like a foghorn. The tracksuited teenagers looked up when they heard her.

'What are you two looking at?' she asked.

'Save it for the match, Maggie,' Noah said.

'You're playing?' the movie star said.

'Yeah, what's it to you?'

'Nothing, but the girls' tournament doesn't start until tomorrow,' he said.

'Then maybe you shouldn't turn up until then,' Maggie replied.

'You're calling me a girl? Wow. That's not very feminist, is it, using "girl" as an insult?'

Maggie's brow furrowed. He had a point. She didn't like that.

'Wait, you're St Mary's?' he said.

'Yeah, that's us,' Noah replied.

'I won't even ask what you're up to, but you're playing us in a few minutes. We're Drumlock Grammar. Here's hoping it's a good game.'

He shook hands with Noah, smiled and waved goodbye.

'I hope we slaughter them,' Maggie said.

There were at least one hundred people on the side of the pitch a couple of minutes before the St Mary's–Drumlock kick-off. It was the biggest crowd Noah had ever played in front of and for the first time in years he felt nervous before a match. He knew he could handle it. A few nerves weren't a bad thing as long as you didn't let them take over. He just hoped his teammates would be able to handle theirs when it came to the crunch.

'It's going to be OK,' Stevie said to his players.

'Really?' Barbara asked.

'Really. You've worked hard; you've done all you can. You're winners just getting to this point.'

Hawk Willis sprinted over to the team. He'd already been to the bathroom twice in the last few minutes and was returning from a third trip. He was wearing his gleaming new white boots with the word 'Hawk' in glittering gold on the sides.

'I don't envy the next person who has to use that cubicle,' he said, patting his stomach for emphasis.

As if on cue, a plaintive wail carried across the pitch from the toilets.

'Fancy Boots, you'd better be good. Only a moron or a star would wear boots like that and you don't look like a star to me,' a voice from the crowd shouted. 'We'll be watching you.'

'That's a bit harsh,' Cormac said.

'Why did I get these boots? It was a huge mistake,' Hawk whimpered.

'Don't worry, Hawk,' Stevie said. 'Take no notice of them. You're going out a nobody, but you're going to come back a star.'

Hawk wasn't the only one in new boots, Noah noticed. Kevin McCooley's battered old pair that had been held together with duct tape were nowhere to be seen. Instead, he was resplendent in a brand-new shiny black pair. Even so, they were the plainest football boots Noah had ever seen, with no trim or labels, nothing to detract from the inky blackness.

'Nice boots. Where'd you get them?' Noah asked.

'In a shop,' McCooley barked, his cheeks flushing red. 'Want to make somethin' of it?'

Noah shook his head. Wow, he's even crankier than usual, he thought. He saw Kevin exchange a look with Maggie. No, Noah thought, she hadn't, had she? He looked in her direction, but Maggie refused to catch his eye. Had she bought the boots for Kevin? Well, maybe there's more to her than being the most annoyingly confident person I've ever met, he thought. Maybe there is a heart in there somewhere!

'Hey, is that St Mary's?' another voice from the crowd called out.

'Yeah, they're the girls. Yoo hoo, want to go on a date?' a first-year boy shouted.

'I thought that odd-looking kid with the stupid fake tattoos was a girl when I first saw him. Look how long his hair is,' a bald old man laughed.

Adam O'Brien reddened with embarrassment. He tried to pull down the sleeves of his jersey to cover up his tattoos, but the short sleeves only barely made it past his elbow.

'Pretty ugly bunch of girls, if you ask me,' someone else said.

'No one's asking you, though, are they?' Maggie spat back.

That shut him up.

'Ignore them,' Stevie said. 'Just go out and play your own game. This is going to be fun.'

Seven extremely pale faces and five slightly more healthy ones stared back at Stevie.

If this is them enjoying themselves, then I'd hate to see them when they're miserable, Noah thought.

Adam and Cormac clapped their support from the sidelines as the team took their positions on the field. They did their best to hide their disappointment at not getting a start, as they really wanted to support their teammates, but with their slumped shoulders and unsmiling expressions they were looking a bit sulkier than they realized. They both gasped when Drumlock Grammar School took to the pitch. The two players Noah had spoken to a couple of minutes earlier led the way. It seemed they were two of the smaller members of the team.

'They're giants,' Sunday cried out to the amusement of those on the sidelines.

'It's not basketball or rugby. It doesn't matter what size they are,' Maggie said.

'Maybe not to you, but I'm only a small lad. If one of them falls on me, it's goodbye, Hawk. I'll be squashed like a bug,' Willis said.

'Focus, everyone,' Stevie shouted from the sideline. He paced up and down, clipboard in hand. He nodded solemnly to the opposition coach. The man looked remarkably like a young José Mourinho – he had the same handsome features and an arrogant sneer on his lips. He even wore a replica of Mourinho's long winter overcoat, which was a mistake as it was a pleasant day, and if Stevie had looked a little more closely he'd have seen the beads of sweat on the man's upper lip.

Stevie checked the clipboard one more time as the referee, dressed in yellow, had a last-minute word with his assistants, two bored-looking youths in T-shirts and shorts.

'Hello again,' the captain of the grammar school said, shaking Noah's hand for the second time.

He waved at Maggie. She stuck her tongue out in reply.

'We must meet up afterwards and you can tell me how you managed to enter the competition under the aegis of a girls' school.'

McCooley growled.

'Did he just growl?' the boy asked.

'Yeah, we're like that.'

'How odd.'

'Odd? What are you doing here, posh boy? Posh boys don't play football,' McCooley said.

'That may be true. Once you've seen the standard of our play, you'll probably think we shouldn't be allowed near a football pitch,' came the chortled reply.

The grammar school won the toss and elected to kick off. The referee blew his whistle and the tournament began for St Mary of the Immaculate Conception School for Girls.

CHAPTER TWENTY-SEVEN

' The World Cup is a truly international event '   John Motson

Noah knew what was going to happen next. Now that he recognized it, he realized the signs had been there since the previous night. McCooley had backed up a couple of metres and was going to charge at the first player who received the ball on the opponents' team. It was one thing putting in a reducer when the opponents were scary men on a bumpy pitch and there wasn't a referee in sight. Here it was different.

'Kevin, don't . . .' was as far as Noah got.

McCooley was on the move the moment the opposition kicked off. The handsome player glanced up as McCooley launched himself towards the ball feet first, eyes blazing. Mr Movie Star didn't panic. He knocked the ball slightly to the right then swivelled to his left. McCooley hit the space between the ball and the man. His boots hit the ground and his studs caught in the turf. He smashed into the ground face first.

'Ooooooooooh,' the crowd moaned in sympathy.

Noah flinched. Maggie covered her face with her hands. It looked painful, but McCooley was on his feet in a moment, not wanting to be seen as wimpy, even though he was groggy and his vision was blurred. Movie Star hadn't paused, though, as Noah realized when he was alerted by a shout from Barbara.

'Drop back.'

The ball was switched left and suddenly Drumlock Grammar School had a three against two situation in the middle. They worked the ball efficiently and at pace and within seconds the striker lashed the ball past Piotr's despairing dive. They were 1–0 up.

'Are you OK, son?' the referee asked McCooley as Piotr picked the ball out of the net.

'Yeah.'

'What colour card am I holding up?' the ref asked.

'Yellow.'

'Good, your eyesight's fine. You're booked.'

'For what? I never touched him,' McCooley said, his arms out wide in a gesture of shock.

'You don't have to touch him. Law twelve of the game. If I consider it reckless or excessive, you're in the wrong. In fact, you're in the wrong four times: you tried to kick, tackle,

jump and charge him all in one movement. If it wasn't the first minute of your first game, I wouldn't be so lenient.'

'What? It's supposed to be a man's game. I played like a man. You're a joke, ref.'

'And that's your second yellow. You're off, son,' said the referee, putting away the yellow card and producing a red.

McCooley was frothing at the mouth. Noah had to hold his teammate back or he'd have attacked the referee. He was quickly joined by Limbsy and Hawk Willis. Between the three of them they managed to hold on to him just long enough for Maggie to arrive and whisper something in Kevin's ear. He calmed down immediately and trooped off the pitch, disconsolate. The crowd on the sidelines parted, wary of Kevin, but he kept walking until he was out of sight.

Stevie signalled to Noah from the sideline, his fingers waving about frantically. Noah got what he was saying. He wanted them to go defensive until he could revise his tactics. Maggie was to drop back into midfield with Noah. Limbsy would have to do all the running around up front by himself.

'You OK with that, Limbsy?' Noah asked.

He got a thumbs up in reply.

They hung on grimly until half-time. The sudden crisis of McCooley's sending off had focused their minds and the ten players left on the pitch forgot their nerves. The crowd didn't matter any more. Making fools of themselves was unimportant. Nothing mattered now except stopping Drumlock from scoring a second goal.

Piotr had a couple of saves to make and Michael Griffin had

to be alert as a pacy winger tried to skin him and send in a cross, but other than that they were all right. Maggie had even tried a few forward runs, but they didn't work out as she lost the ball too easily, much to her surprise. She wasn't used to facing defenders of this quality.

They hadn't been able to create anything, but they hadn't been overrun, which is what Stevie had feared. They stood on the sideline at the break. Sweat dripped down their black shirts as Adam and Cormac did their duty and handed out drinks and offered words of encouragement, even though they were both chomping at the bit to get on the pitch.

'Anyone seen McCooley?' Frank asked between gulps of water.

Stevie shook his head. 'He can take care of himself. We'll worry about him later.'

Drumlock Grammar School changed out of their sweat-stained shirts and put on fresh ones. Hawk Willis blew his nose on his.

'OK, apart from the mess-up at the start, you've been doing well,' Stevie said. 'Let's have more of the same in the second half. Keep them from getting a second goal and see if we can grab something from a corner or a free kick and . . .'

'That's it?' Maggie said.

'What?'

'That's your master plan? After all the tactical analysis and computer programmes and stuff, that's what you've come up with: keep it tight at the back and we'll try and nick one later. That's the sort of rubbish they come up with on Match of the Day.'

'It's better than your tactical trick – take the ball, then run into their defenders and lose it,' Stevie said.

The group went quiet. They'd never heard Stevie being critical like this before.

'I'm giving you the basic analysis because I'd have more trust in a bunch of chimpanzees to follow my instructions. I've held your hands for the last few weeks and I've tried my best to encourage you, but look at you. Kevin hasn't got the discipline to not dive in, in the first thirty seconds. Half of you went and ate chips last night. Chips. The night before an important tournament! And I spent ages writing up notes on techniques for meditation and how to calm down when you get nervous, but based on last night and this morning not a single one of you read them,' he said.

'Bit harsh,' Frank said.

'No, it's not,' Barbara said. 'We took our eye off the prize when we should have been really focused.'

'You're right, Stevie, but we need to get going. Give us the plan,' Noah said. 'Please.'

'Thank you, Noah.' Stevie smiled. 'Listen up, this is what we're going to do.'

They took the field with renewed enthusiasm. Stevie's tactics involved a lot of hard work and some unusual positional changes. He brought Limbsy to the back with the instruction to head anything that came at him in the air.

'With my height and long limbs, I can make things really awkward for them,' he said cheerfully.

Hawk, because of his great pace, was the nominal forward.

Stevie reckoned that the opposition's centre-backs weren't the fastest in the world, which is why they were defending so close to their own goalkeeper. They were susceptible to being caught out, but they had to lull them into thinking they were safe first. He instructed Maggie to do the one thing she hated: pressing the opposition. She thought that with her superior skills she should be allowed to rest and save her energy for wowing the watching crowds.

A few of the parents cheered them on to the field as they took their places for the second half.

'Come on, St Mary's,' somebody shouted.

Stevie felt a presence at his side. It was McCooley. He stared at Stevie. For once, Stevie didn't avert his eyes. He stared back.

'You could have cost us the match,' Stevie said.

'It won't happen again, Gaffer.'

'Right, well, good. You're lucky that it was two yellows. It means you'll miss the next match, but you can play tomorrow, so don't be an idiot and mess it up.'

'I'll make it up to you. I won't let anyone down.'

Stevie smiled to himself and turned his gaze to the match. He felt a hand yank at his collar and McCooley's hot breath against the side of his face.

'Oh, Stevie boy, call me an idiot again and I'll break your face.'

'That was understood, Mr McCooley,' Stevie said.

'Was it?' he said, releasing his grip. 'Guess I'm becomin' predictable.'

The second half was a huge improvement for the team. They didn't carve out many chances, but they pressed and harried and gave it their all. Drumlock grew frustrated. As soon as one of their players received the ball someone was on him. There was no time to take a look at his options or choose a pass. There was no time to do anything except get rid of the ball. This agitated their coach no end and he grew more and more upset on the sidelines, roaring and shouting as his arms windmilled around. If that wasn't enough to distract his team, the players' parents, who had seemed refined and respectable during the first half, transformed into something entirely different in the second when the easy victory they'd been expecting didn't materialize. They encroached on the pitch, they swore loudly and very colourfully. Their eyes bulged and their faces grew puce with rage. And they shouted at their sons. They shouted an awful lot.

'Pass it. *Pass it. PASS IT!* What's wrong with you? Have you suddenly forgotten what *pass* means? It's . . . Now he's going the wrong way. He's actually running in the wrong direction. Why am I not surprised? That boy was eleven before he could tie his own laces, you know.'

'Don't let him get past you. Hit him. Hit him, I said, hit him. What are you afraid of? He's ten times smaller than you. Hammer him into the ground.'

'Go left, Colm. Your other left. You big, incompetent lump . . . Just get rid of it. Why are you trying to be fancy? Just kick it as far away from you as you can. If it's not near you, then you can't make a mistake.'

'That was a foul, ref. How could you not blow that up? You'd better watch yourself if I see you after the match. Yeah, that is a threat. You're a disgrace.'

'You're playing a girls' school. A GIRLS' SCHOOL. They're girls. You're an embarrassment, Drumlock.'

And the more the parents shouted the more anxious the Drumlock players became. Noah could see the colour drain from their faces as the pressure became more intense. The cool, calm, collected demeanour they'd shown in the first half was gone. They may have been a goal and a player up, but they were shaky and anxious, terrified of making a mistake. None of them wanted to take any responsibility, and with time almost up Maggie finally got the chance to take advantage of it.

Two indecisive Drumlock players left the ball to each other near the halfway line. Maggie darted forward and nicked it.

'Go, Maggie,' Limbsy shouted, but she didn't need any encouragement.

A defender rushed at her. She dropped her left shoulder. He was fooled. He mirrored her movement as she flicked the ball to the right and took off. Hawk Willis raced ahead, arcing his run to stay onside, like Stevie had shown him in training.

Maggie released the ball at just the right moment and it zipped right into Hawk's path. He hit the ball like a rocket. It cannoned off the post. The keeper hadn't even moved. A defender booted the ball clear before Noah could get to the rebound. The referee blew the final whistle. It was all over. They'd lost 1–0.

Noah was gutted, they all were, but there was no time to dwell on the defeat.

'Forget about Drumlock. That match is in the past,' Stevie said.

'See, I told you thinking about history was useless,' Hawk Willis said to Frank.

'That's not what he meant by . . . Oh, forget it,' Frank said with a shake of the head.

'Frank, Hawk, focus, please,' Barbara said.

Stevie gave them their instructions for the next match as they started their warm down and by the time they'd finished it was nearly time to warm up again. Since McCooley was banned for this match it was the perfect opportunity to give one of the subs some game time. There was no way Stevie was going to play, no matter how much he wanted to, so the choice of McCooley's replacement was between Adam and Cormac. They both were eager. Extremely eager. Cormac had spent the previous twenty minutes doing stretches and giving himself pep talks while Adam was bouncing energetically on his toes, his ponytail flicking up and down behind him. The two players were so closely matched in terms of skill and effort there was no way to separate them.

'OK, Adam plays the first half, Cormac the second,' Stevie said finally.

Cormac McHugh looked disappointed for a moment until he saw the look on Stevie's face.

'You want to play too, don't you?' he said, when he was left alone with Stevie as the rest of the players took to the pitch.

'Shh,' Stevie said. 'Don't tell anyone.'

'I won't.' Cormac smiled. 'But you should get out there, Stevie. We might never get a chance like this again. I can't wait. This is going to be awesome.'

Adam was so determined to prove his worth that he sprinted on to the pitch far too quickly. He zoomed past everyone before losing control and ploughing into the crowd on the far side, knocking over a couple of spectators. A teenage girl helped him back to his feet.

'I'm good,' he yelled, giving Stevie the thumbs up.

Their second match of the day was against Park Community School. Just like Noah's team, they'd lost their first match too. They'd been well beaten by St Killian's and it showed. Noah knew from the moment the match kicked off they were ready to accept defeat. They hardly showed any enthusiasm at all. It was like the heavy loss in their first match had killed their will to win. He couldn't understand that attitude. It made him angry. Even if his team was losing 7–0 with three minutes to go he'd want to keep giving it absolutely everything until the final whistle blew. Luckily, his teammates seemed to be of the same opinion. St Mary's knew another defeat would mean almost certain elimination from the tournament and they weren't going to let that happen.

Park managed to hang on for a few minutes, but no longer than that. Maggie scored from a lovely pass from Noah, slotting the ball past the keeper with ease. It was their first goal in the tournament and she celebrated wildly, although the celebrations were nothing compared to Hawk Willis's when he scored the second a couple of minutes later.

Nobody ever celebrated his or her first goal in a football tournament more extravagantly than Hawk did at that moment. It took his delighted teammates almost sixteen seconds to catch him and by then he'd already been through three somersaults, fired imaginary guns at the crowd, impersonated an aeroplane and pointed to the non-existent lettering on the back of his T-shirt, which he briefly thought stated his name in big bold letters. Then he started blowing kisses.

'What'll he be like if he scores the winner in the final?' Sunday asked as they got ready for the restart.

Another Maggie goal from an Adam O'Brien through ball made it 3–0 just before half-time. The second half was a doddle and played at a slow pace by the majority of the players, the exceptions being Noah and the dynamic duo, Cormac and Adam, who raced around like whirling dervishes. Since St Mary's were in control at half-time, Stevie had decided to give the exhausted Limbsy a rest and allowed Adam to stay on for the entire forty minutes. He repaid his manager's faith with an all-action display. There weren't any other goals until Maggie claimed her hat-trick with a flying header in the last minute.

Her celebrations were a little less muted than Hawk's, but still over the top. They involved her screaming her own name, including her middle name – Isabella – in the manner of a Portuguese football commentator. It startled the crowd and the opposition, although her teammates appeared to find it perfectly normal.

'Nice way to show it's a team sport,' Noah said.

'You're just jealous. Three goals for me, a big fat zero for you. What does that mean, I wonder? Am I three times as good as you?'

'Three times zero is zero, Maggie,' Limbsy said.

'You'd better make it as a footballer with those academic skills, Maggie,' Noah said.

There was very little conversation on the bus home. Most of the players were practically asleep – heads lolled on shoulders or gently bumped against windows – but Stevie and Noah were checking the printout that Stevie had got from the organizers.

DAY ONE LEAGUE TABLE

Position	Team	Played	Won	Drew	Lost	Goals For	Goals Against	Points
1	Pengardon Academy	2	2	0	0	5	1	6
2	St Mary's	2	1	0	1	4	1	3
3	Drumlock Grammar	2	1	0	1	2	2	3
4	St Killian's	2	1	0	1	3	3	3
5	Park Community	2	0	0	2	0	7	0

It was the day's results and league table. Pengardon Academy had beaten Drumlock in their second game of the day, so they were top of the group with six points. There was a three-way tie for second place between St Mary's, St Killian's and Drumlock who all had three points. Poor old Park had no points at all.

'Mathematically, Park are still in with a chance of qualifying,' Stevie said, 'but it would take an unlikely sequence of results for all teams to end up with six points.'

'They're out. They don't even want to be here any more,' Noah said. 'What about us?'

'We have to win both our matches tomorrow or else our chances are slimmer than Limbsy's legs.'

'We'll win,' Noah said. 'We'll definitely win, but there's something else I want to do first.'

CHAPTER TWENTY-EIGHT

'I can see the carrot at the end of the tunnel'   Stuart Pearce

The St Mary's team wasn't sure how to feel. On the one hand, it had been disappointing to lose their first match, but on the other they were still in with a shout after their great result against Park. Kevin McCooley hadn't apologized to anyone except Stevie, but they all knew he was feeling guilty about his sending off. They'd seen him angry, cranky, belligerent, nasty and violent before, but never so glum.

'Hey, Mr McCooley. Do not worry about this problem. The referee was a very harsh man and you did not deserve to be treated so badly,' Piotr said.

McCooley looked up at him through watery eyes. If Noah hadn't known any better, he'd have thought he was going to cry, but as Kevin had told him once after crashing into a goalpost and injuring a sensitive area during a training session: 'McCooleys never cry.'

'Got it,' Stevie said.

He'd been working on his laptop feverishly since they'd arrived back at Bitsy's.

'I've managed to find out where Pengardon are staying,' he said. 'They're in a hotel about a kilometre from here.'

'Why do you want to know where they're staying?' Maggie asked.

'Stevie thinks there might be a connection between Pengardon and Hegarty. I'm going to go over there and check things out. See what they're up to,' Noah said.

'But you said yesterday that you didn't want to check it out,' Stevie said.

'You don't have to remember every single thing I say, you know, Stevie. Yesterday my gut told me not to check it out – today it's telling me to investigate.'

'You and your gut,' Stevie muttered.

'Why are you investigating? They're hardly likely to have a document lying around the hotel lobby labelled "Evil Plans",' Frank said. 'What are you hoping to find?'

'I don't know, but I feel like I have to do something. I can't just sit here waiting for them to make their move.'

'If they're going to make one,' Darren Nolan said.

'If they're going to make one,' Noah agreed, 'but I'm still going to check it out. You never know, maybe I'll uncover something that'll give us an advantage in the matches tomorrow.'

'We'll all go,' Maggie said.

'That might not be the best idea,' Sunday said. 'Fourteen kids wandering around a hotel is bound to arouse suspicions. And our minders are going to be keeping an eye on things too. Michael's dad is always checking up on us.'

Michael Griffin shook his head sadly.

'Yeah, so it's best if it's just one or two of us that go. You guys can make up an excuse if anyone's looking for me,' Noah said.

'We'll tell them you got the runs, man,' Hawk Willis said earnestly. 'No one ever asks any follow-up questions when you tell them that story.'

'You've used that excuse?' Adam O'Brien said, scrunching up his face in disgust.

'Loads of times,' Hawk Willis said.

'Or you could just tell them I've gone to the shop or something more normal like that,' Noah said. 'Kevin, you want to go with me?'

Kevin McCooley looked at Noah. He didn't even bother to remind him that he should be calling him Mr McCooley.

'Nah, you're grand, Murphy,' he said.

'I'm not trying to be nice. I'm asking a favour. I might need you in case things go wrong,' Noah said.

'Oh, OK, then.'

They changed into white T-shirts and trackie bottoms. Since Noah's tracksuit was particularly shabby and the hotel wasn't, Maggie loaned him one of hers.

'It'll never fit me,' Noah protested, but when he emerged from the bathroom a few moments later he reluctantly agreed that it fitted him perfectly.

Stevie gave them a couple of backpacks.

'If anyone stops you in the hotel, pretend you're part of the Pengardon team. The outfits and backpacks make you look sporty so they'll think you're just back from the day's matches.

Your coach's name is Arthur Slugsley and Cornelius Figg sponsors the team.'

He handed them his iPhone.

'What's that for?' Noah asked.

'There's a street map of Dublin on it. You'll need it to find your way. Now, remember it's a five-star hotel.'

'That means posh, right?' McCooley said.

'Very posh. The thing is to act like you're very comfortable there and you'll be fine, but look awkward and they'll recognize you for what you are . . .'

Darren Nolan grinned. 'A couple of chancers.'

Noah loved the buzz of Dublin. Everyone was busy and seemed to be in a rush to get somewhere else. Cars inched by with impatient drivers behind the wheels. Buses lumbered along in their lanes. Cyclists weaved in and out of traffic. Hundreds of pedestrians walked along the wide, grey footpaths beneath the fading evening sun. It was exciting and thrilling and Noah felt there was so much life here. More than in Carraig Cruach anyway, not that his hometown seemed as bad as it once did, not after the last few weeks.

'Thanks,' McCooley said after they'd walked in silence for some time.

'For what?' Noah asked.

'You know what, now shut up about it.'

The truth was Noah didn't know what he was being thanked for – was it for allowing him into the team in the first place? Or for not giving him a hard time about getting sent off? Whatever the reason, he decided the best thing was to just let it be.

They were passing by two men arguing over a parking spot when McCooley saw the hotel. Noah whistled in admiration, although McCooley wasn't as impressed.

'It's posh,' he said. 'I hate posh.'

The Ailesbury had all the trappings of luxury, even down to a doorman in a top hat and an overcoat with gold-trimmed lapels. Noah resolved that when he made it as a professional footballer he was going to bring his dad and Simone to stay here.

'Remember, act like we own the place and they'll think we're guests,' Noah said.

McCooley was already on his way. He swaggered up the granite steps. The doorman eyed him for a moment, as if deciding whether or not to let him in.

'You goin' to open that door or do I have to do it meself?' McCooley said.

The man hurriedly pulled the door open and McCooley went inside. Noah rushed up the steps after him and thanked the doorman profusely for his help before he followed McCooley into the lobby.

The reception desk was off to their right, across the marble floor. Thick-framed oil paintings hung on the walls and the guests that filtered through the lobby were well dressed.

'What's that smell?' McCooley asked, sniffing the air.

'I think it's perfume,' Noah said.

'It stinks. Right, no point hangin' around here like a bunch of tulips. What's the plan?' McCooley said.

'Erm, well, I . . . Wow, this place is something else,' Noah said, looking around. You could fit my whole house into this lobby, he thought.

'I've never seen a bigger collection of snobs in me life. Makes me sick,' McCooley said. 'C'mon, Murphy, what are we doin'?'

'Let's see if we can find out anything by looking around or—'

'I could knock on every door until we find one of the lads you think might be cheatin' us and then I could threaten him until he tells me what they're up to,' McCooley said.

'That's one way of doing it, but maybe we could try something a bit more . . . What's the word? . . . Subtle.'

'Subtle? OK, not really my kind of thing, but you're the brainy one.'

If I'm the brainy one, then we're *really* in trouble, Noah thought.

He approached the reception desk, McCooley loitering at his shoulder. The pleasant-looking receptionist was tapping at her computer. She looked up and smiled when she saw the two young men standing in front of her.

'Good evening, sir,' she said to Noah.

Noah wasn't sure what to say. 'Er, hello. How's it going? Ahm, Pengardon. Figg?'

'You're looking for Mr Figg, sir?'

Noah shrugged. He dearly wished he'd thought this through before approaching the desk.

'We're with Pengardon. Figg's team,' McCooley said.

'Oh, I see. Yes, you're with Pengardon Academy. I hear you had a good day at your tournament. Congratulations. How can I be of assistance?'

'Lost our room keys,' McCooley said, wiping his nose with the back of his hand.

Noah nudged him with his elbow to remind him that this wasn't how five-star guests generally behaved. The receptionist hadn't noticed. She was busy checking her computer again.

'What room are you staying in?'

'Can't remember,' McCooley said.

'If you just give me your names then and I can . . . Oh, here comes your teammate.'

Noah and Kevin turned round in time to see Barney Figg heading towards the lift. He was lightly tanned and as expensively dressed as always. He strolled across the marble floor as if he owned the hotel.

'Mr Figg, sir?' the receptionist called, waving at Barney.

'What?' he barked.

She smiled and nodded at the two newcomers.

Barney stared back, a little confused. 'Am I supposed to know them or something?'

With a sigh, he sauntered over to Noah and Kevin. Noah didn't believe in judging someone by your first impression of them any more, not since he'd got to know his new teammates, but he really had to fight back the intense dislike he felt towards this Mr Figg character within the first three seconds of encountering him.

'Who are you?' Barney asked.

Noah noticed the sneering look as he took in their clothes, as if he thought he was so much better than they were, which, to be fair, he did.

'They said they were your teammates, Mr Figg,' said the receptionist in a voice that was getting frostier by the second. 'Don't you know them?'

She nodded towards a man in a sharp grey suit. Noah presumed he was security. McCooley must have spotted him too because his hands bunched up into fists.

'No, I don't know them,' Barney Figg said, 'but after all that's happened in the last few months I don't know half of the players on my team.' He frowned at Noah and Kevin. 'Are you new too? When did they sign you up?'

'Yesterday,' Noah said unconvincingly. He wasn't entirely sure what Figg was talking about, but he thought it best to play along.

'Yesterday? That's a bit last minute, isn't it? You enrolled in Pengardon yesterday? At the beginning of the summer holidays?'

'Yes?'

The receptionist signalled to the security man to let him know things were OK.

'Seems stupid to me, but perhaps that's how things are done now. I leave all that administration stuff to Healy. You can't be any worse than the players we've already got, I suppose. Some of them were terrible today,' Figg said.

'But didn't you win both your matches, sir?' the receptionist asked.

Barney Figg glared at her. 'And what, exactly, do you know about football?' he asked.

She didn't reply – she just put her head down. Noah felt sorry for her. His first impressions of Cornelius Figg's son were proving to be accurate. He saw that McCooley's mouth was twitching from the effort it took to remain calm.

Looks like he's thinking the same way as me, Noah thought.

'Have you talked to Healy yet?' Barney Figg asked.

'No, we've been rushing around trying to get—' Noah began.

'I didn't ask for your life story. You'd better come with me, I suppose.'

Noah thanked the receptionist for her help then followed Kevin and Barney Figg across the lobby. He led them through a set of mahogany double doors and down a long hallway. He moved quickly and they almost had to break into a jog to keep up. The hall smelled of fresh flowers and the carpet was so thick Noah felt as if his feet were sinking into it.

'I'm JJ and this is, er, Luke,' Noah said.

'I don't care what your names are. I don't remember names; it's up to you to remember mine.'

'What's your name?'

Noah already knew the answer, but he wanted to confirm it.

Barney Figg stopped walking and turned and faced Noah. He exhaled through his nostrils. 'You don't know my name?' he asked incredulously. 'I'm Barney Figg. I'm the captain.'

'Sorry, it's just been a bit hectic recently,' Noah said. 'So, you said that we're not the only new players?'

'Not the only ones?' Barney said, resuming the walk. 'Real Madrid don't sign as many new players as Pengardon. It's Ireland's top school so I suppose that's why most people want to go there, but it's crazy. The new students aren't exactly what I'd consider Pengardon material either.'

'Lots of new students? Just before the tournament?' Noah was adding two and two together. 'Are these new students any good at football?'

'They're not as good as me, but they're not that bad I suppose. Better than the lot we used to have. They were rubbish. Couldn't pass the ball to save their lives. Here we are.'

They arrived outside room number 241. Barney Figg thumped on the door. Almost immediately it was answered by Plunkett Healy. The room was small and from the papers piled on the tiny desk it looked as if it doubled as an office.

'You'd better not have been asleep, Healy. My father doesn't pay you to sleep.'

Noah couldn't see why Barney would have thought Healy

was asleep. The man was impeccably dressed in a suit and tie and hadn't a hair out of place.

'What can I do for you, young sir?' Healy asked.

Noah could tell that he hated Barney Figg just from the way he spoke.

'These are the new players.'

'New players?' Healy said. His forehead wrinkled up when he frowned.

'Yes, new players. It's your job to take care of them, not mine. I have to go and get some snacks. I'm playing Soccer Blaster X with a couple of kids from LA and London in ten minutes. I'm hoping one of them knows the Beckhams so I can get an introduction.'

He stalked off without saying goodbye. Healy stared at the newcomers.

'I don't have any details of new players arriving and I take care of all the administration. Who sent you here?'

'Mr Slugsley,' Noah said quickly.

'This isn't right. Wait here a moment while I get my phone and give Slugsley a call,' Healy said, disappearing into the room.

Plunkett Healy was only on the phone to Slugsley for thirty seconds when his suspicions were confirmed. The boys at the door weren't new recruits. They were either pranksters or worse, an unwelcome stick in the spokes of the Pengardon wheel. By the time he'd run back into the hall, mobile phone still in hand, Noah and McCooley had gone.

PLAYER PROFILE

Name: William Sheehan

Nickname: When my dad was around he used to call me Billy, but I don't let anyone else call me that.

Age: 12

Position: Midfielder. I'm not an attacking midfielder or a defensive one – I try to do both.

Likes: Football. Action films.

Dislikes: Droombeg Flats, where I live. It's a horrible place. Some of the people are nice, but some are really dangerous. As much as I dislike the flats, though, I don't hate it as much as I hate the Figg family. They're super rich, but they're the worst people I've ever met: spoiled, arrogant and they think they're so much better than anyone else.

Player you're most like: I don't know, but the player I'd most like to be like is Luis Suárez. Not for the bitey stuff, but because of his attitude. He's got skill, he's a hard worker, he always tries new things, he plays for the team and he never, ever gives up.

Favourite player: Kingsley Coman. I'm nothing like him, but I love his power and pace.

Favourite goal: Benteke's bicycle kick against Manchester United.

Messi or Ronaldo: Ronaldo is unbelievably good, but I think Messi is the greatest player that ever lived.

CHAPTER TWENTY-NINE

'Well, I don't like to make outlandish statements . . . but Wimbledon would have beaten them 10–0' Eamon Dunphy

William Sheehan, Pengardon Academy's best player, hadn't planned to eavesdrop. It wasn't as if he was trying to hear what they were saying. It just happened. All he'd wanted was a soft drink from the vending machine, but as he padded down the luxuriously carpeted hallway of The Ailesbury, a few minutes after Noah and McCooley had scarpered, he realized that this wasn't the kind of hotel that would have a vending machine. If you wanted a drink, a smartly dressed man who'd call you *sir* would bring it to your door. That wasn't his kind of thing, so, instead, he decided to head outside for some fresh air.

He wasn't proud of it, but he realized that he'd grown to love his time with Pengardon. He loved the training facilities, especially the perfect pitches and the brand-new footballs, Arthur Slugsley's coaching and the great food that was prepared for them every day. His accommodation had been brilliant too. Everything was top of the range and he never wanted for anything. He was living the life of a professional footballer. True, there were some negatives. He disliked Barney Figg more than any other person he'd ever met in his life, but disliking and complaining about Barney was something all of the Pengardon team had in common. It had helped them bond. It was good to have somebody for them all to moan about.

William had even managed to persuade himself that playing for Pengardon wasn't cheating. So what if he wasn't really a student? He had been registered as one and that made it legal. And, really, how was Pengardon taking the best players from other schools so very different from the way clubs like Bayern Munich or Manchester United or Real Madrid behaved? They were big clubs, they spotted players they thought would improve their team and they paid for them to join. That's all Figg had done: pay for the best players from other schools to play for his son's school. There was nothing wrong with that. It was the way things worked. If it was good enough for the biggest clubs in the world, then it was good enough for him. He was being paid to play football and that was all there was to it. If that was the only wrong thing Pengardon was going to do, then he could accept it.

But two minutes later, when he overheard the conversation, he knew that Cornelius Figg wasn't going to stop there.

Arthur Slugsley and Plunkett Healy weren't aware that William was getting his breath of fresh air beneath the open hotel-room window. If they had been, they wouldn't have said a word. Their voices carried out into the gravel courtyard.

'You're sure the ref knows what to do?' Plunkett Healy said.

'Yes, if we're not winning easily by half-time, then he'll make sure decisions start going our way. He'll send some of their

players off if he has to.' Arthur Slugsley sighed. 'This is wrong, Plunkett. Fixing the groups, paying off referees. I used to have principles. How did we let ourselves get dragged down to this level?'

William Sheehan walked away before he heard Plunkett Healy's reply. He felt like a fool. When he'd first arrived at Figg's house he was playing because he needed the money, but in the last few weeks he'd wanted to lift the trophy because he wanted to be a winner. Not like this, though, not by cheating. He couldn't let them get away with that.

CHAPTER THIRTY

‘ *I would not be bothered if we lost every game as long as we won the league* ’ Mark Viduka

It took some time for everything to calm down. A bunk bed collapsed when McCooley punched it. It groaned once before clattering to the ground. Metal clanged and a loosened bolt rolled along the grubby floor. Stevie fretted that they'd have to pay for the damage. McCooley told him to shut up. Barbara told McCooley to shut up. Voices were raised and there were plenty of unhappy faces in Bitsy's Hostel.

'There's no point in us getting worked up. Things haven't changed. All that's happened is we've found out what's going on behind our backs,' Noah said.

'Allegedly,' Stevie said.

'There's no need to say allegedly, Stevie. There are no lawyers here. We're free to tell the truth. It all adds up. They're dirty, low-down, rotten cheats,' Sunday said.

'No doubt about it,' Cormac chimed in.

Noah and McCooley had arrived back at the hostel twenty minutes earlier having run all the way from the hotel. As soon as they made it to the dorm, they launched into the story of what had happened in the Ailesbury. As far as they were concerned, Cornelius Figg was donating a lot of money to Pengardon Academy and in return they allowed certain football players to enrol in the school. Figg was cherry-picking the best footballers around and making Pengardon as good as possible so that they could win the tournament for his son.

'He's the richest man in the country and he could do loads of good things with his money and instead he tries to rig a football tournament. He makes me sick,' Cormac said. 'Sick as a dog.'

'And he paid Hegarty too. That night when we were in the school. He handed him an envelope, remember? Hegarty said he hadn't given him enough. He had to be talking about money,' Darren said.

'He's paid off Mr Hegarty? Who else has he bribed? This

could go all the way to the top,' Limbsy said.

'To the White House?' Hawk Willis asked.

'No, to the president of the fourteen-and-under Irish schools' football association.'

'Well, that's not really the same thing, but it's still high enough,' Hawk Willis said.

'If I get my hands on him, I'll rip his head off,' Maggie said. 'And I really mean it. I will rip his cheating head off.'

From the look of fury in her eyes, Noah was sure that she would too.

'We should tell Mr McGlinnigle,' Adam O'Brien said.

'Definitely,' Barbara agreed. 'He seems like an honest man and since he allowed us to play in the tournament in the first place that means he's the one person you can guarantee hasn't been bribed. If he had been, he'd have just kicked us out, wouldn't he?'

'Absolutely,' Stevie said. 'That's a good point. We can trust him.'

'But he said he never wanted to see our faces ever again,' Cormac said.

'I'm sure if he knew what was happening then he'd want us to tell him.'

Noah just sat on the edge of his bed, silently waiting for them to calm down. When they finally did some time later, he spoke.

'We're not telling anyone,' he said.

'What?'

'Have you gone mad?'

'We can't let them get away with it.'

303

'We're not going to let them get away with it,' Noah said.

'What's the plan, Murphy? Violence? Intimidation? Stealing their boots?' McCooley asked.

'No, we're going to do what we came here to do. We're going to play football and we're going to play it well. We're going to beat St Killian's and we're going to beat Pengardon Academy and then we're going to win this tournament and represent Ireland in what, Piotr?'

'THE WORLD CUP.'

'You make it sound so simple,' Adam said.

'Why would I want to make it sound difficult?'

'Fair point,' Adam replied.

Noah was still finding it hard to get his head round the idea, but after talking about it with Stevie he was sure there was only one conclusion. Hegarty had kicked him off the team because Slugsley had paid him to. His own principal had betrayed him so that Barney Figg could cheat his way to victory. But there was something else that was bothering him as well, something that he hadn't mentioned to Stevie. If Slugsley had gone around the country looking for the best players and paid them to play for Pengardon, then why hadn't he chosen him? Noah wouldn't admit it to anyone, but his pride was hurt too. It gave him another reason to beat Pengardon and win the tournament. His reasons for wanting to win were really starting to pile up.

'What if they have some other tricks up their sleeve? They could try and hurt us – like they might send some kind of ninja guy in the night to break our legs or something,' Cormac said.

'Or they could have bribed the referees so that all the

decisions go their way,' Barbara said.

Frank jumped to his feet, his eyes ablaze with righteous anger.

'They can try every trick in the book, but they won't get away with it. We'll outsmart them. We'll outplay them. We'll fight them if we have to, we'll fight them all until we're the only ones left standing,' he shouted, pumping his fist in the air.

He was expecting whoops and cheers and applause, but the only response was thirteen pairs of eyes staring at him in astonishment.

'Erm, what was that about, Frank?' Limbsy asked.

'Sounded like you were auditioning for a *Braveheart* sequel there, man,' Hawk Willis said.

'Sorry, I got a bit carried away,' Frank said, slumping back on to the rickety bed.

In the end, when they'd all calmed down, they prepared as thoroughly as they possibly could. Nobody ate chips that night. Nobody went to bed late or stayed up talking. By eleven o'clock all lights were out and as fourteen heads hit fourteen pillows they were filled with one thought – tomorrow they were going to win.

CHAPTER THIRTY-ONE

'It's getting tickly now – squeaky-bum time I call it'
Alex Ferguson

The atmosphere in the sports ground was even better on the second day. Now that there were teams in danger of being knocked out there was an unmistakable air of excitement, and nerves, a crackle of electricity. Of the eighty school teams from around the country that had started the tournament, just sixteen would still be standing by the end of the day. Only the group winners would make it through. There would be four left the following day. The champions of Ireland, the team that would participate in the World Cup in Paris, would be crowned the day after that.

Noah was delighted to see some friendly faces in the form of Simone and Dave when they reached the sports ground. They'd got up at five in the morning to drive across the country to make it in time for the day's matches. Simone still had sleep in her eyes, but she was on good form. Noah would have hugged both of them if there hadn't been so many people milling about.

'I've got a surprise for you, little dude,' Dave said.

He peeled off his jumper to reveal a replica top of the St

Mary of the Immaculate Conception School for Girls jersey. It was the same black colour with the white v-neck and the two stripes on the shoulders. It even had the same crest. It was far bigger than Noah's, of course, yet still too small for poor old Dave. It clung so tightly to him that it showed off every lump and bump on his torso.

'That's amazing, Dave. Is it as tight as it looks?'

'Yeah, it's actually cutting off my circulation and I keep thinking I'm going to pass out,' he said with a grimace. 'It's so clingy I think I'll have to cut it off with scissors later. But it's worth it.'

The team went through its warm-up. They were all focused and as close to professional as a school team could be. Nobody wanted to mess this one up.

Adam's ankle went just before the end of their routine and to his dismay the tournament doctor ruled him out, which meant the only player they now had on the bench was Cormac, unless you counted Stevie, which Noah didn't. Cormac had been happy to give up his place on the team to the returning Kevin McCooley. Stevie wasn't certain whether Cormac was doing it for the good of the squad or if his aim was to avoid the wrath of the team's bruiser. McCooley himself was delighted to be back after his one match suspension and determined to show everyone how good a player he could be when he put his mind to it.

As they lined up and saw that McCooley was in the starting eleven, a couple of the St Killian's team looked anxious. Not Jim Reynolds, though. He looked as eager to play this match as Noah did. Noah wasn't going to mention it to Reynolds, but it felt weird to be lining up against his former teammates. They were all there: Rob Gillespie, Bestie Keenan, Sean McDonagh, Terry Sweeney, Wets, Dermot Coughlan and the rest of the lads. He'd worn the same blue-and-white striped jersey they were wearing so many times, and he'd been proud to wear it, but St Mary's was his team now.

On the referee's instruction, Jim shook hands with Noah, squeezing a little harder than was necessary. Noah's fingers cracked as Reynolds applied more and more pressure. He didn't react, though. He just smiled politely and wished Jim Reynolds luck.

'Why would we need luck? We're playing against a girls' school,' Reynolds said with a sneer.

'Going to be embarrassing for you when you get beaten, then, isn't it?' Noah replied.

Stevie paced up and down the sideline, furiously chewing his fingernails. His eyes darted everywhere, looking for something suspicious, something that Cornelius Figg might be using against his team. He was so wound up it took him a moment to recognize the large man approaching him.

'Well, well, Mr Treacy. Fancy meeting you here,' Hegarty said.

'Hello, Mr Hegarty. Good to see you,' Stevie lied. 'I didn't expect to see you here. I didn't know you were interested in football.'

'Oh, I'm a man of the world, Mr Treacy. I take an interest in many things. For example, one of the things I take an interest in are my pupils, especially the ones who decide to represent another school in a sporting endeavour,' he said. He leaned in closer to Stevie until his jowly face eclipsed the sun. 'Some people might consider changing allegiances like that to be a grave insult, or even a betrayal.'

Stevie gulped. Hegarty's expression was impossible to read, but his words were clear enough. Things were going to be tough for him during the next school year. At least he had nearly three months of holidays before it started. More than enough time to build himself into a frenzy of terror.

'Where's the coach?' he asked in an attempt to change the subject.

'Mr Fleming couldn't make it,' Hegarty said. 'I've decided to oversee things instead.'

'Well, good luck in the match, sir,' Stevie said. 'May the best team win.'

He held out his hand for Hegarty to shake. The principal stared at Stevie's hand until Stevie grew so self-conscious that he stuffed it back in his pocket.

The referee blew the whistle and the match kicked off to a great cheer from everyone gathered on the sidelines.

This is it, Noah thought. Here we go.

St Killian's attacked immediately. They were quick,

aggressive and first to every ball. Their style was very different to when Noah was in the team. They played as if they had a point to prove. Just like St Mary's they had a win and a loss from their opening day, so they needed the three points. A defeat for either team would mean almost certain elimination from the tournament.

The ball pinged around the pitch, but Frank and Barbara marshalled the defence well, aided by several well-timed and enthusiastic shouts from Piotr. Michael Griffin and Darren were working hard to help their centre-backs out yet they also had to cover any attempts by the St Killian's midfield to get down the wing and whip in crosses.

'Man on the overlap, Michael,' Frank yelled.

Griffin got across to the winger just in time to jostle him off the ball.

'Great work, Griffin,' McCooley shouted as Michael cleared the ball down the line.

Michael accepted the compliment with a nod before getting back into position.

Maggie was moving across the pitch, making darting little runs whenever Noah got near the ball. She quickly grew frustrated with the lack of passes coming in her direction.

'Come on, Noah. There's no point in me making all these fantastic runs if you're not going to give me the ball,' she called out.

Noah was doing his best but it was a struggle. Every time he touched the ball a boot crunched in. After the fourth over-the-top tackle his ankle exploded in pain.

'Come on, ref. They're killing him,' Sunday shouted.

The referee held up a yellow card. 'Don't question my decisions, son.'

Sunday was aghast, but smart enough to hold his tongue. There was nothing to be gained from provoking the man in charge.

For a moment, Noah wondered if Figg had paid off the ref, but he shook the idea from his mind. There was no point thinking like that. It wasn't going to help things. He had to keep playing no matter what stupid decisions the ref made.

St Mary's didn't create an attack worthy of the name in the first ten minutes. It was a desperate rearguard action. But although St Killian's attacked and attacked they weren't breaking through and despite all their possession and some trademark dribbles from Bestie Keenan, Killian's most skilful player, they only had a couple of off-target shots to show for their domination.

Piotr placed the ball on the ground for a goal kick. He booted it high and long. Limbsy anticipated it and took a step forward. His marker reacted too slowly and that extra fraction of a second was enough to give Limbsy an advantage. He nudged his opponent, knocking him off balance. The ball flicked off his head and out to the wing where Hawk Willis was lurking. Hawk controlled the ball with an ease that surprised everyone, including himself, and raced forward.

'Yeeeeeooooow,' he yelled. He collapsed like he'd been shot, grabbing his knee.

The physio, who was provided by the tournament's

organizers, hitched up his tracksuit bottoms and lumbered on to the pitch.

'Twisted knee,' he said after a thirty-second inspection of Hawk's leg. 'It'll need at least an hour's rest.'

'Why always me?' Hawk moaned.

McCooley went over to console him. 'Don't you dare cry. Don't even think about it. St Mary's players never cry. Is that clear, Willis?' he grunted.

'Yes,' Hawk whimpered.

The crowd applauded as he hobbled off, his arm round the physio's shoulder.

Cormac jogged on in his place and stationed himself on the right wing.

For the rest of the half, St Killian's worked like demons with a tremendous work ethic. They ran themselves to the point of exhaustion. Sweat poured down their faces. Their drenched shirts clung to them as they pressed and harried and never gave St Mary's a second on the ball.

Somehow, though, through a combination of luck, intelligent defensive work and some fantastic goalkeeping from Piotr, St Mary's struggled on and made it to the break with the score still 0–0.

'I don't know how you're not losing,' a red-faced Jim Reynolds said to Noah as they trooped off for their five-minute rest.

'It's because you haven't put the ball in the back of the net, Jim. Kind of the point of the game.'

Jim couldn't think of a reply in time, which gave Noah

a lot of satisfaction. Stevie gathered his players around in a huddle.

'Stay on your feet,' Stevie whispered.

There were several moans and groans in reply.

'Stay on my feet? I'm dying here,' Sunday said.

'I know, but look at them. Not all of you all at once. You, Darren, make it look natural.'

Darren faked a yawn and glanced over. The St Killian's players were panned out on the ground. Not a single one of them was standing.

'They're cream-crackered,' Darren said.

'Exactly. They tried to blitz us,' Stevie said. 'That was their game plan today. It's not how they normally play. I should know – I've reviewed their matches a hundred times. They gave absolutely everything in the first half and thought they'd be two or three–nil up.'

'You mean they didn't pace themselves,' Barbara said.

'Yes. They were following Mr Hegarty's instructions, not Coach Fleming's. And now they're out on their feet. You lot were magnificent. Kevin, you've been really disciplined, but now it's your time to shine. There's two, maybe more, on that team who are frightened of you. Now they're frightened *and* tired, and we can use that to our advantage. Use your incredible energy to close them down. They'll want to get rid of the ball quickly and when they're tired their execution will be poor. You got it?'

'One hundred per cent, Gaffer,' McCooley said. He grinned. 'I'm really going to enjoy this.'

'Sunday and Noah, move the ball around fast. Drag them all over the place. Cormac, you try and join in with attack when you can. Help Maggie and Limbsy out.'

'Yeah, someone give me the ball. I've been so starved of passes that I've nearly forgotten what it's like,' Maggie said.

'It's that round yellow-and-blue thing that people are kicking about,' Sunday said.

'Gee, thanks.'

'Right, defence, keep doing what you're doing. You've been excellent, but try to vary the passes to keep St Killian's on their toes. A couple of short passes out to Noah, a couple of long balls up to Limbsy,' Stevie said. He checked his watch. 'We have one minute left. I want you out on the field doing a few stretches and looking eager to get the second half started. Do some fake laughing and joking. They'll think you have lots of energy and it'll really wind them up.'

St Mary's high-fived each other then jogged on to the pitch. Even though they were exhausted from the first half, they acted as if they were fresh from the most relaxing and rejuvenating break of their lives. Maggie said a few nonsense words and the rest of the team started laughing as if she'd said something hilarious.

Sean McDonagh and Terry Sweeney from St Killian's looked across the field at their opponents. Both players had given every last drop of energy in the first half and were dreading the second, yet here was the opposition skipping around like they were in a flippin' musical.

'We're dead, Macker,' Terry said.

'You don't have to tell me, Ter. Why are we doing this to ourselves?' Sean said.

'Shut up, you losers,' Jim Reynolds said. 'There's no way we're going to lose.'

'If we're losers then we have to lose. It's kind of our destiny,' Rob Gillespie said.

'We're not going to lose to a bunch of girls,' Reynolds said. 'Or to Noah too-big-for-his-boots Murphy. Get up, get up, get up.'

The teams lined up again. The referee waved to both goalkeepers to check they were ready for the second half to begin.

'Not looking good for your little team, Mr Treacy,' Hegarty said. 'They were quite poor in that first half.'

'Lucky we have another half to play, then, isn't it?'

'Are you giving me cheek?'

'What? No, I meant . . . Sorry, sir . . . I . . .'

Reynolds continued to run around in a fury at the start of the second half. He went for every ball. He chased down every player. He covered every blade of grass. Within five minutes he was on the verge of collapse. It was the perfect time for Noah to take over – and he did.

The next fifteen minutes were amongst the best Noah had ever played. He controlled the entire match. When he received the ball, he never allowed himself to be pressured. Every touch was perfect. When he turned, he swivelled into space, when he passed it was always just in front of a player so they could take the ball in their stride.

Midway through the second half Sunday won a tackle out by the touchline. He rolled his studs over the ball then jinked past Dermot Coughlan, his opposite number, and went straight for the corner flag. It looked like he was setting up to knock a cross into the area, but at the last moment he flicked the ball back towards his own half and chipped it to the edge of the D. Noah was bombing on and caught it perfectly.

It was one of those moments that rarely occurs in life, but when it does it's absolutely wonderful.

Noah knew the second he connected with the ball that it was a goal. He caught it right on the sweet spot. He didn't see it hit the net. He didn't need to. He'd already wheeled away in celebration. He'd only taken a single step when the roar of the crowd exploded in his ears. Two steps later he was wrestled to the ground by Kevin McCooley. There was no escape. Kevin shouted something unintelligible.

The rest of the team piled on top of Noah, squashing him into the turf. Bodies everywhere. He could barely catch his breath. He didn't care. He'd scored a lot of goals in his life, but he'd never felt a rush like this, an absolute sense of joy, of exhilaration. It was as if the rest of the world disappeared. Nothing existed beyond this moment, this beautiful day, this fantastic pitch and these wonderful teammates.

Reality came rushing back when he eventually got to his feet and Limbsy planted a big fat kiss on his lips.

Stevie didn't celebrate on the sideline. He just smiled to himself as his principal swore loudly.

'That was a fluke,' Reynolds said as they lined up for the kick-off.

'What's the score?' Maggie asked.

'Get lost.'

Maggie turned to Noah. 'You've had your fun, now give me a couple of decent passes and I'll show you what a really great goal looks like.'

For the following five minutes, however, it wasn't Maggie who shone – it was the Kevin McCooley show. Every time a Killian's player got the ball, McCooley bore down on him like a rampaging rhino, which panicked the player into kicking the ball as far away from him as possible, usually landing at the feet of a St Mary's defender. Reynolds, exhausted and barely able to move any longer, shouted with rage, but it had no effect. His team were gone and he knew it.

For the last few minutes St Mary's peppered the St Killian's goal. Maggie curled a sumptuous free kick against the bar. Limbsy had a diving header blocked on the line. Sunday wriggled through three players and chipped the keeper only for the ball to land on the roof of the net. Barbara even ambled forward at one point when they won a corner. Unfortunately, her towering header was just wide, but even so she ran back to her position in the centre of defence afterwards with an impossibly huge grin on her face.

'This is brilliant,' she said.

With two minutes left and St Killian's so tired they couldn't even muster an attempt at an attack any longer, Maggie got the goal she craved. A long kick-out from Piotr bounced in front of her. The central defender was just behind her, too close, she knew. He was leaving too much space between him and his goalkeeper. She nodded the ball backwards, just to his left, then ran to his right. He was slow to turn and she was already bearing down on the keeper by the time he gave chase. The keeper rushed out of his goal, intent on clattering her. Maggie was unperturbed.

'Grooaagghh,' the keeper roared as she calmly nutmegged him then leaped in the air to avoid his lunge. He slid beneath her airborne studs and crashed into the defender who was giving chase, flattening him. Maggie tapped the ball into the empty net. 2–0.

She turned back to her teammates, her arms outstretched. The crowd shouted their appreciation. She didn't run off celebrating. She waited for her teammates to come to her. Which they did. As they finished their congratulations, Tony Donnelly leaned in.

'Limbsy, kiss me and you're a dead man,' Maggie said.

He wasn't that reckless.

Less than a minute later the referee blew the full-time whistle. It was over. They'd won. Every one of the St Killian's players made a point of coming over and shaking Noah's hand and congratulating him. Everyone except Jim Reynolds who lay on the ground sobbing, his shirt pulled up over his face.

Stevie turned to shake his principal's hand, but the man had disappeared into the crowds. Everyone was in great spirits afterwards, but Stevie brought them back down to earth when he reminded them that they had another match in just over an hour.

'We'll celebrate when we qualify for the next round,' he said.

CHAPTER THIRTY-TWO

'Without being too harsh on David, he cost us the match'   Ian Wright

It took Mr Hegarty a few minutes to find Arthur Slugsley in the swelling crowds. He managed to locate him just as Pengardon Academy slotted in their second goal against Park Community School. It was William Sheehan's second of the match and, while most of his teammates celebrated, Barney Figg wasn't too happy with him.

'You should have passed the ball to me. Why did you shoot, you moron?'

William Sheehan gritted his teeth. 'I'd gone past two players and was on the edge of the area and you were way back on the halfway line. I thought I had a better chance of scoring than you did and, since I did score, I was probably right.'

Barney Figg snorted his derision. 'Well, maybe I was on the halfway line because I was exhausted from doing all the work for this team. Next time, you pass to me. I'm the captain, so I'm the one in charge. Don't you forget that.'

Sheehan's right hand closed into a fist.

'Great goal, William,' Plunkett Healy shouted from the sideline.

When William looked over, Healy was drawing his hand across his throat, warning him not to go ahead with the pummelling of Barney that he appeared to be planning. Sheehan unclenched his fist and walked back to his own half muttering to himself.

Hegarty tugged at Slugsley's arm. The Pengardon coach seemed surprised to see him there.

'What do you want?' Slugsley asked.

'My money,' Hegarty said. 'My team ran themselves into the ground just like I told them to. They sacrificed themselves to tire out St Mary's. They didn't get the win, but Noah Murphy and his team are going to be so wrecked for the next match your lads will stroll to victory.'

'Keep your voice down,' Slugsley said.

As the final whistle went, signalling a 2–0 victory for Pengardon, Slugsley eased Hegarty away from the crowd. They walked round the back of one of the food tents where they were able to talk more freely.

'I told you on the phone that you'll get the rest of the money when we win the tournament and not a minute sooner,' Slugsley said.

'I don't trust Figg to pay me,' Hegarty said. 'It's not like this is legal. I won't have anyone to complain to if he decides not to pay.'

'I told you you'd be paid and you will when they win. I'm a man of my word.'

'You're the coach of a fixed team. Excuse me for thinking your word doesn't count for very much. If things don't work out for me then I'm going to tell the world all about Mr Figg and his precious little Barney. I'll tell him how you rigged the group—'

'How did you know that?' Slugsley asked.

'Come on, Slugsley. Pengardon end up in the same group as my school and Noah Murphy's team? Eighty teams and that's the way the group falls. Are you trying to say it was a coincidence? You're not pulling the wool over my eyes. How did you do it? Computer hacking? Paying off the man who organizes the tournament? If you'd been smart enough to come to the lovely town of Carraig Cruach earlier rather than waiting until the last minute, you'd have seen how good a player Noah Murphy is. If you'd put him in your team rather than trying to stop him playing, everything would have been nice and simple.

I'd have received a nice fat fee to keep my mouth shut about his transfer to Pengardon, you'd have won the tournament easily and you wouldn't have to spend your time getting stressed and trying to weasel your way out of paying me what I'm owed,' Hegarty said.

'Well, if your miserable little town hadn't been hidden in the middle of nowhere then maybe I would have spotted him earlier, but if I hadn't found it at all then I wouldn't have had the misfortune of meeting you. Now, get lost, you odious man,' Slugsley said.

'I may be odious, but I'm going to get my money one way or the other,' Hegarty replied.

CHAPTER THIRTY-THREE

' No regrets, none at all. My only regret is that we
went out on penalties. That's my only regret, but
no, no regrets ' Mick McCarthy

Noah was really looking forward to the next match. He'd started to believe they could actually win the tournament. A few more parents had turned up and the excitement was building, though he was trying to keep everyone calm and focused. In the end, with McCooley's help, they managed to get rid of the adults and found a quiet corner in one of the marquees.

'Man, my shirt smells ripe,' Hawk said, sniffing the armpit of his jersey. 'We really should have brought spares with us.'

Noah ignored him. 'OK, while our excellent manager was working out our tactics—'

The group gave a little cheer for Stevie.

Noah grinned. 'I got the group table. Park and St Killian's are out.'

Another cheer.

'It's between us, Drumlock and Pengardon. Since goal difference comes into it, we have to beat Pengardon by two goals if we're to stand a chance of getting through. After that it gets a little complicated.'

'No, it doesn't,' Maggie said. 'We just go out there and win ten–nil and we'll be in the knockout round, then it's just a few matches until we're crowned champions and my spectacular goals go viral on YouTube.'

'I'm just going to ignore that,' Noah said. 'Is everybody feeling OK? Other than Adam and Cormac, that is.'

Poor Cormac had landed awkwardly when celebrating Maggie's goal, so he was out for the final. He was distraught, but putting a brave face on it. Adam was out too, but luckily Hawk had recovered quickly from his knee injury and was raring to go. The downside as far as Noah was concerned was that the only fit substitute they had was Stevie. The idea of Stevie having to play against a team of ringers who had won all their matches so far made Noah a little nervous. If it made Noah nervous, it was playing havoc with Stevie's stomach. He wanted to play, he really did, but he didn't want to come on to the pitch for the very first time during the most important match of his friends' lives. He'd mess it up for sure.

'Stevie's looking a bit green,' Darren said.

'He'll be fine,' Barbara said, putting her arm round Stevie's shoulders to comfort him.

'Don't worry, Stevie man,' Hawk said. 'If you have to play, you can just keep talking to the guy you're marking until he falls asleep from boredom.'

'Shut up, Hawk,' Frank said.

'Thanks, guys, but as long as you stay fit and healthy I won't need to play. I'm very confident that'll be the case,' Stevie said as his stomach bubbled furiously.

Twenty minutes later, after Stevie's surprisingly subdued team talk, they lined up for their last group match. The big one. The weather was good and the sun was on their faces. A gentle breeze blew across the pitch, which had held up well despite all the matches that had been played on it in the last couple of days. As the ref counted the players, Noah juggled the football, swapping it from his left foot to his right and back again.

'I know you.'

Barney Figg was staring at him, a quizzical expression on his face.

'Hey, Barney,' Noah said.

'You were spying on us in the hotel! I thought you were there to join our team, but you were spying on us. You're nothing but a cheat,' Figg said.

'One of us is a cheat all right, but it's not me,' Noah said.

William Sheehan moved across the centre circle. He'd heard what Noah had said.

'We're going to smash you into tiny pieces,' Barney Figg said.

'What's with all the hostility?' Limbsy asked.

'That's Barney Figg,' Noah said.

'Oh, *that's* Barney Figg. Got you,' Limbsy replied.

'What are you talking about me for? I'm going to—'

'Be quiet, Barney,' William Sheehan said.

Figg's aggression would have made Noah more determined to win the match if he hadn't already been revved up to the maximum. He was itching to get going now, to show Pengardon what St Mary's were made of, what *he* was made of.

'Where did you buy your kit? At the Oxfam shop?' Barney Figg said. 'Ours was specially designed. It's a fabric that won't be available in the shops until next year.'

In fairness, Noah thought, it was beautiful. A pristine white jersey. He looked around at his team. It was a ragtag, ramshackle affair, all right. Despite Dave's best efforts, their jerseys didn't quite fit them and every pair of shorts was a different shade of white. The socks didn't match either. Still, it didn't bother Noah. So what, he thought. After all that had happened – getting kicked off the school team, getting his own team together, Dig Grimsby, Stevie's training sessions – after all they'd been through, he was starting to feel proud of them. And they were going to win this match fair and square.

After all, fancy jerseys didn't win you matches. Skill, intelligence and effort did.

'When we—' Barney Figg began.

'If you say one more word, you'll wish you hadn't,' Kevin McCooley said, stepping up threateningly. 'Got it?'

Barney Figg shut up.

'Kevin,' Noah said. It was a gentle warning. The last thing the team needed when they were this close to glory was one of Kevin McCooley's berserker rampages. But Kevin winked at him and Noah knew that his temper was under control. For now, at least.

Simone and Dave, who were just to the right of Hegarty, waved excitedly at Noah and Limbsy. They waved back. The crowd thickened as people who had finished watching other matches wandered over to have a look. There were at least one hundred and fifty people watching now, including Cornelius Figg and also Plunkett Healy, who didn't seem happy at all once he recognized Noah and McCooley.

'What's wrong with you, Healy?' Figg asked.

'Nothing, sir. Just a bit nervous.'

'There's nothing to be nervous about. Not unless you've messed things up,' Figg said.

The rest of the St Mary's parents were gathered together on the far side of the pitch. Michael Griffin Senior jumped up and down waving a homemade flag until his wife restrained him.

Noah took a deep breath as the referee tossed the coin. 'Call it,' the ref said.

'Heads,' Barney Figg said.

'Heads it is.'

Pengardon chose to kick off. Barney Figg put his foot on the ball. The referee blew the whistle and St Mary's final group match began.

Figg passed it to William Sheehan who turned and knocked the ball back to McGuckian. Limbsy tried to close him down, but the midfielder was too tricky for him. The opposition player feigned to go left, then flip-flapped right, leaving Limbsy's limbs flailing. The crowd *ooh*ed at McGuckian's skill and *aah*ed when Limbsy hit the deck with his own leg nearly wrapped round his neck.

The ball was switched to the right. Sunday spotted the danger, but before he could get there the player crossed the ball to the opposite wing. The number eleven was in space. He knocked the ball past Hawk who turned quickly. The winger took off towards Darren in the right-back spot. It was a straight race between Hawk and the winger.

'Easy peasy,' Hawk said.

But, as fast as he was, Hawk wasn't able to keep up. He was shocked; nobody had ever beaten him for pace before. Their winger skinned Darren and whipped the ball into the box. Sheehan was there to meet it and thumped a header past Piotr's despairing dive. In less than thirty seconds St Mary's were 1–0 down.

'What just happened?' Maggie asked.

Noah felt as if he'd been hit by a train. Pengardon were good. Freakishly good.

'One–nil, cheater,' Barney Figg said. He hadn't moved from the centre circle since the match had kicked off.

Things didn't improve. As usual, St Mary's worked their socks off, but it wasn't enough. After five minutes, they were 2–0 down, McGuckian slamming one home from twenty-five metres. The crowd were amazed by the quality of the strike.

St Mary's chased shadows for the next few minutes before Frank dived in on the edge of the area and gave away a free kick. William Sheehan curled it into the top corner, just between the angle of the post and the crossbar, the only place Piotr couldn't reach. 3–0.

'Oh yes,' Hegarty shouted from the sidelines.

'Isn't he our school principal?' Michael Griffin's father asked his wife. 'Why is he shouting for a bunch of strangers when some of his own pupils are playing in the match? That's extremely bad form.'

St Mary's managed to contain them until a couple of minutes before the break when Pengardon's number eleven wriggled his way into the area. Darren slipped and his legs flew out, accidentally upending his opponent. There was no yellow card, but the referee pointed to the spot immediately. William Sheehan picked up the ball.

'Whoa, whoa, Sheehan. What do you think you're doing? I'm the captain. I take the penalties,' Barney Figg said.

Sheehan muttered to himself, but didn't bother arguing with Barney. He lobbed the ball to Figg who placed it on the spot. Piotr danced up and down the line.

'Come on, Piotr, you can do it,' his dad called out.

Piotr wobbled his legs so they looked like two pieces of spaghetti dangling from the end of his hips.

'Jerzy Dudek,' Piotr's dad shouted in delight.

'He can't do that. It's putting me off. That's illegal,' Barney whined.

'Just take the penalty,' the referee said.

'Slam it home, Barney!' Cornelius Figg shouted.

Barney took ten steps back then rushed forward. He hit the ball well, so well he surprised his teammates, his own father and anyone else who'd ever seen him play. It rocketed towards the top corner of the goal. It would have beaten any other keeper in the competition, but not Piotr. He sprang to his left, stretching his frame out as far as it would go. He just managed to claw the ball out from under the bar before it crossed the line. He fell to the ground as the ball bounced in front of him. He was back on his feet in a flash, reacting quicker than any of the Pengardon defenders. He grabbed the ball as the St Mary's supporters cheered, but Piotr didn't hear them. He was far too focused.

'You hit it too well if anything. Terrible luck,' Cornelius Figg called over to his son. He grabbed Healy's mobile phone and flung it to the ground in a temper.

Piotr threw the ball out to Noah who had begun to move towards the opposition's goal the second he saw that Piotr was going to save the penalty. He'd signalled to Hawk to do the same. Noah eased past one challenge, then another and now he had time and space. Hawk raced up the wing, putting on the after-burners, his white and gold boots a blur of movement. Caught off-guard and cursing their luck, three Pengardon players chased after him. The left-back moved out to cut him off, which is when Noah, watching Hawk's run, played a reverse pass to Michael Griffin who had snuck up unnoticed on his left. Without breaking stride, Griffin blasted the ball towards the bottom left of the goal.

Boom.

It flew past the keeper. 3–1, just as the referee blew the half-time whistle. Michael Griffin raced towards the side of the pitch, whooping and hollering.

'I loooooove football,' he roared.

A few moments later, St Mary's were gathered together on the sidelines swigging water and scoffing squares of chocolate.

'They were good, we were terrible, but we're only two goals down,' Noah said.

'But we have to win by two if we're going to knock them out, so we have to score four in the next twenty minutes,' Darren said. He was still upset about giving away the penalty even though it had inadvertently led to St Mary's goal.

'Then that's what we're going to do,' Noah said.

'Why isn't Stevie giving the team talk?' Hawk Willis asked.

Stevie was sitting on the ground, his arms wrapped round his knees.

'He's doing a José Mourinho. He's giving us the silent treatment. He knows that we have to figure out what went wrong ourselves,' Noah said.

That was a blatant lie. Noah saw that his friend was in trouble. Stevie was so overcome by nerves that Noah was worried he might faint. The thought of running out on to the pitch as a substitute and making a complete fool of himself in front of all those people was too much for Stevie. I'll deal with that in a minute, Noah thought. First things first.

'So, what are we doing wrong?' Limbsy asked.

'We're not being creative enough. We're reacting to them rather than taking charge of the game. We can't be creative when we're afraid. We can't enjoy playing if we're this tense. We've lost nothing. We've done brilliantly to get here. Six weeks ago most of us didn't even know each other—'

'Gotta say it, not a big fan of the inspirational speech,' Hawk Willis whispered to Frank. Before Frank had a chance to reply, Hawk said it himself. 'Shut up, Hawk.'

Frank nodded in agreement.

'But now we're a team. And we've made it further than we should have. A month ago we had the worst trainer in history and most of us had never played a proper football match before, but look at us now. We have an excellent manager, coach and director of football all wrapped up in one person . . .'

Stevie smiled thinly.

'. . . and we came here to win. So we're going to win and we're going to do it by playing football that's exciting. When we were little kids and dreamed of scoring in a Champions League final, we never thought of going one–nil up and then defending for eighty minutes. We dreamed of scoring a crazy last-minute winner as the crowd went wild. We imagined excitement and glory and sliding across the pitch on our knees. None of us will make it to Wembley or the Camp Nou—'

'Speak for yourself,' Maggie muttered.

'– but that doesn't matter. Today's our day in the sun.'

At that very moment the rain began to fall. A sudden burst that seemed to come from nowhere. Noah began to laugh. 'We're from Carraig Cruach. We play better in the rain anyway.'

As the rain teemed down, half the crowd rushed away for the shelter of the tents and marquees. The spectators who remained were those who were used to going to outdoor events in the Irish weather. They pulled on their plastic ponchos and opened their umbrellas.

'Let's get out there and win this thing!' Noah shouted.

'Yeah!'

'Woo hoo!'

There were cheers and applause and fist bumps. They all felt different. None of them believed a word of what Noah had said about winning, but they knew he was right about not coming all this way to be overwhelmed. If they were going to go down, they were going to go down fighting.

Noah let the others go out on to the pitch before him. He needed to have a word with Stevie.

'Hey, buddy,' he said.

'Sorry. I wasn't really up to giving the talk,' Stevie said. 'When the chips are down, I'm always found wanting.'

'No way, Stevie. You've been brilliant. All of this,' Noah said, spreading his arm out to indicate their place in the tournament, 'is down to you. So what if you're a bit nervous of playing? Don't worry about it. You don't have to play if you don't feel like it.'

'But what if someone gets injured?'

'We'll play with ten. And no one's going to get injured. We need you on the sideline. That's your place. You were never much of a player anyway.'

'Oh,' Stevie said, relieved and disappointed at the same time. 'Wait, is this some sort of reverse psychology?'

'No, you're too clever for that. I'm telling you the truth – you know I've never rated you as a player.'

'Oh. Wait, is this a double bluff? Are . . .'

But Noah was already on his way to the centre circle. Just before the referee began the second half, Noah called Limbsy and Maggie over to him and whispered to them, 'I've got an idea.'

CHAPTER THIRTY-FOUR

*'I don't believe in luck . . . but I do
believe you need it'*   Alan Ball

Hegarty twitched nervously on the sideline. There were only about fifty people left watching the match now that it was pouring down, but there was no way he was leaving his spot. There was far too much at stake. He'd spent the half-time break working out the permutations of the league table. By his calculations, St Mary's needed four goals in the second half if they were going to qualify.

'There's no hope of them scoring four goals in the second half,' he said to the man nearest to him. 'Pengardon are definitely going to win the group.'

He must have looked a little scarier than he realized because the man began to edge away from him.

'Everyone ready?' the referee asked.

Limbsy stood over the ball in the centre spot, facing his own goal. Noah was beside him and Maggie was just on the edge of the circle. On the referee's whistle Limbsy tapped the ball to Noah who flicked it into the air. Before anyone knew what was happening Limbsy threw himself to the ground. Half a moment later everyone knew why. As the ball dropped, Maggie hit a thunderous volley. If Limbsy had remained upright, it would have smashed his face in. It flew straight towards the goal. The keeper, who hadn't fully settled himself yet, stuck out a hand. He got his fingers to the ball, but not enough to deflect it from its path. It arrowed into the back of the net. 3–2.

'They only need three goals now,' the man said to Hegarty.

To Noah's surprise, Maggie didn't go wild in her celebrations. She'd just scored from the halfway line and she didn't run around or stand there with a smug look on her face or declare herself to be the greatest player that ever walked the earth. Instead, she turned and shouted:

'We are the Mighty Dynamo!'

The rest of the team cheered.

'How did you know?' Noah asked.

'Stevie told us, doofus. Now, let's continue to be inspired by your wonderful half-time speech about friendship and dreams.'

'You're being sarcastic.'

'You bet I am. That speech was terrible. This is real life, not some Disney movie for toddlers,' Maggie said. 'But Mighty Dynamo is different. That led to all this. And this is cool.'

'You know what? For the very first time, I agree with you,' Noah said as the rain began to bleed some of the black from his jersey. 'This is brilliant. Mighty Dynamo!'

After all their excellent play in the first half, Pengardon were distraught to find themselves only one goal ahead. Instead of attacking, they began to drop deeper, scared of letting in another goal. The weather wasn't helping them. As the pitch grew more and more saturated, passing accurately became tricky and they stopped taking risks. They knew if they just hung on to their lead they were guaranteed to qualify for the next round.

Pengardon defended valiantly, but they were handicapped by the presence of Barney Figg. With so many men behind the ball, they needed an outlet for their clearances and they placed Barney up on the halfway line where they thought he could cause the least amount of damage. Every time they booted the ball away it was retrieved by one of the St Mary's team. Barney Figg would half run, half walk towards the ball, but it always evaded him and he grew tired of making the effort.

'Keep your head up, Barney!' Cornelius Figg shouted from beneath the designer umbrella that a sopping wet Plunkett Healy was forced to hold over him. 'What's going wrong, Healy? I thought you said the referee was going to be on our side. This one doesn't seem to be giving us any decisions.'

'I don't think it's the same referee,' Healy said.

'Are you sure?'

'Pretty sure. Unless he's shrunk and grown a full head of hair in the last twelve hours.'

The man Healy had bribed was tall and bald; today's ref was short and had a fine head of curls.

'Perhaps our referee was taken ill, sir,' he added.

'So you gave money to the wrong man? My Barney is out there killing himself for the sake of his team and he has to rely on his own skill and talent? You really are an incompetent, Healy,' Cornelius Figg said.

He turned to his coach. 'Do something, Slugsley,' he ordered.

Slugsley waved his arms wildly and shouted encouragement, followed by a few threats, but his words had no impact.

'You're useless too, Slugsley. I'm taking over. If you want something done right, then do it yourself. Healy, hold that umbrella higher. The water's going down the back of my shirt.'

Stevie was pacing up and down the sideline, shivering in the cold and wet. St Mary's were starting to get on top. He didn't know quite how they were doing it, but they were. He looked at his watch. Ten minutes left. Three goals. Surely not.

'Barney, drop back! McGuckian, you take his place,' Cornelius Figg roared through cupped hands.

'I'm not a defender,' Barney moaned.

'We need your skill back there. McGuckian is about as useful as a chocolate teapot so he can run around up front.'

'Nice one, boss,' McGuckian said.

Within seconds of Barney moving back, St Mary's had them pinned on the edge of their own area. Noah was at the centre of things, pinging the ball around with nice crisp passes along the rain-sodden surface, hoping to drag someone out of position to give him enough space for a through ball. Pengardon were well organized, though, and St Mary's were finding it almost impossible to break them down.

Noah played the ball out to the right. Hawk Willis took a touch and then passed it back to Darren who was moving forward at pace. He tried to cross the ball, but didn't make a great connection and underhit it. It dropped down on the edge of the area.

'Barney's ball,' Figg called.

Barney swung wildly at it, slicing it high and backwards. Limbsy leaped up and the ball connected with the top of his head and looped into the top corner to make it 3–3. Limbsy went crazy. He ripped his shirt off to reveal the skinniest torso in Northern Europe and swung his jersey round his head. He didn't stop grinning even when the ref gave him a yellow card.

Watching from the sideline, Dave celebrated by sliding on his knees through a series of puddles. He couldn't wipe the smile from his face either. Not being a great fan of football he wasn't quite sure what was happening, but he knew that his brother had scored and that this was a good thing. He ran back to Simone and swept her up in his arms.

'I'm in trouble, man,' Hawk Willis said as they trooped back to their own half for the restart. He looked devastated. 'I'm injured again. I won't be able to keep going.'

'You sure?'

'Even walking's killing me. I could stand there, but not put any weight on the foot, if that's any good to you.'

'Thanks, Hawk, but there's no point making things worse.' Noah jogged up to the ref. 'One of our players is injured, ref. We need to bring on our sub.'

'OK, go ahead, young man.'

Stevie thought Noah was joking when he told him.

'But you said I didn't have to come on if I didn't want to,' he said. 'I figured it was a quadruple bluff which meant I was in the clear.'

'You don't have to come on,' Noah said. 'Nobody's going to

force you to play if you don't want to. But you're going to play because you're not a jerk and you're not going to leave us out there with just ten players.'

'You said I wasn't any good. You've always said I'm rubbish,' Stevie pleaded.

'Yeah, but how sweet would it be to prove me wrong?'

Stevie peeled off his tracksuit. His legs were like matchsticks and whiter than milk. 'I hope my health won't suffer for this.'

'They're bringing on the big guns now,' Hegarty said mockingly to his neighbour, who ignored him.

'Hurry it up,' the ref called out.

The remaining supporters, squashed together under their umbrellas, clapped as Hawk Willis double high-fived Stevie, and the manager of St Mary's strode on to the field to become the only player-manager in the tournament.

Noah glanced across at the thinning crowd. Simone was talking to someone – a man covered up by a poncho. His heart began to race. It was a scout. It had to be. Why else would he be talking to Simone? She didn't know anything about football.

'You show them how it's done, Stevie,' Dave shouted.

The cheers of the crowd encouraged him, but Stevie's first ever touch of the ball in an organized football match wasn't a good one. Maggie had dropped back into midfield, taking Hawk's place and Stevie went up front even though he protested he'd do less damage as a defender. Noah passed the ball to him, a nice simple one that only required him to tap the ball back to his friend, but he was too nervous and left it short.

'They've got David and Goliath up front,' Hegarty called

out with a laugh, referring to the difference in height between Limbsy and Little Stevie.

'Seriously, what is up with that man?' Michael Griffin's dad asked, scowling at their head teacher.

William Sheehan was on to Stevie's lax pass immediately. He played a fine ball up to McGuckian who was up front on his own with four defenders ahead of him. He spotted Piotr off his line and chipped the ball.

Piotr backpedalled furiously, splashing across his area. He leaped up. His fingers grazed the ball. It was just enough to turn it on to the bar. McGuckian followed it up and was about to blast the ball home when Barbara slid in with a last-ditch tackle, taking it off his toe and sending it to the right.

Darren controlled the clearance and knocked it down the line to Maggie who spun past her marker. Noah made the angle for her, but instead she knocked it forward to Limbsy who, with his back to goal, controlled it beautifully. He played it out wide. It wasn't the greatest pass in the world, the ball slowing on the soggy ground, but it was a fifty-fifty between Sunday and the right-back. Sunday moved faster than he ever had before, dragging up energy from somewhere deep inside. He nicked the ball away from the left-back who went sliding past. Sunday was in the zone now. Everything seemed to be happening in slow motion for him. He knew where everyone was on the pitch without looking around and he was two moves ahead of them. He slalomed past the first centre-back as an image of his father's hero popped into his head – Jay-Jay Okocha. Sunday rainbow-flicked the ball over the next defender and curled the ball round the outside of Barney Figg. It smacked off the post, but before the crowd had time to *ooh* or *aah*, Sunday was on the rebound, slamming it home to make it 4–3.

'You beauty, Sunday,' Maggie cried in delight.

Hegarty buried his head in his hands as the ball spun around in the goal, rippling the white net.

Cornelius Figg was furious. 'Healy, I swear if we get knocked out, I'll have you transferred to some godforsaken part of the world so fast . . .'

'As long as I won't ever have to see your face or hear your voice, I'll take it, sir.'

'*What?*'

'Nothing,' Plunkett Healy said.

'You absolute morons,' Barney Figg roared at his teammates.

There were only two minutes left when Pengardon kicked off again. Two minutes to find one more goal, Noah thought. They'd surely get one last chance. Pengardon were trying to kill time. They moved the ball out to the left-hand side of the pitch. Their number eleven who had been so impressive in the first half wasn't attempting anything as outrageous as scoring a goal. He took the ball into the corner to try to waste a few seconds. No matter what Darren and Maggie did, they couldn't get the ball off him. They had him penned in by the corner flag. There were only thirty seconds to go when McCooley thundered over to them. He shoved his teammates out of the way and growled. The winger, a cultured chap, got such a fright he lost control of the ball and knocked it out for a throw.

Piotr sprinted to the sideline and gathered the ball. He

threw it almost to the halfway line. Noah took it down in one movement. He looked up. Maggie and Darren were bombing down the right wing, but they were being covered. It was the same on the left – Sunday and Michael weren't being given any space. Limbsy was double-marked at the edge of the area. The only one who was free was Stevie, soaked to the skin, but moving around. He was being loosely shadowed by Barney Figg, William Sheehan having coaxed his captain into taking care of St Mary's least dangerous player.

Out of the corner of his eye, Noah saw the ref check his watch one last time. He was about to put the whistle to his lips. Why not, Noah thought. After everything that had happened, why not? He played the ball forward. As usual, his pass was accurate. It slid along the slick, wet surface right into the penalty area. It was perfectly weighted. Stevie saw it coming. He dummied, letting the ball run under his legs, and turned. He was free and clear. Only the keeper to beat. He swung back his leg . . . and his face hit the ground.

The referee's whistle *peep-peep*ed. Stevie had been fouled. Barney Figg had leaped in with a two-footed challenge and sent him flying. The referee didn't hesitate. He pointed to the spot. It was a penalty.

'What? What? I didn't even touch him,' Barney Figg cried. He turned to the referee. 'No way was that a penalty. What's wrong with you, ref? Are you blind or stupid, or both?'

The referee held up a red card.

'You can't send me off,' Barney screamed. 'Don't you know who I am, you absolute idiot?'

Because of the protests from Hegarty and Cornelius Figg, who had to be held back by Plunkett Healy as Barney was dragged from the pitch kicking and screaming obscenities, it was a full minute before the referee was ready to allow the penalty to be taken. Stevie had recovered from the challenge that had sent him sprawling.

'Great bit of skill,' Noah said.

Stevie beamed. He didn't think he'd ever been happier in his life. 'I just got lucky.'

'Luck had nothing to do with it, Stevie.'

'You guys can talk about how much you love each other later. We've got more important things to do. Give me the ball. I'm taking the penalty,' Maggie said.

'No, Maggie. This one's mine,' Noah said.

He put the ball on the spot with such authority that Maggie didn't even try to argue.

The keeper was doing his best to put him off. He jumped up and down, slapping his hands against the crossbar. Noah swept his hair back from his eyes as the rain rolled down his face. His socks were full of water now. His jersey was soaked through too. He took three steps back. He was slightly to the left of the ball.

Barney Figg paced up and down on the sideline biting his perfect nails.

'Shoot left,' someone behind Noah called out.

'No, blast it down the centre as hard as you can.'

McCooley stopped them from talking after that. Noah didn't need any advice. He knew what he had to do. The referee blew the whistle.

Simone couldn't bear to look. She grasped the arm of the man in the poncho. Hawk Willis covered his eyes too. Michael Griffin's father said a silent prayer. Hegarty looked like he was on the verge of a heart attack.

Noah ran up. The keeper didn't move until the last moment when he dived to his right. Noah struck the ball powerfully. It flew past the keeper's outstretched gloves and hit the inside of the net. The referee blew the final whistle. It was all over. They'd won. 5–3.

And everyone went crazy.

CHAPTER THIRTY-FIVE

'Beauty comes first. Victory is secondary. What matters is joy'   Socrates

Darren and Michael Griffin hoisted Stevie on to their shoulders. Hawk Willis hopped on to the pitch on his one good leg. Limbsy began to sing 'We are the Champions'. Barbara did a robot dance while Sunday ran one way, then the other, without knowing quite where he was going or what he was doing. McCooley punched himself in the head and roared and roared. Maggie dropped to her knees and Piotr did a backflip. Adam headbanged, his hair whipping back and forth. As for Noah, he just collapsed on the ground with joy and relief. It was over. They'd done it. For the next three minutes everything was beautiful chaos.

Hegarty began to pound his fists into the now muddy ground in frustration. All that money he'd been promised. Gone. Just like that. Because St Mary's had knocked Pengardon out of the tournament. He swore loudly.

'That's no way for you to behave, swearing in front of children. In fact, your behaviour throughout this match has been bizarre, grotesque—' Michael Griffin's father began. He

345

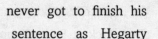

never got to finish his sentence as Hegarty clambered to his feet and swung a muddy fist, knocking him to the ground.

'You assaulted that poor man. I'm calling the police,' a woman said.

Hegarty didn't wait around for the authorities. He disappeared in the direction of the car park.

On the pitch the celebrations continued as Michael's dad got back on his feet, gingerly nursing his jaw.

William Sheehan was the only Pengardon player to come over and shake Noah's hand.

'Well played,' he said with a wry smile. 'Great game.'

Simone, Dave and the man in the poncho were making their way towards the victorious team when Stevie spotted something from his perch on Darren and Michael's shoulders. There was something happening two pitches away.

'Let me down,' Stevie cried.

'What's up?' Barbara asked, stopping mid-robot.

'We forgot about the other match,' Stevie said.

Noah led the way as they raced across to the pitch, one with a small crowd around it. Limbsy had to carry the injured Hawk on his back so they were the last to arrive.

Even though both matches had begun at the same time, the Drumlock v. Park Community School match was still taking place. One of the players had suffered a fractured leg during the second half, which meant there was a lot of injury time still to be played.

'What's the score?' Noah asked one of the supporters.

'Four–nil to Drumlock.'

Stevie did the calculations. Drumlock were going to finish on the same number of points as St Mary's, but they'd be level on goal difference. St Mary's would still be in the next round though as they'd scored more goals.

'We're OK,' Stevie said. 'We'll still make it unless Drumlock get one more.'

'How much time is left?'

The supporter checked his watch. 'It's just about up.'

They only had seconds left. Noah crossed his fingers. He wasn't superstitious, but today he'd take any help he could get. As long as the score remained as it was, they'd be safe.

'Come on, come on,' Maggie said to no one in particular.

One of the Drumlock midfielders had the ball. He looked up and spotted the keeper off his line.

'Look out, he's going to try a Maggie,' Limbsy said, referring to Maggie's shot from the halfway line.

And that's exactly what the player did try. The St Mary's team held its collective breath as the ball arced through the air.

'It's going in,' Barbara said.

'No, it's going to drop short,' Noah said.

347

It was too. It was going to drop right into the goalkeeper's hands. They were safe.

Or they would have been if the keeper hadn't slipped on the wet surface at that very moment. He fell backwards and the ball smacked him on the chest. It bounced out past the eighteen-yard line where Mr Movie Star was waiting to rifle it home.

Drumlock's forward wheeled away in celebration. The score was 5–0. They were top of the group and St Mary's were down to second place.

'There's still a chance. If Park manage to score, we'll win the group,' Sunday said.

He was grasping at straws. There was barely enough time for Park to get back on the ball. A moment later the referee ended the game. Drumlock were through and St Mary of the Immaculate Conception School for Girls were out of the competition. The dream was over. All the joy and celebrations of five minutes earlier had been for nothing. Noah couldn't believe it. After all they'd been through, they were out.

He slumped to the ground. Maggie sat down beside him. She had tears in her eyes. As the Drumlock players celebrated their win, St Mary's were stunned into silence.

'I'm still not sure what's going on,' Hawk Willis said.

Noah went over and shook the Drumlock captain's hand.

'Well played – you deserved it,' he said.

As they gathered up their belongings, Stevie's phone beeped. Stevie checked the text then passed the phone to Noah. It was a photo of Dig Grimsby smoking a cigar.

'He said he'd celebrate when we failed, didn't he? How did

he even know the result?' Stevie asked.

'Who cares. And we didn't fail. We did more than we should have. We were brilliant,' Noah said.

Dave trotted over to where they were standing.

'Well done, Mighty Dynamo,' Dave cheered.

'Not the right time, big guy. We didn't make it to the next round.'

'Sorry, dude,' he said.

CHAPTER THIRTY-SIX

' *I've never wanted to leave. I'm here for the
rest of my life, and hopefully after that as well* '

Alan Shearer

No one spoke for the next few minutes. There was nothing to
say. They just sat there trying to make sense of everything that
had happened. They'd come so close, but it didn't matter now.
They were out of the tournament and there was no way back.
The dream was over. Noah was on the ground again, soaked
and lost in thought, the rain still washing over him when he
heard the voice.

'Well played, young man.'

It took him a moment to recognize the face. The old man
was swathed in oilskins. 'Mr McGlinnigle?'

'I'm glad you recognize me, Mr Murphy.'

Noah got to his feet and shook McGlinnigle's hand.

'I have to say, your team were excellent. A very spirited
performance. Five–three, what a scoreline. I loved every
second of it.'

'Two good teams,' Noah said.

'But only one who played by the rules,' McGlinnigle said.

Noah realized he must have looked alarmed because

350

McGlinnigle began to chuckle before turning serious again.

'Not your team, Mr Murphy. I'm well aware of your attempt to bend the rules. It's Pengardon Academy I'm referring to – they're a disgrace.'

'How did you—'

'I received a very interesting email last night. It pointed out a couple of anomalies with the Pengardon situation. It mentioned a Mr Figg. Our paths have crossed in court on a number of occasions. I have won more often than I've lost.'

Stevie, Noah thought. Stevie must have emailed McGlinnigle even though he'd asked him not to do anything.

'Just to be on the safe side I switched the referees at the last moment so that there wouldn't be any – how shall I put it? – impropriety,' McGlinnigle said.

Suddenly, Darren was at Noah's shoulder.

'You've got to see this. Everyone, come on.'

Nobody else wanted to move – they were too exhausted – but Darren was insistent.

'You'll want to see this too, Mr McGlinnigle.'

'Well, I did have a couple of other things I wanted to say to Mr Murphy, but it does sound urgent and it's not like a young person to get overexcited by anything,' he said with a wry smile.

'And somebody bring a phone,' called Darren before haring across the pitch. On the far side was one of the large temporary car parks that was currently home to hundreds of vehicles.

'You go, I'll follow you on at my own pace,' McGlinnigle said.

'I'll walk with you,' Stevie said. 'Here, Noah.'

351

He threw his phone. Noah caught it and took off after Darren, with Maggie and the rest of the team not far behind. Noah squelched across the muddy pitch, summoning the energy from somewhere. He covered the distance in just over ten seconds. He had no idea what he was looking for, but as he got closer to the cars he spotted someone he recognized – Simone. She was standing on the edge of the car park, waving her hands frantically. Was she in trouble? But then Noah saw her put her finger to her lips to signal quiet. And Darren was doing the same.

What's going on? he wondered.

Noah slowed down and let Darren take the lead. The rest of the team behind him must have got the message because they too were suddenly a lot quieter. Quieter than they'd been since Noah had first met them.

'Shh,' Simone said as Noah reached the edge of the car park.

He stopped behind a white Range Rover Evoque. On the far side of the vehicle he spotted the large and distinctive head of his principal, Mr Hegarty. He was shouting at somebody.

Simone mimed at Noah to start filming with the phone. He'd almost forgotten he had it tightly gripped in his hand. He sneaked past her and moved down the side of the Evoque, keeping just out of sight. Now he could see that Hegarty was arguing with two people – a man and a boy. Cornelius and Barney Figg. And further on, standing behind the red Ford Fiesta that looked like Slugsley's car, was the man in the poncho, the scout. Noah glimpsed a salt-and-pepper beard beneath the hood and began to wonder why a scout would be standing there watching the argument before he was distracted by Hegarty's words.

'I did my job and now I want to get paid,' he said.

'You did your job? It couldn't have gone any worse. Look at my poor son, practically in tears because of you.'

'It's not my fault your team was such a miserable failure. And, just let me say, your son is possibly the worst footballer I have ever seen in my life.'

'How dare you insult him, you incompetent moron!'

Hegarty ignored Cornelius and turned his attention to Barney.

'You lost to a team with girls in it, Barney boy,' he said. 'Do you know how embarrassing that is? Almost as embarrassing as your father buying the tournament and your team still failing miserably. He bought players to play for your team and you *still* lost.'

'Why you—'

Cornelius Figg swung wildly at Hegarty and missed. He slipped and fell on to the muddy ground. Barney made no effort to help his father up and Cornelius Figg slipped another couple of times before he managed to get back to his feet.

'Did you really pay people to play for Pengardon? All those new players? You actually *paid* them?' Barney said, shocked.

'No, no, no, of course I didn't. Don't listen to a word that fat liar says,' Cornelius Figg spluttered.

'Yes, it was just coincidence that all those new players turned up right before the tournament. I don't know what's worse, Barney – that you're so thick you believe your dad's lies, or that your dad tries to trick you by playing a team of mercenaries,' Hegarty said.

'Dad?' Barney whined.

'Shut up, Hegarty. Do you know who I am?'

'Yes, you're the man who owes me over ten thousand euro. You asked me to get rid of Noah Murphy and I did and now I want to get paid.'

'Except you didn't get rid of him, did you, you buffoon? He turned up for that girls' team and knocked my son's team out and now Barney's traumatized for life.'

'Tell me the truth, Dad, or I'll make things really difficult at home,' Barney said.

'Fine, fine,' Cornelius said, wiping his filthy hands clean on his designer suit. 'I did it. I paid for them to play.'

Barney's tanned face twisted itself into a spitting, snarling rage.

'You paid a bunch of players and those were the best you could find?'

'What?'

'You're rich. You could have got a lot of top-class players from South America and no one would have been able to tell the difference and instead you got that bunch of nobodies. Not a single Galáctico among them. You're a useless father.'

Barney stormed off. Unfortunately for Noah and the rest of the team who were gathered behind him shivering in their sopping wet jerseys and shorts, he stormed off in their direction. He stopped dead when he saw them all gathered there, gaping at him.

'Dad, that horrible team that beat us is lurking here and they're filming our conversation.'

Hegarty and Cornelius Figg forgot their differences and joined Barney in record time.

'Murphy?' Hegarty said.

'Give me the phone, boy,' Cornelius Figg said. 'Give it to me now.'

Noah passed the phone to Adam who in turn passed it to Stevie.

'Now, let's be reasonable here, Murphy,' Hegarty said. 'We've both done some things we're not proud of, but if you just delete that video then I'm sure we can have an amicable chat about how we see your second year in school going.'

'I think it's too late for that, Mr Hegarty,' Noah said.

'Too late? It's never too late. All you have to do is—'

'The video's online,' Stevie said.

Hegarty's face fell. 'No, it can't be. Not already—'

'One of the many good things about this tournament,' Stevie said. 'Great Wi-Fi.'

'I will make your life a living hell,' Hegarty said.

'Not sure you'll still be in a job, then,' Maggie said.

McCooley laughed.

'You've just made a huge mistake,' Cornelius Figg began. 'I'll sue every last one of you. You'll lose your houses, you'll lose your—'

'Oh, pipe down, Cornelius,' Mr McGlinnigle said as he arrived at the back of the group of players.

'McGlinnigle?'

355

'I see you remember me. And you know what I can do in court, so you might want to reconsider those threats.'

'I . . . Barney, let's get out of here,' Figg said, dragging his son by the arm just as he was in the middle of forming a rude gesture specially for Noah.

As the Figgs departed, Hegarty remained where he was, his face growing redder and redder until it reached volcanic level.

'You're a sneaky, horrible, nasty little boy, Murphy. Just the sight of your stupid, skinny face makes me sick. No wonder your father left you—'

Noah watched in shock as the man in the poncho rushed forward from his hiding place and placed a meaty hand on Hegarty's shoulder. Hegarty spun round in a fury, but when the man pulled back the poncho hood and revealed his weather-beaten features all the fight left the St Killian's principal. His face transformed from red to white in a heartbeat.

'Who's that?' Cormac asked.

Noah didn't hear the question, but he supplied the answer.

'Dad,' he whispered, turning as white as Hegarty.

He couldn't believe it. He wanted to, but he couldn't. This had to be some kind of trick. Or maybe I'm dreaming, Noah thought. But as the rain continued to bucket down he knew he wasn't. His father really was standing there in front of him. He looked a bit older, a bit hairier than when he'd last spoken to him on Skype, but it was him. Noah just stood there gawping. He didn't know what to do. He didn't know how to react.

'Want to repeat those words, Mr Hegarty?' Noah's dad asked politely.

'What? Ha, ha. No, no. I was joking of course, Joe. You know me. I speak first, think later. I'd never really threaten a child.' He smiled nervously. Joe Murphy's hand still rested on his shoulder.

'I'll give you three seconds to get out of here, Mr Hegarty, or else I won't be responsible for my actions. One. Two . . .'

Noah had never seen a big man move as quickly as Hegarty did at that moment. He slipped and skidded, bashing his chin on the roof of a car before scrambling to his feet again and running off into the crowds.

'Dad? Is . . . is . . . that really you?' Noah asked. His heart was racing and the bitter taste of adrenalin filled his mouth. He could hardly contain his excitement. Please don't let me be wrong, he said to himself. Please.

'Sure is,' his father said, his face wrinkling into a broad smile. 'Had to come back and see what all the fuss about this girls' team was.'

'St Mary's,' Piotr bellowed.

Joe Murphy reached across and grabbed his son, wrapping him up in a bear hug.

Nothing else in the world mattered to Noah now. His dad was here. He wanted to shout the words: *He's here!* Normally, a public display of affection would have embarrassed him, but as he buried his face in his father's shoulder, as the rain lashed down, he couldn't care less what anyone thought of him. His family was together again. He thought he was going to explode with joy.

Hawk turned to McCooley. Kevin didn't look quite right to him.

'Hey, are you . . . are you *crying*?'

'No. Shut up,' McCooley said, wiping his eyes with a sopping sleeve.

'You are! You said McCooleys and St Mary's never cry and—'

McCooley gave Hawk such a thump that he didn't know what had happened to him until he was flat on the ground, tasting mud.

'Hawk down,' he mumbled.

'You had to have been expecting that,' Maggie said.

It took Noah a long time to calm down. A very long time. He'd never experienced emotions like this before. He could hardly think straight. Nothing made sense. His father was really there. He was home again. It was wonderful.

His dad had hoped to make it back in time to see both matches, but his plane had been delayed and he'd only arrived in time to see the second-half comeback against Pengardon. Noah didn't care. He was here now.

'I thought you didn't have enough money to come home,' Noah said.

His dad smiled, his eyes crinkling at the corners.

'I'm not complaining,' Noah added quickly, in case his father got the wrong idea.

358

'I know you're not. In a way, I wouldn't have been able to return if it wasn't for your friends,' Dad said.

'My friends?' Noah was confused.

'I know why you played in the tournament,' his father continued. 'To get a professional contract and bring me home.'

'Who—'

'Stevie told Simone. She thought you were throwing yourself into football because you loved playing it again, not because you wanted to help our family.'

'That's why I started doing it, Dad, but once I began playing . . .'

'I know.' His dad smiled. He understood. He'd played enough football when he was young. It was fun. 'Anyway, once I heard that, I knew I couldn't stay in Australia. Of course, I couldn't just leave – I still needed the money. The last six months and Simone's two jobs have helped hugely, but we still have money to pay back. I need a job. I did a Skype interview with OCH, a company that's starting up in Carraig Cruach in a couple of weeks. The pay's not half as good and it'll take us a little longer to get fully back on our feet, but it's work.'

OCH? The name was familiar, but Noah didn't care about that now. He wasn't certain: was his father really saying what he thought he was saying?

Noah's dad wrapped an arm round his son's shoulder. 'It's not your job to take care of me – it's my job to take care of you. And I can do that better when I'm here at home.'

'You're staying home?'

'I'm staying home,' his father said with a smile. 'This is where

I want to be. This is where I have to be.'

Noah could hardly believe it, but it was true, even if it would take him days before he finally accepted it.

When the commotion had died down and after they'd all had piping hot showers and a bite to eat, the St Mary's team piled on to the bus for their journey home. Players collapsed into their seats, their legs aching, their spirits drained. They had given everything and they were wrecked. Despite his protestations, Noah's dad managed to persuade him to go home on the bus with St Mary's while he took a spin with Simone and Dave.

'From what I've heard, Stevie, Maggie, Kevin and all the lads couldn't have done any more for the team,' he said. 'You can't let them down now. You have to go home together. Don't worry, you'll be sick of the sight of me soon enough.'

'Never,' Noah said, and he meant it.

Noah and Stevie were about to board the bus when McGlinnigle hobbled over to them.

'I'm glad I caught you before you left,' he said, a little out of breath.

'Me too. I wanted to say thanks for your help earlier. After Mr Hegarty and Mr Figg left, things got a bit hectic and I didn't see you,' Noah said.

'Your thanks are unnecessary,' McGlinnigle smiled. 'I should be thanking you. You've helped restore my faith in young peop—'

He was looking at the bus window. McCooley had Adam O'Brien in a headlock and the long-haired player's face was

360

pressed up against the glass. A stream of drool rolled down the window.

'Erm, Stevie,' Noah said hurriedly, 'Mr McGlinnigle got your email about Pengardon.'

'My email? I didn't send any email,' Stevie said.

'Oh no, that was from a William Sheehan. I believe he was one of the Pengardon players. Must have had an attack of conscience, poor lad. Can't blame him. When he heard about the plans to bribe referees into giving decisions Pengardon's way, he grew outraged and wrote an email to me. This whole situation has been a terrible mess. Pengardon won't be allowed play in any schools' tournament for many years to come. Bribes to principals and referees, paying players to play, illegal payments to the school, getting committee members to arrange the groups in his favour. This one will run and run.'

McGlinnigle reached into his coat pocket and took out a business card. He handed it to Noah.

'It's for a contact of mine. He scouts for a club in England, not at the top level, but high enough. You've got some good players on your team, but you're an excellent talent, Mr Murphy, and I've already raved to him about your ability. Next time you organize a match, give him a call and he said he'll come and watch you. Some of the others too. Can't make any promises, mind you. The professional game's a tough one to break into.'

'Thanks a lot. I really appreciate it,' Noah said. And he did. He didn't *need* to be a professional footballer now, but that didn't mean he didn't want to become one. He couldn't climb aboard the bus without asking. 'What did you think of Maggie? Number nine.'

'An undoubted talent,' Mr McGlinnigle said. 'Unfortunately, I don't think the men's game is liberal enough to allow women players just yet. But the women's professional game has really taken off recently. Miss O'Connell may yet receive the recognition she craves.'

'I don't know. She really has her heart set on playing against men,' Noah said. 'If anyone can make it through, she can.'

'That I *can* believe.'

As McGlinnigle said his goodbyes, Noah put two and two together and for once managed to come up with four. Miss O'Connell, McGlinnigle had called her. He'd almost forgotten that was her surname.

'Stevie, you know lots of boring stuff, don't you?'

'Oh yes, knowing a vast amount of information about the world we live in couldn't be considered anything but dull,' Stevie replied.

'Exactly. So, what's the name of Maggie's dad's company?'

'OC Holdings. Stands for O'Connell Holdings. Why?'

O'Connell Holdings. OCH. That was it.

'Her dad offered my dad a job. You don't think she had anything to do with it, do you?'

'The thing about Maggie is she puts on this tough front because she thinks she has to be self-centred and ruthless to make it in the world of professional football. She believes that showing you care is a sign of weakness,' Stevie said.

'But under that tough front, she's actually soft?'

'No, under that tough front, she's cranky and intolerant and more than a little arrogant, but I've seen her help people too. Usually, she insults them at the same time, but she's not entirely unfeeling.'

Noah thought about Kevin McCooley and his new boots.

'I wouldn't mention it to her, though. If you really believe she did your family a favour, I mean,' Stevie continued. 'She wouldn't like you bringing it up. It would embarrass her. In fact, she'd probably punch you.'

'She wouldn't punch me.'

'No, you're right. She's an excellent footballer. She'd probably kick you. Say nothing, Noah.'

The mood on the bus began to change as they were about to set off. Noah took Stevie's advice and didn't mention anything to Maggie about her father or his. Instead, he told her what McGlinnigle had said about her. Feeling an unexpected warmth towards her, he left out the solicitor's opinion on her chances of making it all the way in the men's professional game.

'An undoubted talent?' She was excited, but tried to hide it. 'He couldn't have said anything else, though, could he? I mean the man has eyes and anyone with eyes could see . . .'

Barbara interrupted her. 'Maggie, just this once, please.'

'Yeah, all right,' Maggie grinned. 'That was fun, wasn't it? The tournament, I mean.'

'It was brilliant. *We* were brilliant. It was the best two days of my life,' Frank said. He was about to sit down beside his sister, but she shook her head.

'Sorry, bro, this seat's taken,' she said to him.

363

'Who's taken it?'

'That'd be me,' Stevie said.

He apologized as he squeezed past Frank and sat down beside her.

'Shame it's all over. We had a chance of winning it,' Limbsy said.

'We came so close,' Cormac said.

Michael Griffin nodded in agreement.

'There's always next year,' Sunday said.

'Yes, we will win the World Cup next year. I can guarantee it,' Piotr boomed.

The bus passed through Ballymun and joined the M50 as the rain eased off. It was going to be a long journey back to Carraig Cruach.

'Some of us will be too old then,' Adam O'Brien said. 'It wouldn't be the same team.'

'There's an under-sixteen tournament on next year. I saw it online,' Darren said.

'A lot of us will be too young for that. The organizers mightn't allow it.'

Noah looked at Stevie. 'I think I might know somebody who can find us a way in.'

'Don't look at me. My days of organizing are over. There's no way I'm going down that road again,' Stevie said.

Kevin McCooley leaned across the aisle and growled at him.

'Although, I might reconsider under certain circumstances.'

St Mary of the
Immaculate Conception
School for Girls

St Mary of the Immaculate Conception School for Girls

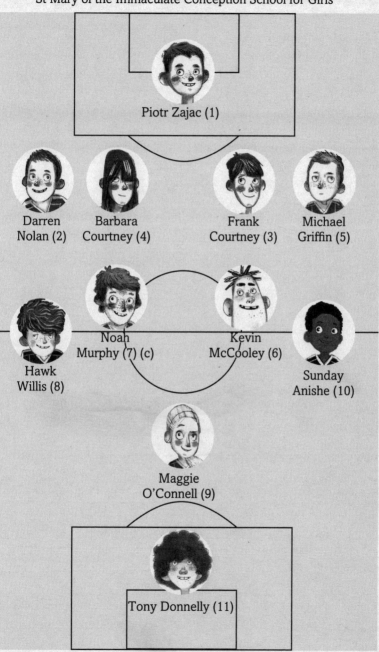

Piotr Zajac (1)

Darren Nolan (2)

Barbara Courtney (4)

Frank Courtney (3)

Michael Griffin (5)

Hawk Willis (8)

Noah Murphy (7) (c)

Kevin McCooley (6)

Sunday Anishe (10)

Maggie O'Connell (9)

Tony Donnelly (11)

Manager: Steven Treacy

Substitutes: Cormac McHugh (12) Adam O'Brien (13) Steven Treacy (14)

DAY ONE TOURNAMENT RESULTS

Drumlock Grammar	1	St Mary's	0
St Killian's	3	Park Community	0
Pengardon Academy	2	Drumlock Grammar	1
St Mary's	4	Park Community	0
Pengardon Academy	3	St Killian's	0

TOURNAMENT SCHEDULE

Sixteen groups, each group consisting of five teams. Each team plays four matches to determine the winner of the group. Winners of each of the sixteen groups qualify for next round of the tournament (a round of sixteen). Teams placed from second to fifth in their group after the four matches have been concluded on Day Two are knocked out and will take no further part in the competition.

Day One (Thursday):   Group Matches 1 and 2

Day Two (Friday):   Group Matches 3 and 4

End of Day Two – only group winners remain.

Day Three (Saturday): Round of 16, followed by quarter-finals

Day Four (Sunday):   semi-finals, followed by final

Tournament winners represent Ireland in Schools' World Cup

ACKNOWLEDGEMENTS

Special thanks to my agent, Marianne Gunn O'Connor, for all her hard work, enthusiasm and support.

Thanks also to my wonderful editors, Venetia Gosling and Anna Roberto. And to Paddy O'Doherty for all her help (and patience).

And, as always, thanks to Dee for the endless hours you spent reading the story, for all the helpful suggestions you made, and for, you know, putting up with me.

ABOUT THE AUTHOR

Kieran Crowley is a children's writer from Mallow, Co. Cork. His debut novel, *Colm & the Lazarus Key*, was shortlisted for the Bisto Book of the Year Award in 2010. The follow-up, *Colm & The Ghost's Revenge*, was published in 2012.